The Clockwise Carousel

Merry Christmas
2019

Louise Gorday

LOUISE GORDAY

The Clockwise Carousel

ISBN: 1533532699

Cover design by Kit Foster

Printed in the United States of America

This book is dedicated to three Irishmen
who worked for the Baltimore and Ohio Railroad:
Patrick James Lalley, my great grandfather
James Patrick Lalley, my grandfather
and
Michael Francis Lalley, my great uncle

Also by Louise Gorday

The Pickle Boat House

Bayside Blues

Contents

CHAPTER ONE

The Healthy One

M oira Byrne closed the shades just as the western horizon sucked the last wisp of pink from the sky. Opening the side-table drawer, she pulled out her tattered Bible, its black cover worn to white in patches, the top edge split and curling. She handed it to the young woman huddled under a red plaid blanket on the settee.

"Is this it, Nora? It's the only one I could find."

Nora nodded, leafed through the first few pages, and stopped at the one titled "*Family Record – Deaths.*" The earliest entries were documented in the careful, even pen strokes of parish priests long accustomed to recording births and deaths. Later entries, scribbled by family members in a hurry to complete a duty they had not practiced, lacked the same smooth shapes and spacing. She turned to the next page—only half-filled—and scanned the entries.

"Pen?" she asked, looking up.

Moira handed her a pen and sat down beside her as she entered in the first free space: "*Harry Cooley, died March 9, 1901 (Nevis, Maryland), age*

1

twenty-five, three months, twelve days." Her hand trembled a little as she wrote, so she bore down harder to keep the numbers legible. Finished, she put the pen in the book seam and clutched the Bible to her breast.

"Harry, my Harry," she said, rocking and sobbing as if recording the event had somehow made it final.

Moira wrapped an arm around her and murmured a few gentle words. Then, after a moment, she eased the Bible away with the other hand. She got up and walked back to the side table by the front door, where she left the book open to the entry—an official announcement of the latest passing in the long line of Cooleys.

"Patrick, we're going upstairs," Moira called to her brother in the next room. She put her arm around the crying widow and guided her toward the staircase. "You can take care of this until we come back down in the morning?"

Patrick Byrne came out of the parlor. "It's all under control. Go." He tipped his head toward the parlor. "I don't see him giving me any trouble. Frank and Connor will be in later to keep us company." He took out his pocket watch out and checked the time.

"Bad luck," Moira said. "No running clocks in here. Turn that thing off or put it outside."

"You don't stop a railroad watch, and no self-respecting railroader goes without." He gave his sister a kiss and hugged Nora. "Go. I'll take care of him."

Patrick walked back into the parlor and sat down in the chair by the head of the coffin. He looked down at Harry, his best friend, and tried to picture how he had looked before he died in the tunnel accident. It might have been an easier loss to bear had he not warned Harry away, tried to keep him from taking the temporary assignment. He had dreamed the accident in all its vivid gruesomeness, clear as anything in his waking moments, only two days before. They said he had the second sight, but they were eejits, of course. It was nothing but an old wives' tale he had been saddled with since he came into the world with the caul still covering his face. He had heard about it countless times from maiden aunts who cooed over its importance and his specialness. If the sight was to be like this, God was welcome to have it back.

Moira, his only sister, was apparently keeper of the caul—he had never seen it—and responsible for burying it with him when the time came. If he ever found the damn thing, he would burn it to a cinder—which was probably why Moira never discussed it with him. *Specialness?* Seeing your friend die twice was nothing but a curse, pure and simple.

Harry was bunged up for his 27 years, but not as bad as some railroaders. His hands, once strong with a hearty, viselike grip, were folded now to hide the stump of a mangled thumb. Patrick looked down at his own hands, splayed out on his thighs: ten perfect fingers. In his line of work, he was a lucky man.

He studied the dead face. It was relaxed, without a single line, but it was not a good look. He wanted to put his fingertips on those pallid cheeks and pull the sagging skin upward. It was not the Harry he knew: twinkling eyes, the cock-and-bull rolling off his tongue. He envisioned his own face in the pine box, staring up at him: the handsome features and curly brown hair. He ran his fingers through his mop. He was glad he had postponed his haircut. It looked better longer. And the small ears, he mused, reaching toward Harry but hesitating to touch him. He breathed easier as the facial features drifted back to become Harry's once more.

Why Harry? There was no sense in it. He was the healthy one, the one not living on borrowed time. The one who never let Patrick forget that life was a blessing. "*What blessing?*" Patrick would snarl back at him. And he would reply, "Paddy, you know the value of a day, and you can squeeze every drop of goodness from it. Stop planning so much, or you'll

Louise Gorday

waste the last day of your life canning tomatoes you'll never get to taste." Patrick shook his head and sighed. He'd start counting his blessings when he could get off the tracks. In the autumn, maybe. He had an in.

The night was going to be long. He pushed his chair back, stretched his legs out, and closed his eyes. He must have drifted off, because a soft rapping on the front door startled him awake. Some friend he was—couldn't even give Harry a few hours. He got up and let in his brother and Connor.

"Hey, Harry," Frank said. He set a half-empty bottle of Jameson down on the coffee table, leaned over, and peered into the coffin. "Looks pretty good, don't he, Pat?" he asked, turning back to his brother.

"Yeah, picture of health. You bring the cards?"

Frank pulled a deck out of his pocket and tossed it on the table. "Whose deal?"

"I got it," Connor said, palming the box. "Do we let Harry win the first one, or leave him dangling for a while?"

"First one, before he gets bored."

"Okay. Deal him his aces and eights so the chariot can cart him off happy."

Connor dealt the corpse in, and they played loose and free until Harry won the hand.

Frank grabbed the Jameson and poured three glasses. "To Harry. May the Lord keep you in his hand and never close his fist too tight." The three clinked classes and knocked their liquor back.

"Ah," Frank said. "It don't get smoother than that. Water of life, indeed. Deal."

A handful of games and many drinks later, Patrick could not even outsmart a corpse. "Jesus, Mary, and Joseph," he muttered, slurring his words, "no luck tonight." He slid his empty glass aside and took a swig from the bottle. "But I'm feeling good about the next hand. Deal."

4

When Connor failed to respond, Patrick kicked his boot under the table. "Pay attention, Connor. It's your deal. 'Sa matter?"

"Hold on," Connor said, staring bleary-eyed at the corpse. "Something's off about his hair. Didn't he part it on the other side?" He thumped his glass down, not quite sloshing it, pulled a brown celluloid comb out of his back pocket, and walked over to Harry.

"You're changing his hair? Shit! Nora will know we messed with him. Don't." Patrick got up and followed him over to the casket.

Connor snickered. "Harry needs to look his best." He changed the part to the right, then leaned back and studied the face. "Matter of fact, I think he'd feel much more comfortable at the table. What'd ya think?" He winked a glassy eye.

Patrick and Frank exchanged slow glances, then each grabbed a shoulder. The three pulled Harry out of his box of eternal repose, snorting and giggling as they heaved and pulled. When they got him out, they propped him up in a chair, curved his hand around a drink, and dealt him a few winning hands. The stories and liquor flowed well into the wee hours before a stupor settled over them.

"Bloody hell, get off me!" Patrick swiped again at the hand shaking him by the shoulder. He cracked one eye to find Moira looming over him.

"Where's Harry?" she screamed in his ear.

"He's in the . . . ," he began, lifting his head up and gesturing toward the empty chair at the table. "Harry? God, where's he gone off to? Swear to God, he was right here last I saw him."

"You're in so much trouble, Patrick James Byrne! Now, you get your scuttered friends up, find Harry, and get him back in that box before I bring Nora back down here in half an hour. *We'll* talk later."

Patrick kicked Frank's chair leg. "Get up. Where's Harry?"

Frank returned a bloodshot stare. His eyes darted to Harry's empty chair and back to his brother. Patrick could see mild panic setting in—not a good sign. He lunged over the table and shook Connor awake, cursing and babbling about what Moira would soon do to him if Harry did not turn up at once.

"I'm telling you, I don't *remember* where we put Harry," Connor said. "Frank and I walked him outside, and that's all I can remember. I'm sure we put him in a good, safe place, though. He'll turn up; you watch."

"Relax, Pat," Frank said. "He's here somewhere. Did you check the bathtub?"

"He'll turn up, all right—in the next twenty-five minutes, potato heads. Get your bottoms off those chairs and help me find him before Moira comes back down and flays me alive."

Frank grinned. "Look, he couldn't have moved from wherever we put 'im, so he's not lost permanently. Someone's gonna find him."

"Not someone—*us*. Now, move your bones." Patrick tipped over his brother's chair with his foot, spilling him onto the floor.

They began in the attic and made a frantic sweep of every room but Nora's, all the way down to the root cellar. Nothing. Patrick shoved them out the front door and headed toward downtown, where they ruled out the businesses still shuttered from last night. He was not at the depot or sitting out in front of their favorite watering hole or at any of the other handful of places deemed worthy venues for a proper send-off of poor Harry. Pat turned to his brother, a good five inches shorter than he, and lifted him up by his suspenders.

"Think!" he growled.

Frank grimaced, probably more from the exertion on his brain than from any real pain inflicted by his brother. "Well, there is one place we haven't checked. I can't see us carrying him all the way to the edge of town, but he could be . . . at Sally's."

"You took Harry to the *brothel*?" Patrick loosened his grip and began to laugh. "If he's there, you're never going to breathe a word of this. Got it?"

Business was not exactly booming at Sally's, so early on a weekday morning. There was a line, however, starting with Harry. He sat on the porch, propped up by the door with his cap pulled down over his eyes. He looked asleep, but no amount of shaking would have gotten him up for the occasion.

"Jiminy," muttered Connor. "We hauled him all the way down *here*?" He slapped Frank on the back. "Good job, Frankie."

Connor cradling his shoulders and the other two grabbing legs, the three hauled Harry back to Harry's house and settled him in his box, where Patrick resumed his vigil in the chair alongside and waited for his sister. He kept his eyes on Harry, and his ears cocked for his sister. The other two wisely skedaddled.

Patrick gazed at the corpse, trying to soak up the essence of Harry Cooley in these, their last private moments. They had known each other since they were in diapers in Philadelphia, and until this moment, Patrick had felt only disbelief at his death. Their last adventure together, to Sally's, had been cold and impersonal, and the conversation necessarily one-sided. Only now he felt the aching emptiness, from somewhere so deep within that he bent his head under the weight and sobbed. Harry had slipped from their mortal grasp. The healthy one had moved on.

CHAPTER TWO

Boom Time

Flat caps pulled low against the sun's glare, Patrick and Frank Byrne lounged on straw bales stacked near the newly constructed rail depot, and studied the waterfront. Boom time. Across the bayfront, laborers toiled away, cutting and hauling into place the infrastructure for the next great thing—or, perhaps more accurately, the greatest thing ever to come along to the small, withering Chesapeake Bay community of Nevis. Even after eight months of double shifts, things were still barreling along with no apparent end in sight. A New York partnership had bought 120 acres of shoreline and hardwood forest, with a grand scheme of turning ramshackle homes and boarded up fish processing warehouses, empty lots, and woods into the modern amusement park of Bayland. With the railroad itching to expand weekend business, and a bored middle class looking to be entertained, failure was impossible.

The scene reminded Patrick of ants swarming over a dropped Berger cookie. As he watched, three wagons with "Zugel" painted in red on their sideboards pulled up to the boardwalk with freshly hewn logs, their teams of draft horses shifting in their collars as the wagons stopped.

There would be no colored or Irishmen in the Zugel group. The Germans who settled here decades before had made it clear enough that the newly arrived railroad crew of Irish and coloreds was unwelcome. Life remained calmest when the Germans stayed in their half of town and the rail crew didn't venture far from the hastily constructed shantytown along the foggy bottom, and the few scattered crew houses from Nevis to Upper Marlboro. For Patrick and the rest of the Irish crew, discrimination was to be expected—they had been no strangers to it up North. But he and the Chesapeake Railway Express took all comers willing to put their back into a good day's work. It was simply good business.

Patrick grabbed the edge of his shirtsleeve and wiped a gnat out of the corner of his eye. "Too bad Harry won't see this," he said.

"Aww, God'll make sure he sees it all and places we ain't never even heard of," Frank said. "He'll be a regular old world tour guide by the time we see him again." Frank Byrne eyed his brother as he chewed thoughtfully on a piece of straw. "How's life?" he asked, talking around the stalk.

"A headache, and I'm parched," Patrick said. "If that's your way of asking how big an argument Moira and I had after the funeral, you can drop it. We didn't get into it, and I'm sleeping in the depot till it blows over. Hopefully, she'll find something else to distract her. Last thing I need right now is another temperance lecture. The woman should have enough to do without running around trying to take away everybody's liquor. She's become a regular Frances Willard."

Frank rolled his eyes. "Don't look at me when you say that. And whatever you do, don't get into a discussion about a woman's right to vote. She was swinging a number seven skillet at my head by the time I got to the front door. I got no patience for all that. But *you*," he said,

9

wagging the wheat stalk at his brother. "Never thought I'd see Patrick Byrne a whipped boy. What happened to the lad who ran off to Chicago to try the whores out before he was even out of knickerbockers? Ha! Worried that his sick ticker would quit on him before he ever lost his cherry. I turn around, and he's wooing every young lady at St. Peter's."

"Not all of 'em were ladies," Patrick said. "Docs don't know everything. The day I can't make it to work is the day I'll start worrying."

"Need to pace yourself. I noticed how out of breath you were, lugging Harry last night. You got nothing to prove. Let your crew do the heavy lifting."

Patrick leaned back into the bale behind him. "Tell me, Frankie, what kind of respect would I get out of these guys if I sat on my duff all day and watched them sweat?"

Frank chuckled. "Like I tell all the pretty ladies, *I'll* still respect you in the morning." He looked out across the wharf at the labor gang. "Spirited bunch, aren't they? We could use that kind of energy fixing track."

"Nothing new or exciting about railroad ties, Frank. It's those pavilions and boulevards that are pulling together dreams. Tycoons, haberdashers, con men—hundreds of families will pour into Nevis when the park opens. This resort will be big, but it's not happening without us. Material, machines, labor—if it doesn't come on the Chesapeake Railway, it'll have to walk."

"And you're the man."

Patrick put his arms behind his head and leaned back into the bales. "Yep, getting Harry's job, I'm the man. My stretch of track, my men, my rules."

"And yet, you're the glummest fella I ever saw. Moving up from assistant foreman should make your life a whole lot easier—longer, too, maybe. And you're that much closer to getting off the tracks—maybe a desk job here with the Chesapeake."

"Burying your best friend will do that. Makes you stop and think."

"Well, yeah, but I think ol' Harry's sending a pretty clear message: do what makes you happy, because you never know." He pulled his legs up underneath him on the bale. "I need wider horizons. We both do. We should ditch all this and go west—slow boat to China, or at least somewhere more exotic than Nevis."

"China's *east*. And anyway, leave Moira to take care of things?" Patrick shook his head. "I can't run off like that. I think what Harry's telling me is to be patient. It won't be Charlie Broderick's desk job, though. Harry said the man was never going to retire. No, my future is with the Baltimore and Ohio. They'll be hiring in the fall. That's the only place I can get a fresh start: where my boss doesn't hate me. The B and O gets a sizable chunk of freight in Baltimore. They'll pay me more. All I need's a grubstake to pay the rent and tide me over till my first check. I got a nest egg, just not enough yet. One day, one day . . ."

"Yeah, well, nobody's got the luxury of time—least of all you," Frank said, looking his brother over. "You're really feeling okay, right? Losing Harry was a shock. I don't need you following in his footsteps anytime soon."

"I never felt better. Worry about something else." Patrick turned his back and looked to the west, away from the waterfront and back toward town, where the storefronts were. "They say there's cheap eats up there," he said, pointing toward Seventh Street. "You hungry?"

Frank shoved his hands into his empty pockets and pulled them inside out. "If you're buying. Otherwise, I'm not hungry till payday."

Patrick snorted. "Seriously, what do you do with all your money?"

"Sally, drink, food, Dad." Frank shrugged.

"If you know what's good for you, you'll give up the first two."

Frank tucked his pockets back inside his pants. "Which part of 'Irish' don't you understand?" he asked, laughing.

"Just you, moron," Patrick replied. "Come on. The joint's down a few blocks—Dilly's Diner."

The brothers skirted the dock and headed toward the stockade fence encircling the rail yard. The fence served a dual purpose: keeping layabouts and pilferers out, and valuable equipment and materials in. Halfway up the hill, Frank stopped and grabbed Patrick's arm. "Quick! There, above the fence. See 'em? Bouncing heads—kids. Run 'em out of the yard a couple times already."

Patrick put his finger to his lips, and they sneaked up along the fence until they were underneath the bobbing heads. They waited, listening as shoes scrabbled against the wooden fence. Soon enough, a towhead reappeared and stayed there as a youngster clambered up and straddled the fence.

Patrick grabbed the youth by the arm, and he and Frank dragged him down from his perch. "Come here, you little rascal." The boy, in denim overalls, was maybe 10. He cowered against the fence. "What's your name?"

"Karl Peters, sir."

"Catch you in here again, Karl Peters, and I'll throw you in a mail pouch and hook you on the outside of the postal car. Now, go on, git." He let him loose and kicked the bottom of the fence. "Rest of you better make it outside that yard before I make it around the other side."

Frank kicked the fence and began to laugh. "Hear 'em skedaddle? Won't stop till they hit home. Hell, they're probably not doing anything we weren't doing at their age."

Patrick leaned over, picked up a round chunk of wood off the ground, and fitted it back into the knothole it had been poked out of. "Rail yard's no place to play. If a grown man like Harry can get himself killed, how much easier for those little demons! Gonna get hurt, and I don't want it on our watch. Let 'em play on the docks. They can't get hurt there, long as they don't drown."

"I'm impressed. Since you've taken over from Harry, you're sounding more and more like a company man. Another few months, you and Christian Miller should be downright chummy."

Patrick put his index finger to his temple, miming the barrel of a pistol. "You have permission to shoot me if that day—"

He dropped his arm. Across the dock road, standing well away from the crane lifting timbers from the Zugel wagons, a group of uppity-ups had gathered to admire the grand progression of things. Patrick had inadvertently drawn attention to himself by looking directly at Lawrence Carr, master planner of Nevis's grand new scheme. Their eyes locked, and Carr motioned him over.

"When Mr. Carr wants to talk, everybody better pretend to listen," Patrick muttered. "Come on. We both might be waiting till payday to get some grub. This should be as exciting as a temperance lecture from Moira."

CHAPTER THREE

Bonus

They crossed the main thoroughfare to where the big wheel and his people stood. Lawrence Carr cut an elegant figure in his four-button black suit. He held the purse strings to the Bayland venture. Patrick need not like him, but life was too short to be finicky about who put dinner on the family table.

The only woman in the group was a looker, the type Patrick would have expected to be with a man like Carr: small waist, big bosom, hair pulled back in a knot below a wide-brimmed hat protecting what he imagined to be flawless skin. Her large green eyes gave him a quick once-over. She whispered to the young assistant in a dark-blue suit, who responded with sweeping hand gestures and lots of nodding. Directly behind them stood a freckle-faced young gent with brilliantined persimmon hair, his black suit coat falling open to reveal a gray waistcoat, and his necktie loosened from his high-collared starched white shirt. Hands clasped behind his back, he was attentive in the way that a hawk is attentive, and had a natural elegance in the way he stood. The woman turned and tugged on his coat sleeve, pulling him closer to whisper in his ear. Only then did his expression soften, and he laughed, nodding in apparent agreement.

"Weren't you on the tour of the train station the other day, in the group of rail reps?" Carr asked when the Byrne brothers drew near.

Patrick pulled his cap off. "Yes sir, Mr. Carr. Patrick Byrne. I'm not in charge—only the track foreman from here to Ducketts Mill Bridge. Anything you need, let Mr. Miller know. He's vice president of operations on the southern leg of the Chesapeake Railway Express. With a little notice, we can accommodate anything you'll need on the track." He cleared his throat and pulled Frank forward. "This is my brother, Frank Byrne—also out on the line."

Carr pumped Patrick's hand, then Frank's. Though Patrick expected a dead fish, he got a firm, no-nonsense grip.

"What do you think of that station?" Carr asked, cocking his head toward the rail yard. "I convinced them to bring in Joseph Hadley, Frank Furness's man. You've seen Furness's Chestnut Street Station in Philly? Remarkable. City's full of geniuses."

Patrick shook his head. "I haven't seen it, but Hadley is a genius if he builds 'em all like this one. It's eye catching, for sure."

"What I'm paying for. Once our plans are in motion: *boom!*" Carr snapped his fingers. "We'll be running your trains round the clock. Get ready! There's a nice little bonus if our Bayland beats the opening of the Sandy Springs park in Baltimore and the new Glen Echo park."

"B-bonus, you say?" Patrick's heartbeat quickened. Frank stepped in closer.

"Oh . . . maybe I've spoken out of turn here," Carr said with a chuckle. "But in the end, we can't make money if we let the competition get a leg up, can we? We'll be bigger, newer, higher-quality attractions, two for every one of theirs." He pointed his cane across the water. "You can't beat the bay. This is a dream come true for everyone involved. There will be so much, Patrick—a little something for everybody. Get a little horse track in here," he said, turning away from the shore to point to a grove of hickory trees that two-man teams with crosscut saws were busy leveling. "And maybe a baseball diamond over there on the outskirts," he continued, his cane wandering a few degrees left. "We'll be all set—except, of course, for the heat." He shrugged out of his suit coat and held it out in front of him. The assistant darted forward, took the coat, and folded it neatly in half before rejoining the buxom young woman. The freckle-faced man with the glistening red hair smirked and gave Carr a nod.

Carr ran his finger around the inside of his tall collar and pushed his sleeves up. "They say this weather is unseasonably hot. Of course, if it's hot here, it's hot in Washington. Bathhouses all along the pier here should bring them in by the trainload."

"Yes sir," Patrick said, hoping the talk would come back around from bathhouses to bonuses.

"Saw you reading my flyer on the post down there. In the next six months, we'll have the two best carousels on the Eastern Seaboard. Know anything about carousels?" he said.

"Not much, sir. None around here. Maybe further up toward Baltimore? I recall seeing them in Philadelphia when I was younger."

"Baltimore, eh? Ever hear of Gustav Dentzel?" Carr asked, throwing the name out as if the man were his next-door neighbor. "German out of Philadelphia—the place to go if you want a carousel. I say I need two carousels; he tells me they can make one. I wave double money at them—all cash, too—but they tell me business is good and I can only have one." He shook his head. "Not good business, right?"

"No sir," Patrick said, wondering how he might gracefully cut the conversation short and get to Dilly's. He could hear Frank's empty stomach grumbling. His eyes wandered to the black automobile parked a few feet away, still gleaming even after the mile of rutted dirt road it had traveled to reach the shoreline.

"They're too busy working on a ride for Sandy Point," Carr droned on, seemingly unaware that he had lost his audience. "But they'll sell me the coaster Coney Island doesn't want. No good businessman would pass that up—including Sandy Point if they'd got the offer. No sir, Sandy Point will not hold a candle to us. Can't—*won't*—have that." He clapped his hand on Patrick's back. "Money moves mountains, Mr. Byrne—and roller coasters. I'll find someone to build the second one, and it'll put Sandy Point's to shame. Mark my words."

"Yes sir." Patrick nodded absently, unable to keep up with all the names the man was slinging around. He stole another glance at the car. Money certainly could move people. He'd never even seen an automobile up close, and he'd damn sure never own one, either. A rail pass would take him anywhere he wanted. Still, it was a beauty—varnished to a high sheen and gleaming like polished ebony.

Carr came up for air and caught the young Irishman looking. "Impressed? It's an Olds. I had her brought down by rail. Curved dash, gasoline powered—number seven off the line. I paid six hundred dollars for it, but it's worth every dime. We're heading up to Detroit in autumn to watch Alexander Winton at the races. Ransom Olds is sponsoring it. I'm sure you've heard of him. Personal friend of mine."

He turned and looked toward the tree clearing. "Might not even be a bad idea to race *here*—plenty of land, bring in lots of money. Cars. A rich man's sport, but even poo—um, the less affluent—like to watch. What's the use in having money if you can't spend it on nice things? Come," he said, waving Patrick toward the car. "I'll show you this beauty. I'm sure you can appreciate what a step removed it is from *your* occupation. I've already put in a word for next year's model. Even more impressive, if that can be believed. Mary, A. J.," he said, turning to address his companion and the redheaded assistant. "Can I tear you away?"

She shook her head and went on whispering. A. J. raised his palms and shrugged.

Patrick caught the brief flash in Carr's eyes, but then the man laughed. It all happened in an instant, and Patrick marveled at the smooth recovery from an awkward moment. Obviously a complex man and capable of masking his true feelings. No doubt, years of backroom backslapping and palm greasing would have taught that. Clearly, this was someone you didn't trifle with.

Carr turned back to him, beaming a smile. "Women and machines— what can I say? Complains about the wind in her hair." He thrust his chin toward the freckle-faced man, whose attention seemed to have shifted from the grand construction plan entirely to her. "Do you know A. J., there, Patrick? James W. Packard's nephew?"

"'Fraid not, sir."

"Packard's making some lovely cars, too. Owns the Ohio Automobile Company. A. J.'s a young one, but he's smarter than many twice his age, and a go-getter. Good man."

Carr's demeanor suddenly lightened, and he pushed past Patrick. "Here's a man I'd love to shake hands with. Your boss, I believe," he said, smiling at a man who approached from the direction of town. "Christian Miller, you old rascal, how is the railway business?"

Miller removed his hat, revealing a ruddy complexion and a head of curly hair beginning to mat down with perspiration. "Mr. Carr. They said I might find you here. Things are excellent, thank you—better than expected, in fact."

Patrick looked at Miller's stylish black bowler, three-piece black linen box suit, and spit-shined two-tone shoes. Miller had obviously dressed to impress someone, but, as Patrick noted with amusement, with little regard for the sultry heat. That he had dandied up to schmooze a man like Carr was not surprising. Although he kept his nose—and everybody else's—to the grindstone, Miller had not gotten where he was by hard work alone. More of a surprise was the pleasant, smiling expression—ill-fitting on a man whom Patrick and his rail crew could only describe as the most cantankerous, back-stabbing, manipulative son of a bitch God ever made. Seeing Miller bow and scrape and sweat could prove entertaining. Patrick decided to stick around a bit and watch the show. Retelling it would be good for a pint or two at the Bottle and Berth.

Carr pointed his cane at the brand-new, sprawling Bayside Hotel directly behind them. "Now that my hotel's done, I'll be down here frequently. Had to come to town and make sure it's up to snuff. I'm staying all week, maybe longer." He turned back to the construction along the bay. "I must say, it's looking good down here. I was going to show Patrick here my new automobile. Come take a gander."

"Oh, it caught my eye from way back there," Miller said. "A lovely sight, but of course, we wouldn't want to see you give up the rail system *entirely*. It is still the backbone of commerce."

"Oh, mercy me, no," Carr said with the same affable smile he had used on Patrick. "It's all in fun. I don't see any sense in being at the forefront of industry and not enjoying what it produces."

"I can't argue, Mr. Carr. Have you ventured any farther than here? If not, let me amaze you with what is happening out there. I got a tour yesterday. Then we can get in out of this heat." He swiped a hand across his forehead.

"Enthrall me, Mr. Miller—and Mr. Packard here, too. You know James's son?"

"Pleasure," Miller said, tipping his hat at the younger man. "And the lady?"

"Mary Partridge?"

"Excellent," Miller said, giving her a thorough twice-over. She glanced his way with what might have passed for a smile.

"Be delighted to show you about, Mr. Carr. If you'll excuse me for a minute, though, I need to have a word with Mr. Byrne. I'll meet you down by the pier?"

"Yes, sir. Front and center with my little entourage here. I'll introduce you around."

"Looking forward to it," Miller said. He gave Patrick a penetrating look and moved away from the retinue. Patrick followed along until they were out of Carr's earshot.

"What mischief are you getting into out here, talking to Mr. Carr?" he asked. "Hopes of rising above your station, Mr. Byrne?"

"Well, no sir," Patrick said. "Frank and I were minding our own business when Mr. Carr waved us over. I thought it would be rude—"

"Leave Mr. Carr to other people, and just you keep the rail line all shipshape, okay? I have another way for you to keep Mr. Carr happy." He pointed toward the wharf. "See the skinny young fellow in the white shirt and straw boater, leaning against the post? Carr's nephew, Albert Harmon—the newest member of the Chesapeake Railway Express. I want you to take him under your wing and show him the ropes. He loves railroads. I promised I'd have you look after him."

"All right," Patrick said, not liking the sound of it. "Any experience?"

"Fresh out of university—accounting." Miller slapped Patrick on the back. "He's a fast learner. Now, I know you can handle this. Give him a good show, but don't let anything happen to him. Carr adores the lad's mother, but you know how sisters can be."

"Yes sir. He'll be here all day?"

"Heavens no! You can have him for the next four months. I mean for you to get him on solid footing."

"Christ, Mr. Miller," Patrick said, throwing his hands up. "I'm kinda' busy right now. I can't be nursemaiding some rich brat in the middle of all this."

"*Nursemaiding,* is it?" Miller said. He took off his silver pince-nez, wiped it on his handkerchief, then shook it at Patrick. "If Carr's sister, Fannie, isn't happy, I don't get to be happy. And if I'm not happy, you won't be, either." He slid his glasses back onto the gleaming bridge of his nose and snugged them in place. "Your mission in life, like mine, is to keep all this humming along."

"Unfortunately, sir, I'm not hearing any humming—groaning and moaning is more like it, and Mac's chanting. That's what's waking me up in the dead of night. Curve number three—it's a problem. The bed runs low through there, and the ground close by is wet . . . with the Piscataponi Creek there, and all. The ground all through there is saturated and unstable. I need to shut things down and haul in some ballast, build it all up. The roadbed'll take a beating once Mr. Carr's heavy loads start coming in. From experience—"

"And I do appreciate your experience, *son.* That man over there can buy and sell us ten times over. He's paying me, and I'm paying you to keep this line open."

"But if we get an unusual weather, *sir,* we'll have lost the opportunity to get ahead of it."

Miller waved him off. "Figure it out without shutting the line down. If that means working at midnight, do it." He glanced in Carr's direction. "You keep up your end so I can keep up mine."

"But—"

"Now is not the time, Mr. Byrne." The two men locked eyes for a moment, and the steeliness in Miller's eyes softened. "Let's not add any needless pressure to such a fine day. I have perfect faith in you. Now, I'm off to give a tour and, just maybe, ride in that beautiful Oldsmobile."

Patrick watched the old weasel scuttle off to join Carr, seemingly without a care in the world. So be it. Patrick would do what he must, and if it didn't go well, he would make sure Miller went down with him.

"Damn fool," Frank said, coming up behind him. He held up his hand, forefinger and thumb almost touching. "We were *this* close to getting a look inside that beauty. He sighed. "Damnation."

"Damnation," Patrick echoed.

"Do you still feel like the man?"

"That man," Patrick said, nodding back toward Carr, "spent more on an automobile than I make in a year. I'd say that makes him *the* man."

"You think we can keep up with number three?"

"God help us if we don't. Come on, brother, we need to skedaddle. Those folks'll never eat in a place like Dilly's. We can squeeze in half an hour of peace before we need to get back on the track. I don't want the crew thinking we're using Harry's send-off as an excuse to dodge work."

Frank nodded toward Harmon who was still in the same spot as he studied the waterfront with a pair of binoculars. "What are we gonna do about him?"

Patrick blew out a deep breath. The B&O could not come soon enough. "Make him feel welcome, like he's one of us. Let him shovel ballast for a half a day, and he might decide on a new profession. He goes everywhere we do, including Sally's. If getting a bonus means we have to nursemaid him, then so be it."

"Don't let that bonus talk go to your head, Paddy," Frank said over his shoulder as he headed for Carr's nephew. "Rich people always talk money, but they didn't get that way by throwing it around."

"With that bonus, I can get to Baltimore a whole lot faster. You'd see that if you ever held on to a dollar long enough to do something important with it. Just get Junior and we'll hook him up with a rail buddy." Patrick turned toward Seventh Street.

CHAPTER FOUR

Dilly's

D illy's stood at the end of Seventh Street. It was not a flashy place—Nevis didn't have much need for fancy. With the sudden influx of rootless, hungry manual laborers in town, it needed to put out a square meal at a reasonable price. The best butterscotch pie and raisin bread south of Upper Marlboro was a bonus.

George Dilly had chosen the location against the advice of naysayers who were blind to the potential of a backwater like Nevis. But the diner prospered, its success a testament to George Dilly's foresight, ingenuity, and reliable sources regarding Carr's business ventures. Laborers building the Chesapeake Bay resort filled his coffers, and the promise of trainloads of vacationing city dwellers whispered of more to come. For a town that had been threatening to sink back into obscurity as the fishing industry turned belly-up, the business had an auspicious beginning. But sudden wealth hadn't changed Dilly. He was still the same brash Englishman who had hoboed into town with a hundred dollars in his pocket, to find his way amid the cocky Irish and headstrong German immigrants, all of them scrabbling to get ahead. From day one, he treated them all the same: pay up or get out. For Byrne and his crew, it was refreshing to see an eatery without "No Irish Allowed" plastered on the front door.

<hr />

Frances Jane Mitcham and Mary Alice Bohanan stood at the diner window, transfixed by the three men swaggering down the street. Their friend Anna, shut out from the view, pressed in from behind.

Frances sighed, "Heaven, right outside." She pushed her raven hair away from her face, sending corkscrew ringlets cascading down her back. She bit at the ragged edge of a broken fingernail.

Anna pushed down on Frances's shoulder, trying to get a better view. "The tall one in the middle—have we seen him before?"

Frances shook her head. "Patrick Byrne, new section foreman between here and Ducketts Mill Bridge. The shorter one, that's his brother Frank."

"How do you know all this?" Anna asked. As Frances turned toward her, Anna wedged her shoulder in and slid closer to the window.

"Hey! I was here first!" Frances flicked Anna's honey-blond bun. "Everybody knows he's taking the place of the man who died—everybody except *you*. But it is hard to keep up with 'em all. Lots of Paddies running around. Never seen the dandy before, though."

They stared at his shiny pointed shoes, tweed jacket, and high-collared white shirt—clothes as foreign to their fathers' and brothers' chest of drawers as the gold watch fob that looped from his button to his vest pocket.

Mary Alice agreed. "The skinny one, dressed all fancy—he's new. I've seen the other two at church. There's half a dozen Byrnes living over there in Foggy Bottom. I think it's all one family."

Anna sighed. "*Patrick Byrne.* I'm going to marry him."

"Sure, you are. Right after me, Mary Alice, and every other girl in town. 'Cept he's not the marrying type. I've heard he's been places." Frances started to work on another nail.

"Lordy Moses, look at those shoulders!" Mary Alice breathed. "They don't get any broader. I've heard he knows every girl down at St Peters."

"I'm gonna marry him," Anna repeated.

"Anna, you can't marry him," Frances said, prodding her in the back. "He's Irish Catholic. Your daddy would pull out the robe and have him lynched."

"*Shh!* Not so loud, big mouth! They don't lynch. They just don't give 'em jobs. And I don't care. I'm marrying that man."

"I'll believe it when I see it," Frances murmured.

"If you're taking him, I'll take the other one, *Frank* Byrne," Mary Alice whispered. "He's kinda cute. Think of it. We could be *sisters.*"

Frances took her pinkie out of her mouth. "Oh, God, one's headed in here. Hide!"

The girls fled the window and took refuge behind the kitchen door. Safely out of sight, Frances leaned forward and shoved Anna back out into the restaurant and refused to let her back in the kitchen. "Say 'I do,'" she whispered, and she and Mary Alice erupted into giggles behind the door.

Anna felt wobbly in the knees. Was her apron clean? She could not bear to look down. Or up. Was her hair even combed? Every breath she took sounded raspy and loud. *Breathe,* she thought. *Oh, dear God . . .*

As the man of her dreams walked alone into the restaurant, Anna worried that he would hear the thudding of her heart. Tall and lean, he had bronze skin, and burly shoulders strengthened by years of lining track along the Chesapeake Railway. He had an air about him that seemed to demand respect transcending heritage or occupation. He slapped his paperwork down on a table by the window and sat down. As he did, he noticed Anna, standing frozen in the middle of the room.

"Good afternoon," he said.

"Good afternoon." She felt her feet thaw. "Coffee?" She scurried behind the counter.

"That'd be great. And whatever's left of the lunch special. Two of 'em if you've got it."

Without a second glance, he fished a pencil stub from his shirt pocket and began jotting figures. Freed from his gaze, Anna brought his coffee without sloshing a drop, then beat a path back behind the counter again. There was a lilt to his voice, almost a brogue . . . She tried to sear it into her brain as she stole a glance.

Once, he looked up and caught her, but he just smiled and returned to his work. It mattered not a whit whether he was rascally man-about-town, or even a papist Bog-trotter. She had made up her mind. One day, she would be his wife. Today was but the first step. She cleared her throat and opened her mouth. Not a sound came out. She inhaled deeply, reminded herself that it was merely another small step, and began again.

"Did your brother not want to eat?"

The pencil stopped moving, and he looked over at her, a frown creasing his tanned forehead. "I'm sorry, were you speaking to me?"

Anna felt like crawling into a hole and pulling it shut over her. "Your brother," she said, a little louder this time. "Did he not want to eat?"

"He had other business. How did you know he was my brother?"

Anna's eyes grew large, and she could think of no better reply than to shrug.

Patrick smirked and nodded. "We look a lot alike." He went back to his figuring.

"You work for the railroad?"

He looked back up. "Between here and Ducketts Mill Bridge."

"So you moved here recently?"

"No, been here a while—just didn't have any need to come up this way."

"So now . . ."

This time, the head did not come up. He grunted and shook his head as the pencil kept moving.

Anna turned away. She looked toward the kitchen, eyes beseeching her friends to rescue her from her misery. The kitchen door edged open, and she fled.

———◆◆◆◆◆———

Patrick sat scribbling a while, only momentarily glancing up when Frank and another young fellow approached the table. With their dark tans, faded overalls, and faded blue neckerchiefs, they looked every inch the rail men. They sat across from him and waited silently as he finished writing his entry. Then he turned to his brother. "Did you find Connor?"

"Yup," Frank said. "And I told him exactly what you told me to tell him: 'Nursemaid this dumb ass Harmon. Make sure he gets really dirty and sore so he doesn't come back tomorrow.'"

"Christ, Frank, tell me that isn't what you said!"

Frank chortled as his eyes took in the simple decor of the little diner—heavy straight-legged wooden tables covered in blue-and-white checkered gingham, and a counter lined with pressed-glass cake safes filled with pastries and a cake with white icing. "Not a bad place," he said. "Not bad at all. Did you order? Cute waitress," he said, eyeing Anna, who had ventured back out but kept to the safety of the counter. "I could take her places."

"Yeah, girls just love broke guys."

"I have lots to offer."

Patrick rolled his eyes. "Seeing as I'm paying, I already ordered yours. Blue plate, and if you shape up your act, some butterscotch pie over there. Jack, sorry—didn't know you were coming."

Jack Glynn pushed back in his chair. "Don't give it a thought," he said, patting his midsection. "Full up from Harry's spread. You shoulda stuck around for the wake. Family did his passing proud. Nope, just here for the conversation before heading back out—long as it's not about Miller, ballast, or how my shoes still haven't dried out from slogging through curve number three."

Patrick side-eyed the shoes and nodded. "Let's see. That leaves the weather, fickle women, and the odd fellow with the shop full of useless equipment down past Doc's."

"Odd one he is," Frank agreed. "Sneaks around the pier at night with a telescope. And it's not so much the telescope—he talks to himself, and he looks like he smells."

"Work starting on the racetrack," Jack said. "What do you do to get some java around here?" he murmured, looking around.

"Make it two," Frank said, looking toward the counter. "Bro here's killing me with these double shifts. Where'd you hear about a racetrack? There's already one at Marlboro. Makes no sense putting one here."

Jack shrugged. "Where money's concerned, everything Carr does makes sense, else he wouldn't bother. Temperance league is all over New York racetrack betting, and the bookies are saying they're gonna run all horse racing, including the Preakness Stakes, right out of the state."

Frank cut eyes at Patrick before turning back to Jack. "And how did you get to be this fount of knowledge?" he asked. "We haven't heard nothing, have we, Pat?"

"'Cause you don't have a cousin Riley who runs the numbers up there," said Jack. "He says Carr's trying to snag a deal to bring the race here. Chesapeake rail will bring 'em right from Washington and dump 'em off at the park, like the New York, New Haven and Hartford's doing right now at Gravesend racetrack on Coney. It's like shooting fish in a barrel. Preakness belongs back in Maryland anyway, where it started."

Patrick leaned in toward Jack. "Where money's concerned," he said, "nothing Frank does makes sense."

Frank took the toothpick he had been gnawing on and threw it like a dart, just missing Patrick's ear. "You talking behind my back?"

No, right in front of you, baby brother." Patrick threw the toothpick right back and ticked him on the chin. "Track betting is one more hole for you to throw money into."

"*Phew*," Frank said, rubbing his chin. "Talk about something else. It's sunny today. Okay, weather's covered; now let's talk about women. I was down—"

"Ups, make way, food coming." Patrick shoved the paperwork into his notebook and put it on the floor to make room for the plates the young blonde waitress carried on her arm. He reached out and took a shaking plate from her. "Rough day?"

"Little bit," she whispered. She handed the other plate to Frank and returned to the counter without looking at either of them.

Frank nodded in her direction and cocked an eyebrow at his brother.

"No pie for you, dummy," Patrick said. "Cute, but too young and innocent. Go see Sally." He looked over to make sure he had caught Frank in time and hadn't added to the girl's unpleasant day.

Anna had her back to him as she held the door open for a man carrying a box. He thumped it down on the counter and left in a hurry, returning a few minutes later with an armload of smaller packets. Perspiring from his exertions, he dumped those on the counter, too, then stuck his head in the kitchen door and called everyone out.

"Who came in first this morning?" he asked the three girls.

Anna raised her hand halfway. "Me," she peeped.

"Did you make all these pastries, too?"

She nodded.

"And when I came in, you were the only one I saw doing anything. What have you other two got to say for yourselves?"

"Cooking, sir . . . in the back," Frances said, hitching a thumb toward the kitchen door. Mary Alice took a step behind her and nodded.

"Well, God forbid you're cooking out *here*." He turned back to Anna. "Miss Zugel, you can go home now. Other people here need to earn their keep."

Patrick's head whipped around. Michod Zugel's daughter? Never mind her tender years—no Irishman need apply for her dance card. He would have to clue Frank in before he got himself lynched.

CHAPTER FIVE

Bayland Partnership

The Chesapeake Railway Express train rolled past fields sprouting with young Maryland tobacco. The train rocked gently back and forth to the clackety-clack of steel wheels over rail joints. The Bayside Limited partners relaxing in the parlor car were delighted with the progress of Bayland Park's construction, no doubt seeing its rise as a monument to their personal vision and shrewdness.

Lawrence Carr stood up and surveyed his heavy-eyed, impeccably turned-out audience seated at the long oak conference table in the luxurious parlor car. They were men of considerable means and respectable backgrounds, and he had expected more from them: more moxie, more vision, more interest. Their complacency was unsettling. Wallace, Bush, Browning—all trust-fund babies from wealthy steel, rail, and shipping families—flush with cash but apparently with no inherited business sense. When the partnership moved past the need for large influxes of money, he would force them out. It was nothing personal, just his own good business sense—sense that any self-made man developed early on.

And then there's Wilfred, Carr mused, glancing to the man at his left, at the end of the table. Wilfred Pettigrew had been an annoyance ever since they played together as young children in Central Park. Carr would have to put up with him a bit longer, even as he watched the man gloat at his every misstep and hesitation.

Pettigrew peered over the rims of his spectacles and ran an index finger under the cone-shaped tip of his small nose. "So we have other options, another carousel up our sleeves somewhere?" He seemed to enjoy the pickle they found themselves in: an amusement park without a carousel. He made a face as if he smelled something rancid. The others laughed.

Carr let them laugh, even joining in briefly to show his good-humored tolerance for other opinions—although, from Pettigrew, it was never so much an opinion as a general intent to make Carr look bad whenever possible. "I'm not saying we don't have the Dentzel carousel, only that his main warehouse on Fifth Street is a total loss from the fire. We are not certain where *our* carousel is housed. There is a possibility—another facility, perhaps. All is not yet lost."

Pettigrew persisted, easing back in his chair and addressing the other partners as if winning them over to his opinion would earn him points in some unspoken game. "But in the worst imaginable case . . . the park doesn't have a carousel?"

Carr sighed and shook his head, sitting down as the train whistled a warning to the town of Owings—a necessary stop to take on water. He decided to talk to the ceiling for a while. "We need to wait and see—hope the carousel we were offered is being warehoused somewhere else. My first choice, of course, is Gustav Dentzel. His machines are the best, the crown jewels. If our carousel was torched, he will have to build us another. If it arrives after opening day, we'll build it up as something so fine it took longer to get it designed, et cetera, et cetera. If Dentzel does not come through for us, quite frankly, I'll be in the mood to run his little business into the dirt—I won't care who he is."

Edwin Bush stirred from his apparent slumber, sliding his sleek black leather notebook several inches away from him. "We've been in touch, Lawrence. He is taking inventory. If it was destroyed, he said we'll have to wait six months for him to replace it. He's offered to find craftsmen to add to the few carved figures he does have on hand. The only other game in town would be E. J. Morris—a smaller, less prestigious company, but from Philadelphia nonetheless."

"Nobody likes second-rate, Edwin," Browning murmured. He ran his hand down the buttons of his vest, brushing off a few errant Berger cookie crumbs. "Let's accept Dentzel's proposal to cobble something together. We can still call it a Dentzel, and who's to know the difference?"

"Agreed," Bush said. "The uncertainty of the whole affair is making me—and my wallet—uncomfortable."

Carr nodded. "Agreed, then. If our carousel was damaged, we immediately go with the partial Dentzel. Hop on it before anyone else can snatch it." He pulled a cigar from inside his jacket. "But, gentlemen, let's not let this crush us. What we need now is to sit on this—a vow of secrecy until we know for sure about the warehouse. We don't want to give the impression Bayland is second rate in any way. The key to success here is to appear positive, on schedule, everything well in hand."

"Looks like a public-relations nightmare to me," Pettigrew said. He lit a Romeo y Julieta of his own and casually blew smoke in Carr's direction. Then his eyes narrowed to slits. "Who's going to come to a park that can't compete with Marshall Hall and Cabin John? Don't they both have carousels? Cabin John has a Dentzel, if I'm not mistaken, and they're building a scenic railroad that will pull in herds of people. What about Glen Echo? Isn't a carousel going in there when they reopen?"

"Well, yes," purred Carr. "All true, but as I understand it, the Baltzley brothers are out of their depth in Glen Echo. I hear they're going under."

"Yes, but the Bobingers are going hell's bells at Cabin John," Pettigrew said. "The trolley from Washington is a sweet ride—drops patrons off right at the entrance. Why would those same patrons want to change their routine and come here for less, Lawrence?"

Carr sighed and pulled the unlit stogie out of his mouth. "The Chesapeake Railway will match their little trolley system and up the ante, I assure you. Our bay and swimming facilities will be matchless: modern bath facilities, golden beachfront, and sparkling bay vistas. There will be a permanence here the other parks could never hope to compete with. When we develop the north end of Nevis, tear down all those old fishermen's homes along the bayfront, they'll snap up the summer homes we build there like they were the last houses in Shangri-La. Even when all the others fail, Bayland will still be standing—a monument to the business acumen of the men sitting right here at this table." Carr paused and made eye contact with each of them as he spoke. "Something your grandchildren and their children will come and enjoy." Carr's gaze settled last on Pettigrew, and it was now one of warning rather than reassurance.

As silence fell over the room, Carr looked casually about for any sign that opinion had shifted in his favor. Pettigrew still looked smug, while Bush and the rest kept their poker faces, characteristically waiting for their silence to prompt someone else onto breaking cover first.

And as usual, Pettigrew took the cue. "I don't suppose you'd like to discuss the *second* carousel we've promised for the park. God knows, we haven't even begun to discuss that there will be two of them," Pettigrew said. "The troubles in getting hold of the first one should have been thoroughly vetted before we promised *two.*"

Pettigrew wafted a smoke ring in Carr's direction. The other partners fidgeted, and the silence hung heavy.

"I have it!" Carr slammed his hand down on the tabletop. "Why don't we run a contest for a second carousel? This town is *full* of wood and woodworkers. The winner will be unlike any of the others made by Dentzel and all the rest. It'll be fresh, special."

Carter Wallace rolled his eyes. "Furniture makers, yes, but *carousel* makers?" he asked with disdain. He consulted his pocket watch and returned it to his pocket. "Germans are best at making beer and sausage."

Bush shifted in his seat. "All the best designers are German. They learn it early, like with cuckoo clocks and beer steins."

"There is a better way," said a quiet voice from the far end of the conference room.

All bodies rotated toward the red-haired man sitting away from the table, in a back corner of the car. Carr brightened at the new voice and at the novelty of hearing any constructive suggestion from this bunch. "Mr. Alexander Joseph Packard," he said, rising, "in case you haven't been properly introduced," knowing full well they had not. Packard had been on the receiving end of raised eyebrows and sidelong glances since the meeting started. "I've brought A. J. in as a consultant. Impeccable credentials, knows all about how things run—uncle owns the Ohio Automobile Company. I coaxed him away from Steeplechase on Coney Island because he knows more about the business end of developing amusement parks than anyone else I know." He nodded toward the young man. What would you like to add, sir?"

Packard rose from his seat. "Instead of dealing directly with the carvers, we should consider hiring an intermediary to procure the second machine."

"And where would we find such a convenient person?" Pettigrew asked, glaring at the newcomer.

"William F. Mangel's your man. He himself doesn't carve. He commissions carvers and then mounts the figures on his own machine base.

I've met him. Woo Mangel and let him do the legwork for you. He'll pull from the best, and you can take advantage of the latest advances in design. As I understand it, he has a mechanism that makes the animals move up and down as the whole contraption turns. It's patented. Glen Echo's animals are all stationary—not a jumper in the bunch."

"Sounds German," Bush said. "It just might bloody-well work."

"We could still include the woodworkers in town," A. J. said, nodding at Carr. "I doubt we'll get anybody trained in this type of carving, but it's a great human-interest story. The town will invest in the idea. Just think of it: one of their own creating the carousel they all love to ride! It'll be word-of-mouth free advertising. Mr. Mangel can put out a call for sketches or whatever he deems necessary, and then he separates the wheat from the chaff. He assumes responsibility for the final product. Should the town craftsmen not be able to compete, Mr. Mangel, not us, will have to answer for it. All the better, really."

The idea smacked of success without any expenditure of personal time or extra thought, and the partners naturally warmed to it. Their unanimous vote sent the redhead off to another car to check his personal availability for a trip to Philadelphia. Pettigrew went off to pout, and Lawrence Carr sat back and marveled at his own brilliance in hiring such a golden young protégé as A. J. Packard.

CHAPTER SIX

Tests and Tested

Now that the rail workers knew that bonus money was tied to an on-time opening day for the park, they took every delay as a personal omen that they would be left out of the Bayland windfall. Autumn had been dry and the winter unusually mild, but when unusually heavy spring rains delayed the clearing of land, boardwalk construction, and shipment of materials and arcades, they took it as a sign that not only did the Germans and uppity-ups want to oppress them, but that God himself was against them.

At the section house five miles north of Nevis, the day crew milled about, waiting for the last straggling gray clouds to clear. Patrick hung back under the protective overhang of the section house's metal roof. His feet felt clammy in boots still damp from yesterday.

Frank sat off by himself on a makeshift bench cobbled together with barrels and a two-by-twelve. He was quieter than normal—a grunt or two early on and nothing much since. It seemed he had on his mind something too weighty to talk about. Patrick counted it as a positive.

Frank would have a handle on it by midday, and then he would be impossible to shut up. The lad was goodhearted but maybe a little too complicated for his own good, and, at 24, sorely lacking anything that resembled a life plan. Perhaps, he needed a good woman to anchor him down and keep his head screwed on straight, but if he had one who lit a flame in his heart and not just his loins, he kept it to himself. Patrick wished he could give Frank stability. Whether Patrick jumped companies to the B&O and lived long enough to play with his grandchildren, or God called him home early and the doc got to say *I told you so,* Frank would need someone down the road.

Of course, Patrick could say much the same about himself. Aside from Sally and her bunch, there were two kinds of women: the kind you dated and the kind you married. There were plenty of the former, but he had yet to meet the latter. He had thoughts about the marrying kind: smart looking and regal like Lawrence Carr's lady, but also one capable of creating a home he could escape to at the end of a hump-busting day shoving rails—someone like Anna Zugel, only older and not a Zugel. Unlike Frank, he had a life plan: B&O and *then* settle down.

"Pass all your tests?" Patrick asked as he watched Frank shuffle a handful of railroad certification cards for the umpteenth time.

"Nope, think I got one more." Frank fanned them again, like a dealer looking for the joker in a deck of playing cards. "Yeah, don't see rules and regs. Damn, I hate that one. I can't half keep up with all the changes."

"The notices on the depot bulletin board? Read 'em. Five minutes a day—that's not too hard. Use the five minutes you take in the office to finish getting dressed. Don't ever expect to make foreman if you can't keep up with it."

"Take a hike, Mr. Perfect. I have bigger plans, and they don't involve making *foreman.* I'm not slogging away my life in some pissant backwater like this taking orders from a jerk like Christian Miller. Here I'm just one more mick sweating it out on the rails. I need wider horizons. Maybe the merchant marine—see the world. Don't you ever want something else? Nothing says you have to be just another Irish knucklehead working the rails. We can do other things."

Patrick watched the crew move about as the sky cleared to blue. Some disappeared inside the section house while others dragged equipment out to one of the wagons. "The B and O is all I want. But I'm not yakking it around. I don't want anyone speculating or planning business around me. If I ever get a chance to get off this crazy train, I'll go on my own schedule and terms. If we get a bonus, it would give me enough cushion to go to Baltimore and hit up the B and O. Johnny Doyle says they'll be hiring soon, and people move up all the time. Said they're so big that a year after getting on, I'd have a shot at a desk job."

"B and O, B and O, B and O," Frank growled. "You have some crazy uppity notion that the B and O's better, but it's all the same shit job. Besides, Johnny doesn't know uptown from shantytown. Stop fooling yourself and make the most of what you have right here. Stop canning tomatoes." Frank fanned out the cards once more. "How many of these do *you* still need?"

"Done. Hate stuff hanging over my head. Want all the paperwork straight when I jump to Baltimore."

"Well, I reckon I can card the last one by the end of next week. That leaves the physical. Why didn't you remind me when you went?"

"Uh, lemme see . . . because I have better things to do than keep track of you? Yeah, that must be it." Grinning, Patrick pulled out his notebook and a pencil stub.

Frank collapsed the fan of cards in his hand and looked hard at his brother. "Pat, when did you . . ." He smacked the deck down on the two-by-twelve. "I'll be damned! Lying to your brother. You haven't *had* a physical yet, have you?"

"Last week. Passed with flying colors."

Frank stood up from the bench and closed the space between them. "You're lying. You're afraid you'll flunk, aren't you?"

Patrick consulted his pocket watch and made some notations. "Be busy here in a little bit. Roller coaster supports and cars coming in anytime now."

"Aw, come on, Pat. *Seriously?*" Frank glared, but Patrick refused to meet his eyes. "Fine, Mr. Foreman. Go ahead and ignore me like you're too busy. Whatever you *don't* say, *sir*. Ever heard of a working stiff, bro? You're taking it to a whole other level. Unless you've had some magical vision that has you bouncing a grandkid on your knee, borrowed time—that's all it is. Borrowed time . . ." Frank saluted his brother and walked into the section house.

Frank always walked a fine line, and with a mouth like his, someone was always tempted to take a swing at him. Patrick had resisted the urge so far, but it wasn't always easy. And if anyone else had been in earshot, he would have sat on him harder so nobody else got the idea that being mouthy was a good idea.

Still, he could do worse in the brother department. Few tangled with the Byrne boys. When you took one on, you knew you'd have to reckon with the other. In fact, serious tangling with any Irishman in Nevis was likely to mean tangling with them all. They protected their own.

Besides, this morning Patrick had a more worrisome problem than making an example of his brother. That problem came in the person of Albert Harmon. A decent enough fellow, he was quick to take directions and genuinely interested in what was going on around him, but he didn't have much to say and he took a lot of watching. Patrick couldn't see any of the crew getting close to him. With luck, he'd grow tired of the imposed solitude and get his uncle to find something more in keeping with his skills—like an office job, doing accounting.

❖ ⊷•⊶ ❖

Patrick was wrong. By midday, *everyone* wanted to get close to Harmon, but not in a good way. He watched with a mixture of horror and fascination as Harmon hoisted the end of a chain over his shoulder and dragged it back toward the rail runner. Halfway down its twenty-foot length, it curved back toward the handful of gandy dancers taking a water break, cutting into the legs of the one on the end.

"Aw, Jesus, watch the ankles!" one of them yelled, jumping back. He turned around and yanked the chain hard, tumbling Harmon onto his back and sending the rest of the crew into peals of laughter.

"Sorry, sorry," Harmon said, getting up and dusting himself off. Then he picked the chain up and dragged it along past the rest of the laughing workers.

"Jumping Jehoshaphat," Patrick murmured, looking back down at the dispatches he had been sharing with Frank and Jack. Harmon was not cutting it. Part of the problem was the resentment any laborer would have harbored for someone coming from money and suddenly deciding to become a common man. And it wasn't long before the crew discovered Harmon's family background and how he came to be here. Even if they hadn't, the man's carriage and his woman's hands would have marked him as a refined gentleman unaccustomed to manual labor. The man had no muscle. The biggest problem, though, was not his station in life or his physique; it was his utter lack of horse sense. Apparently, money could buy you a university degree, but not wisdom.

"Damn," Frank said, gawking as Jack Glynn stood chuckling beside him. "You gotta get rid of that train wreck, Paddy. First thing I ever heard him say: 'sorry.' Pretty well says it all, don't it?"

"Yeah, but where?" Jack asked. "I wouldn't want to get on Miller's bad side."

"Send him back to Daddy," Frank muttered, "before he gets himself or somebody else killed. Pat, they're all refusing to work with him. They had him lubricating all those switches at the Solomons crossing, but Christ, oil was going every which way. He took so much watching, they didn't get their own stuff done—never even got to the angle bars and joints."

Patrick batted a sluggish fly out of his face. "Who last inventoried the section building at mile marker ten?"

"The new one? Nobody. Shouldn't need checking anytime soon."

"Send Dingbat and Connor over there. Pull all the full-service checklists for them to fill out. When that's done, I want a complete inventory of all the parts in the shed, and if they aren't labeled, label 'em. I don't want to see those two again till it's done."

Frank put his hands on his hips and gave his brother a hard look. "Aw, Connor's gonna hate you. He's been grousing the loudest as it is."

"Well, maybe next time Connor'll keep his gob shut." Patrick turned his attention back to his paperwork.

"If it can be marked with an X, Connor can handle it. Anything more complicated, and you'll need someone who can write."

"You volunteering?" Patrick asked, looking up.

"Uh, no."

"College Boy can handle it. Tell Connor that Harmon is to have a pen and paper in his hands at all times. When Connor needs a break, he can send Harmon over to the depot to monitor the dispatches. I'll give Sean a heads-up to keep him busy with nothing. That should keep him out of trouble, and all of us safer."

"Does he know Morse code?"

"If you'd been reading the bulletin board, you'd know dispatches are now coming in by both telegraph *and* telephone. All he has to do is man the phone. Sean'll handle the real stuff."

Frank flushed, but instead of directly engaging the slight, he huffed off. "Don't kill the messenger, Connor," he said, just loud enough to be overheard by the others. "I'm all for booting his bum out of here, too. *Nursemaids* is all we are."

Strike two, Frank Byrne. Patrick clenched his jaw and walked away. They would have it out before the end of the day, hopefully in private—a public chewing-out would only make it worse for Frank. Sometimes, he just didn't give enough of a damn about the politics of the situation. Bad attitude would prevent him from ever being promoted to foreman. The job was mostly about good judgment—never one of Frank's strong suits.

CHAPTER SEVEN

Got It in Writing

As Dr. Bagley poked and prodded, Patrick took a deep breath and looked out at the whitecaps on the bay. The infrastructure was complete—grid for the amusement park marked, rail line laid—and finally, after months of preparation, something great was rising. Construction had moved on to finer details of the grand scheme. In a matter of days, the boardwalk had rolled down a mile of shoreline, and new sideshow, concession, and arcade buildings, in muted earth tones, were popping up like mushrooms all along its length.

"Like what you see?" Doc asked, shifting his stethoscope.

"Keeps me out of the bread line, Doc. Mr. Carr and company are pushing hard to finish by summer. Once the buildings along the board-walk are up, we'll be hauling freight like crazy. You can already feel it picking up."

"Lots of talk about the scaffolding down near the end, Doc said," moving the stethoscope again. "Breathe."

"Roller coaster," Patrick said, taking another breath. "You didn't see the big metal pieces we hauled in here late last week?" He watched the horde of workmen around the area designated for the roller coaster. "They say bigger than the one at Coney."

"Like to see that. It's growing higher and longer by the day. Beginning of the week, we couldn't see any of it from here. I might try it. Don't much think Alice would be up for it, though. What else you heard?"

"As far west as you can go," Patrick said, tilting his head in the general direction, "they've cleared a large section of woods. Know where I mean? Racetrack and stables going in there. Fancy ballroom and dancing and liquor over there, too."

"Gambling, too, I expect. The missus *definitely* won't be going there." Doc paused to listen, then moved his stethoscope back to a place on Patrick's chest he had listened to earlier. "Whole lot of ladies won't want to see all that vice coming to town."

Patrick started to shrug, but Doc's hand on his shoulder stilled him. His interest shifted to the stickball game in the open field at the end of Fifth Street. "Have you seen the baseball diamond Carr built? It's soggy from all the rain, but finished. Bleachers, lots of grass—as fine a ball field as I've ever seen." He sized up the stickball players. The teams appeared pretty even: a few string beans a head taller than the rest though probably not much older, a couple of half-pints, and the rest in-betweeners. One of the bigger kids lined up at home plate, doing his best Honus Wagner impression.

"Honus," he mumbled.

"Wagner?" You like baseball?"

"Oh, yeah," Patrick said, pulling back to look the doctor in the face. "Honus Wagner—best shortstop ever. Saw him play for Pittsburgh at an exhibition match in Baltimore last year, when I was knocking on B and O's door. Rough-and-ready field, but packed—wall-to-wall people, you know? Game ended in a big brawl, fans and both teams in on it. It was great!"

Doc leaned forward and tapped Patrick's chest, making quiet thumping sounds as he moved across. "Carr could do worse than pump up attendance at the park by bringing in an exhibition game or two. The Baylanders—what do you think?"

"I could ride that train. Supposedly, Carr's gonna let us all watch a game for free. That'd be something, but he didn't get rich by giving things away." He looked back out the window. Somehow, the Honus impersonator had gotten on base. If this were his house, Patrick would have run the ballplayers down the road a piece. Not that they were interfering with anything going up in the vacant lot, but the outfield was on the town side, and windows were expensive. He had broken a few in his time but never had to pay for one. He ran with a tight bunch; nobody ratted.

"Mm-m." Doc's hand tightened on Patrick's shoulder.

He glanced at Doc's face: focused but unreadable.

Dr. Bagley moved his stethoscope higher on Patrick's chest. "Haven't seen you in here in a while, even though I told you to come back and see me in six months. Don't suppose Harry Cooley's passing put the fear of the Lord in you?"

Patrick shook his head and checked the game again—two men on base. "Ten hours a day, one day off—it's all I can do to keep my head above water, Doc. Good man, Harry. Nobody knows when God's gonna punch their ticket."

Doc withdrew his stethoscope, and Patrick studied his face again. It mirrored his own: concern and apprehension. But maybe there was also something there he couldn't share.

Doc shook his head. "Sometimes God gives us a little wave—like a catcher throwing signals. It doesn't sound good in there," he said, tapping on Patrick's chest. "Murmuring, heart working hard, sounds like inflammation—"

"But better than before, right, Doc?"

"Shortness of breath?" Doc asked, draping the stethoscope over his neck.

Patrick's gaze returned to the game outside—bases loaded. "Nope. I've never felt better."

"How old are you?"

"Twenty-six."

Doc sat down at his desk and scratched a few notes on his writing pad, then pushed back in his chair and sighed, fixing the young railroad man with a look of concern. "If you don't slow down and take it easy, you won't see twenty-seven, dangerous profession or not. It's simple: less stress, no physical labor. You're beginning to wheeze, and your heartbeat is irregular. What the rheumatic fever destroyed, I can't repair."

"You'll sign my clearance, though, right? Patrick looked him square in the eye with a hopeful smile. "They've temporarily offered me Harry Cooley's position. More money. But you've got to sign the form or they'll find somebody else."

A noncommittal "Mm-m" was the only response he got as Doc swiveled in his chair and wrote another note.

"Listen, Doc, I've got five mouths to feed. I am *this close*"—he pinched his thumb and forefinger together—"to getting an office job with the Baltimore and Ohio. But it won't happen if you don't sign the blessed form. *Please?* This is all going to work out so I can ease back on the heavy lifting, but only if you help me out here. I promise. Please, Doc, I don't have a death wish. I'm pacing myself, delegating the tough stuff." He waved the railroad medical form at the doctor.

Doc snatched the form, scribbled across the bottom, and shoved it back at the dogged Irishman. "I wish I could say you were going to be around long enough to be the death of me. Better have a desk job next time I see y—"

The sound of shattering glass sent both men ducking for cover under the examining table. Patrick peeked above the windowsill. The ball game was over, and youngsters were scattering in all directions, the scoring potential swept away with one bad swing. Should have lined up better.

"One of mine?" the doctor asked.

Patrick motioned next door.

Relief showed in Doc's face. "On second thought, this is the last time we negotiate. You be back here in four weeks or I'm contacting the railway board. Now, scoot on out of here." He stood up, shoved his stethoscope and a folder into the leather satchel, and lifted his bowler off the hickory hall tree by the door. "Alice!" he yelled up the stairs. "I have to head over to the Ryans' and deliver a baby. Don't know when I'll be back. Number three—shouldn't be too long."

Patrick scooped his hat off the table and slapped Doc on the back as he walked out. "Four weeks it is. Never count an Irishman out, Doc. And this time next year, I'll have a new doctor in Bal-ti-more." He sauntered out with the air of a man who had been given a new lease on life, even though it was only on paper.

CHAPTER EIGHT

The Wesson

Five months into construction, the Bayside Park Limited Partnership appeared to be content with the 120 acres it owned. With one exception, it had not tried to push northward into the established town of Nevis. The only incursion was on the town's southern fringe, where railroad, legal, and other professionals settled into several new two-story brick office buildings across from the depot. Did Lawrence Carr covet the area beyond? Like King David pining for Bathsheba. He had big plans for the whole area, but his ambitions to the north would have to wait until the park was completed.

Ascribing to the maxim that nothing introduced lawsuits and other complications as swiftly and surely as large sums of money, the firm of Wesson, Pepper and Smith moved in at the same time ground broke on the park. They leased several offices on the ground floor of the corner structure eventually referred to simply as the Wesson Building. Chesterfield Pepper practiced as Mr. Carr's personal lawyer, and Myron Smith was a newly certified public accountant. The jury was still out, so to speak, on Wesson. Apparently a silent partner or figurehead, he had not been seen or even mentioned since the firm moved in.

The rail line leased space on the second floor, directly above Wesson, Pepper and Smith. Other occupants of the upper floors included other equally important names and titles related to park business, none of whom had reason to interact or concern themselves with a common railroad man or townsfolk.

Normally, from this section of town, there was an unobstructed view of the morning sun when it rose above the horizon, setting the calm gray bay water alight in sparkling shimmers. Not this morning. Unlike on the previous days, which had begun with blue skies and ended with heavy clouds and downpour, today's rain had come before sunrise. The Byrne brothers sat on a green slat depot bench halfway between the ticket window and the end of the porch.

"Hit it again," Patrick said, passing his coffee mug back to his brother.

Frank picked up a copper kettle off the porch and refilled the cup, pushed the kettle back behind a paper sack, and passed the cup back.

"Sean know you've got that out here?"

"Hell, no—took it when his back was turned. He's good for another hour."

Patrick sighed. "I'll make myself scarce till I meet with Miller at nine thirty."

Frank leaned his head back against the depot's clapboard wall, closed his eyes, and said, "If I didn't have to be in town till nine thirty, I'd a' slept till nine."

"Can't sleep for worrying about things not getting done," Patrick said, nodding toward the track.

Frank gave a snort. "Don't flatter yourself. It'll survive until you get there. Nobody's irreplaceable—except me, of course. If you hadn't put me in depot hell with Sean after Murphy took a swan dive off that ladder, I could sub for you out there. Lift the load. Think about it next time you fob me off on some crap assignment."

"I know. Makes my heart bleed, it really does." Patrick studied the building across the street a while, then reached down and picked up a marble-size rock off the decking and lofted it up to the Chesapeake offices right above Wesson and Pepper, where it bounced off a window shutter. "Someday, I want that office right there—Broderick's."

Frank half opened one eye. "Not satisfied with section foreman? Been what, almost two months since Harry passed? Lots of other people would step forward for Broderick's office. Don't get your heart set on it."

"Yeah, but not everybody's thinking about it, angling for it every day of the world."

"Get your feet back on the ground and deal with what you've got. Charlie Broderick ain't never leaving."

"Not what I'm hearing."

Frank opened both eyes. "They're promoting that old codger?"

"Retiring come summer," Patrick said with a grin. "Then moving to Shee-ca-go. Least, that's what I'm hearing. I'm gonna bust my butt for that job." He was silent for a moment, staring at the window. "Then B and O," he added, almost as an afterthought.

"Well, if it's anybody around here, I hope it's you, but don't count on it. Not if Miller has any say. *His* office—that's the one we need somebody new in." Frank picked up a pebble and side-armed it toward the other second-story window. It hit the window pane, shattering the glass and eliciting a string of profanities from inside. Frank bounced up and hotfooted it back into the depot. Patrick darted down the steps and into the middle of the street, where he stood, hands on hips, staring up at the window. Somebody was in the office, but it seemed too early for Miller. Seconds later, Miller's pink face appeared at the window, glowering out through the shards of glass still hanging in the sash. His scowl settled on Patrick.

"Byrne!" he shouted. "Need to talk to you." Then he was gone.

Patrick approached the building with the enthusiasm of a steer on market day. It was a rare day that Miller decided to come to town, and his showing this early couldn't mean anything good.

———•◦•———

Patrick muttered to himself as he climbed the stairs to the rail offices. Christian Bartholomew Miller, lord high muck-a-muck of the Chesapeake Rail Express line in southern Maryland, had started out as a man of moderate means. But the right family social and political connections had enabled him to skip the grimier rank-and-file jobs in the company and burrow his way into a powerful desk position at the Chesapeake's East Baltimore freight facility. When he remained there, everything in Nevis ran smoothly, but when he came to town, everything went south for Patrick's crew. And it tended to stay that way until he moved on to other things and allowed subordinates enough time to institute work-arounds to his ill-conceived, typically inept procedures.

Patrick knew how to play Miller, but it would be exhausting. He took off his hat and entered the austere office with a little less swagger than usual.

"You wanted to talk to me, sir?"

"Hmm." Miller kept his eyes on his paperwork. "Who broke the window?"

"Hard to say, sir," Patrick said, looking past his boss to the triangles of glass still puttied into the window sash. "Maybe kids. There's been a bunch hanging around playing ball. Broke a window down near Doc's the other day. What's going on?"

Miller looked up and glared. Patrick kept his mouth shut and waited, slowly turning his hat in his hands.

"Got a red ball coming in Friday, day after tomorrow, and one next Friday," Miller said, returning to his papers. "Make sure markers go out down to Ducketts Mill Bridge, especially Brickhouse and Old Solomons Island crossings. Don't want any of the locals running livestock across there at an inopportune time."

"Yes sir, standard procedure. Can't have cows shutting down the line. What kind of priority freight?"

Miller picked up a yellow manifest from the desk. "On the Eight seventy-three this Friday morning, May tenth, there will be steel girders, three flatcars of lumber, two barrel organs from the North Tonawanda Barrel Organ Factory in New York, six crates from Mills in Chicago packed with such niceties as three Twentieth Century slot machines, three Mills Owl slots, one Dewey Chicago Twin, one Jockey poker machine. Criminy sakes, hope they can control all this gambling," he murmured, shaking his head.

"Yes sir," Patrick said. "If Bayside Park generates enough money, somebody besides the partnership may want a piece of it." Like Miller, the unspoken thought of thugs from Chicago muscling into Nevis was not a comfortable one. Thugs from Philly might be okay. Patrick had grown up with quite a few Irish lads who came by their living less than honestly, but overall, they were reasonable as long as you stayed out of their business. But Chicago? Seeing as how they'd be Italian . . . "That all, sir?" Patrick asked, stirring from his thoughts.

Miller shook his head. "From Detroit's Caille Brothers Company," he continued, running his index finger along the page, "we have five crates, including two Centaur Lone Star Twin slot machines, five jumbo counter slots, peep shows, a musical floor machine, an Angldile Springless Automatic Scale traveling with a sign that promises 'honest weight,' and an assortment of Adams gum vending machines including tutti-frutti and honey flavored. A little tame for the powers that be in Chicago, wouldn't you think? And last but far from least, *ponies and other animals.*" He lifted a well-manicured hand. "You get the drift."

Patrick stifled a snort and looked down at his hat, rotating it another quarter turn. "Must be some special ponies if we couldn't find any around here," he said, avoiding Miller's face.

"Don't know, don't care. If Mr. Carr wants to throw his money away on ponies that waltz and fart fairy dust, *we* don't care. Anything he wants."

Miller put the manifest down and pulled out another yellow sheet from the same stack as the first. "Friday morning, May seventeenth, on the eight-seventy-three: three crates from the International Mutoscope Reel Company packing a Liberty Bell Striker, Mutoscope (Indian), and various peep shows; seven crates from the Mills Novelty Company in Chicago, contents unknown; and eight crates from the American Radiator and Standard Sanitary Corporation. The park is going to be a modern wonder, with the best pissing and crapping facilities this neck of the woods has ever seen." He tossed the page on top of the first one and raised an eyebrow at Patrick. "Puzzled? Questions? Comments?"

"No sir. Well, yes sir, but not about the shipments. I wanted to ask . . . well, Charlie Broderick . . . he's leaving."

"How'd you find out?" He waved the question aside. "No matter. It won't be vacant long," he said, nodding toward the office next door as he swiveled in his chair. "I've been tasked with making a recommendation—someone who knows our system and this area."

Patrick felt his heart gallop. Pain radiated out across his chest in a tight band that traveled around to his back. He took a slow, shallow breath. Broderick's job was exactly the respite he needed—less physically taxing. A desk job would expand his skills and make him more marketable with B &O.

"If it's not too late," he said, staring Miller square in the face, "I would like to be considered for the job, sir. Throw my hat in, so to speak."

Miller looked thoughtful for a moment, although it was not clear to Patrick what inspiration might come from staring at a blank wall. Miller stood up and walked around the glass shards on the floor, to the damaged window. He looked out toward the masonry archway now partially constructed at the park entrance. "I don't need to tell you we're moving into a critical period for the park: heavy shipments of steel and lumber and fragile, damageable goods like the carousel and all these arcade games. I know I'm leaning on you, but please understand, I'm under enormous pressure right now. I don't think it needs saying that you're the linchpin on my track out here." He turned and faced Patrick. "I've decided to recommend *you* for the job—on a temporary basis, mind you. Purely a *trial* run. *Make it work.* You do a good job, I'll recommend we make it permanent."

Patrick blinked. Miller being *nice*? Maybe when hell iced over. He glanced toward the window. Nope, something didn't add up. He had missed something. His thoughts galloped.

"Of course, you'll have to continue your foreman responsibilities until it's all approved. I do have the payroll to appoint an assistant foreman to ease the transition. Do you want to recommend someone, or should I—"

"Frank Byrne," Patrick said without hesitation. "Harry and I've been training him for a while. He's ready, sir."

"You're recommending your *brother*?"

"Only because he's the best choice, sir. Nobody else comes close."

"Very well," Miller said, sitting back down and scrawling something on a tablet. "Tell him, but make it clear it's temporary until everything shakes out. Got it?"

Patrick nodded, still wondering what Miller's game was. Should it matter, though, as long as he and Frank came out the better? The answer was a resounding no. This would be a good time to make a quick exit. "I'll have Sean tell 'em to slow it down around number three," he said over his shoulder.

"Stop. I thought I told you to keep ahead."

Patrick turned around. This man was the child even a mother could hate. "We are, but you can't go open throttle on the section we just repaired. The speed and all the rain are ripping the roadbed up like a buzz saw. Something about that section isn't right. We can keep on it all the time, but the story'll be the same: centrifugal force pushing those rails out, and the saturated ground is making it worse.

"If you trust me enough to give me Broderick's job, you need to let me do things the way they need done. The whole area needs reworked—right-of-way and onto some private farmland next to it . . . Mrs. McClelland's farm." He returned to the desk. "Someone needs to talk to her about getting on her land and making some changes. If we could get permission to dig a swale and create a berm on the farm side, it would catch and control the overflow if it floods in there. Simple fix, pending the owner's permission. I'd be glad to go talk to her myself, if need be."

"I'll see what I can do, but no promises."

"Actually, the safest bet would be to delay those shipments," Patrick said, recklessly pushing forward, "because I can't guarantee everything will hold out there when they want to run full blast—it being wet and all."

Miller pushed back in his chair and rolled away from the desk in a smooth, calm motion that belied the anger boiling up in his eyes. "We're not here to play it safe, Mr. Byrne. Why am I paying you all this money if you can't deliver? I've been clear from the beginning: if you can't meet the deadlines, someone else can. Christ, I would have thought the bonus and the chance at Broderick's position would speak for themselves. If that doesn't motivate you, I can't imagine what would."

"Sure," Patrick said, bobbing his head, "money is always a motivator. But even with a bonus, all this rain we've been having . . . If you send a train barreling through there and it washes out, you're risking the rail workers' lives, the trains, Carr's cargo, and a timely opening. I want my conscience clear. At least deadbeat 'em for a while to pound it all down."

"Listen here, Mr. Byrne," Miller said, punctuating each word with a jab of his index finger, "running empty cars doesn't fill the coffers. Carr has thousands of dollars riding on this project—setting it up and opening on time. The Chesapeake will stand behind its commitment, so *get . . . it . . . done.*" Miller pulled a pen out of the cup on his desk and pulled the paper stack at his elbow closer.

The man was too pigheaded to listen to reason. The shipments would still come in as scheduled. Patrick would do the best he could, and pray about the rest. He was turning to leave when a thought popped into his head. "Hey, what's the story with the C and O?"

Miller stiffened and put down his pen, eyes narrowing as if a beam of sunshine had suddenly blinded him. "You've heard something?"

Patrick's question had the effect he intended. He watched, fascinated, almost seeing the wheels spinning frantically in his boss's head.

"They're close to buying us out," Patrick continued. "The Chesapeake Railway, that is, and all the corporate people are running for the exits, scared they'll lose their jobs. Leastways, that's what I'm hearing."

"Poppycock," Miller said, shifting his eyes back to his paperwork. "Ignore it. The only people spreading those rumors are the ones not busy *doing* their jobs."

"*Whew,* that's a relief." Patrick offered an insincere smile and headed for the door.

"Hold up," Miller said. "One more thing before you run off. Who else handles the till besides Sean?"

"Till? No one, sir. Why?"

"Go find me Sean. Oh, and about the window—I want a name."

"Yes sir, but Sean, he's the only one on the tele . . ." Patrick stopped and began again. "Harmon can take over for a while. He's been real handy helping out. Took to office work like a duck to water, sir. I think he's ready to move on to bigger things."

He left before Miller could reply. "*Special ponies,*" he mumbled as he closed the office door. What the snoots wouldn't come up with next! He headed down the hall to the payroll office.

Looking after curve three was going to be a real bastard. May as well set up tents for the crew and keep them out there all week. Maybe they could handle it. If not, Miller would blame Patrick and can him. The only possible bright spot to that would be that he could then go beg for a job with the B&O, where he wanted to be anyway. They might even can Miller, too. The thought made him smile.

As unpleasant as his dealings with Miller were, Patrick *had* learned two things of value. First, Miller was an easy man to read, and right now he did not feel secure in his position. As far as Patrick knew, there were no rumors about a buyout of the Chesapeake line, but he sure had Miller buying it. Second, like manna from heaven, a new assignment for Harmon had just come to Patrick: mucking out the incoming livestock car.

CHAPTER NINE

Ticked Off

T he depot was busy for a Saturday. In a business built on punctuality, where policy mandated that timepieces maintain accuracy to within four seconds a day, the ten o'clock express was an almost unthinkable half hour late. An antsy crowd of frazzled mothers, fidgety youngsters finally outdoors after a week of rain, and pressed-for-time entrepreneurs jostled for space around the ticket window. The newly formed Nevis Temperance League added to the hubbub as it marched and waved hand-stenciled signs condemning the evils of alcohol and offering salvation to anyone willing to abstain from the devil's own brew. As they drew near the depot steps, they seamlessly shifted from a funereal "Amazing Grace" to an equally somber rendition of "The Drunkard and His Family" before turning and marching off in the opposite direction.

By contrast, the inside of the depot seemed as calm as a graveyard. The big round clock hanging on the front wall tracked the lateness of the express. The teletype was unusually silent, and Harmon sat at the ticket window, nervously licking his lips and repeatedly glancing at Sean for any calming word to give the peevish, anxious patrons. Sean kept his nose in his ledgers and ignored him as the tension within him tautened with every second the clock ticked off.

As the impatient crowd lay siege to the ticket window, three youths added to the commotion by tossing their handball up on the mansard roof and scrambling through the crowd to catch it as it skipped and bounced off at odd angles.

Frank pressed up close to Harmon and looked at the faces hovering inches from the ticket window. He was sick of the confusion. Even on a normal day, he detested the confining work of the depot. Only a bookworm like Sean could warm to it. The rain had stopped, at least. Eyeing the shirtwaisted, gore-skirted women as they marched by, Frank leaned toward the window.

"Sean, who are those old biddies with the placards?"

Sean glanced up. "Temperance League. Nevis is going all in. If I hear 'Stand firm for temp'rance, nobly stand' one more time, I'm going to pull the bottle out of that bottom drawer and empty it in my coffee. Is the tall bulgy woman with the gray hair still out there?"

"Right in front," Frank said, picking her out right away.

Sean looked at Harmon who had inched his chair back away from the noisy clamor at the ticket window. "Harmon, might want to watch out the freight door for the express. It'll be smoky just over the tree line." He turned back to Frank. "It's that old battle-ax Camilla McClelland." She got wind of beer concessions going in the arcades, and now all the church ladies are out to save everybody. Never mind that half the population in town is German and already brewing their own at home, and the other half single Irish men, turning in every night with a whiskey bottle tucked next to 'em. Old broad has nothing but time on her hands since her old man kicked the bucket. Somebody needs to wed and bed—"

"Frustrated old spinster," Frank agreed. "That's her dairy farm, isn't it, out there before the bridge, fence posts leaning every which-a-way? All hell will break lose someday if that herd wanders outta there and ends up on the tracks. Everybody'll be in trouble."

"Maybe, but I heard it's tobacco keeping her place afloat."

"Hmm," Frank said. "But they could modernize some equipment and get something going. Smart man would marry her and start shipping milk outta there by rail. They can refrigerate it now, you know—milking machines, too."

"And you know this how?"

Frank sighed. "I'm not gonna walk ties forever. Always looking, Sean. Something else for me out there somewhere."

Sean leaned back in his chair. "Good for you, but don't do it. Don't marry the old hag. Still, you might want to watch what you're calling an 'old biddy.' Thought I saw your sister Moira out there leading the parade this morning."

"Aw, jiminy," Frank said, taking off his hat and sliding his fingers inside along the sweatband. He put it back on with a tug of the brim to pull it tight. "Why are they over here pestering us? They should be across the street, making Carr's people miserable."

Sean got up from his desk and joined Frank at the window. "Moira said they're trying to slow him down, hit him where it hurts: wallet and timeline. Don't be hard on her. She means well."

Frank fixed Sean with a glare. "Sean Michael Murphy, if I didn't know you better . . . Stay away from my sister, for both our sakes."

"*Talking*, no courting," Sean said. Blushing, he went back to his desk.

"Maybe I should let you have her. She'd make a new man out of ya."

Sean brightened, and Frank turned away, scowling. He studied the marchers, trying to locate Moira. "Patrick look a little under the weather lately?" he said. Tired? Dragging around?"

"Not particularly," Sean replied. "Then again, I never see him anywhere but in here. Why?"

"No reason." His shoulders froze in mid shrug as he watched a green handball spatter mud on three young girls. He bounded for the door. "It'll be our jobs if somebody gets run over by an incoming train." He swung the door open and pounded down the wooden porch steps toward the ballplayers. "You kids are gonna hurt someone!" he growled. He pointed down the street. "Get in that field if you want to horse around. Any ball I catch, I'm keeping."

He turned to see Albert Harmon motioning him toward the freight door. The train was on its way. Under the eyes of the exasperated crowd, Frank grabbed the thick pulley rope, hoisted the door aloft, and came back inside for the mailbag and outbound packages. Sean would wait for him to finish before announcing the train's approach. Not that it mattered anyway. About a mile out, the engineer would let loose with a single whistle blast announcing his approach.

Frank threw everything into a handcart and pushed it near the siding. "Line up," he called out to the crowd, waving them back a safe distance from the track.

"Mine! I got it, I got it!" one of the youngsters yelled, backpedaling across the lot, eyes locked on the arcing handball.

A man in a suit and bow tie skittered backward, trying to avoid the hurtling boy and a large mud puddle. As the ball smacked into the boy's outstretched hand, he toppled the man, and both went down.

The youngster lay where he fell, gasping for air, while the man scrambled to his feet. "What the devil!" he snarled. "Come here, you!" He yanked the wide-eyed youngster up by an arm and shook him. "What's your name?"

"Martin Byrne, sir," the boy stuttered. He turned and spat mud on the ground. "Sorry, I didn't see you, sir."

"Damn Irish see what you want to see. Not learn any manners down there in the Foggy Bottom, Martin Byrne? Your father too drunk to discipline you? I could do him a favor—"

Frank closed the distance in three strides and grabbed the arm holding his younger brother. "I suggest you turn the lad loose," he said. "I didn't learn any manners down in the Bottom, either, and I'd hate to give you a proper drubbing on behalf of his sorry Irish dad."

The man let go and stepped back a pace as Martin scrambled out of the way on all fours. "Martin, go home," Frank said. The boy took off, followed by a half-dozen others, caps in hand, shirttails flapping.

The man scanned the faces in the crowd. "You and who else, Byrne?" Now Frank could hear the German accent. "I don't see anybody around to stick up for you." He took a step forward. "How well do you Irish boys do on your own?"

The noise around the ticket window grew quiet as the crowd drew a tight circle around the two. Reliably, a few voices started agitating for a fight.

Frank smiled and took a step backward. "Go on, folks. Show's over. Nothing to see here."

He turned to follow his little brother, who was lurking on the steps of the Wesson Building. He didn't look hurt, but he needed a talking-to. And better a lecture from a brother who had been down the same path than from an absent-minded father who often could not recall where he put his glasses.

"Big words," the man taunted. "The bigger they come, the quicker they turn tail and run."

Frank turned and swung. His fist caught the base of the other man's jaw, and he fell like a rock.

"Next time a man takes a step back from you, duck."

The man didn't get up, but three others stepped forward with fight in their eyes. Not liking the odds, Frank bolted.

Patrick came to a halt halfway across the street and did a double take at the sight of his brother, running full tilt with three burly, cursing Germans not far behind. It seemed that only the greater age of his pursuers was keeping Frank from the worst beating of his life.

Bemused, Patrick watched as Frank circled the block, peeled back toward the depot, and vaulted the stockade fence into the rail yard and gave them the slip. Patrick waited a minute to make sure they didn't double back, and then he, too, jumped the fence. Frank had ducked behind a stack of lumber, but took off again when he caught sight of his older brother coming hell-bent his way.

"Aw, God, Frank, you've got a pattern here." Patrick grabbed his younger brother by the top of his arm and slung him up against the fence. Frank's right hook went wide, and Patrick doubled him over with a knee to the midsection. "Christ, kid, stop fighting me! I'd be the only friend you've got right now."

"Ease up," Frank gasped. "I'm done."

Patrick let go and watched his brother sink to the ground, back against the fence, chest heaving.

"Bit off a little more than you could chew, smart aleck? What'd ya do this time?"

"I didn't do nothing."

"Mouth off? When are you gonna learn?"

"Over at the depot, Peter Glass—he was mouthing off about Dad and he had his hands all over Martin. What was I supposed to do, let him whup the poor kid? They were playing around, that's all."

"You can't fix ignorance with violence. He was baiting you, and you're too thin-skinned to ignore it. How bad did you hurt him?"

"Like Granddad taught us: good shoulder, and all my weight behind it."

"Save the bragging for later. What I'm asking is, they gonna send for Doc Bagley and the law, or is this now a case of bad blood?"

"Dunno. I didn't stick around long enough."

Patrick put his hands on his hips and took a breath to calm himself. "You'll be the death of me. Get out on the track and don't come back till I get you. See if you can stay out of trouble for a while. Sean can make do with Harmon."

CHAPTER TEN

The Switch

The train whistled its departure warning. Patrick frowned and checked his watch. The express forty-five minutes off schedule? Still sitting in the station was a blue passenger coach trimmed in bold silver lettering: *Chesapeake Railway Express*. Yep, it was the 405, with Wasserman engineering and Smithton shoveling coal. Wasserman was never late. Patrick had half a mind to circle around and see if someone else was up in the engine cab today.

He began a mental inventory: track problems, siding delays for higher-priority trains, a careless dispatcher not taking his job seriously. Track problems could mean *he* was the careless one, and curve number three came soaring to the top of his list. A week of on-and-off heavy rain had been doing the devil's work on the track between Nevis and Ducketts Mill Bridge. With all the freight coming in, the last thing he needed was a washout of that busy section. Roll 'em in and get 'em out—that was all anyone understood. His crew had gone out early every day for the

66

past week, trying to stay ahead of nature. Miller was useless, so unless Patrick scrounged up help from somewhere else, his was a losing battle.

By the time Patrick completed his mental inventory, the express had pulled out and was fading into the distance. The engineer blasted the whistle one last time as it rounded a curve in the track and disappeared beyond a stand of oak and scrub pine at the northern city limit.

The depot yard was a peaceful, deserted place. Patrick saw no evidence of the bad blood he had witnessed just moments ago—no dead bodies, and no cops. He counted Frank's blessings for him. It looked as though any resentments had been shrugged off, bundled onto the train, or buried for future reference.

He pushed through the depot door to find Sean, at his desk in the corner, probably transcribing the latest telegraph dispatch. All those dots and dashes—Patrick got lost in them. The telephone system was good to have in reserve, but the railway would never trust the precise information on times, freight numbers, and locations to a telephone. He surveyed the room and wondered where Harmon had gotten off to.

The small potbelly woodstove in the corner pumped out heat like a blast furnace. Patrick filled a cup with hot water from the battered copper kettle sitting on top. "God, Sean, it's like an inferno in here. Is hot tea worth all this?" He yanked his red bandanna off and undid two shirt buttons. Then he hunted down Sean's discarded tea ball and dunked it in his cup until the water turned honey brown.

"Good morning to you, too," Sean said without looking up. "And the answer is always *yes* to hot tea."

Patrick took a sip of tea and wandered over to the counter, near the telephone. "What's all this nonsense?" he asked, running his fingertip across a mysterious lump shrouded under a gold linen cloth. "Father Paul been by?" He flipped up a corner of the fabric and peeked, expecting to see a chalice underneath instead of the glass container and strange-looking piston device shoved down into it.

"It makes coffee. D'ye know nothing?" Sean mumbled, still absorbed in his paperwork.

"Dear God, don't let any of the men see this." Patrick shoved it into the nearest cabinet and slammed the door. "And *this*?" He picked up a red and white can with a picture of a turbaned man in a flowing robe. "*Hills Brothers. Highest grade java and mocha,*" he read. "*San Francisco, California* . . . Harmon?"

"Harmon."

"*Two pounds?* Christ, you'll have a regular old coffee klatsch in here before you know it. When are the Germans coming over?" He tossed the can up next to Harmon's newfangled contraption and parked himself on the oak stool near the desk. From here, Patrick had a clear view of the freight room through a large window beside the freight roller door. Harmon was there, sorting the head-high stack of new crates, baskets, and boxes.

"All that come in on the express?" Patrick asked, nodding toward the room.

"Things picking up. Wait till everything's open and people are renting cottages down here. Might need a bigger room—and another Harmon."

Patrick laughed. "God help us. Until then, I'd say he's going to have to put some effort into it to get things shipshape before quitting time."

"And if he gets it all done," Sean said, a note of mild irritation in his voice, "he can get up tomorrow and look forward to repeating it with the next shipment."

"Why was the express late?" Patrick asked, rolling the stool toward Sean. He reached around him and pulled the latest train schedule out of his box. "Something I need to add to the list?"

"Nope, not us." Sean ground the tip of the pencil into the paper he was writing on, and tossed the pencil aside. "Late from the Washington end."

"Excellent." Patrick stretched his long legs and studied the schedule, written out in Sean's large, elegant hand. Then he sailed it back into the box, nearly clipping Sean's ear in the process.

Sean brushed the top of his ear and pulled down a leather-bound ledger from the wooden shelf above the desk. "How do you do that? All those ten-digit numbers—you worry me to death. I make a copy for you every morning. Take it."

Patrick shook his head and laughed. "Everybody's got a skill." He glanced toward the storage room in time to see a stack of empty boxes topple in Harmon's direction. "Well, almost everyone. Dots and dashes for you, numbers for me. I trust you, you trust me, and everything runs smoothly. No need to ruin a beautiful thing."

Sean made a single notation in ink and shoved the ledger back in its place. "Yeah? Then what's this rumor I hear about you wanting to jump train to the B and O?"

"Just rumors. Where'd you hear it?'

"I have my sources," Sean said.

"Tell Frank to quit talking out of school and mind his own business. He gets everything bass-ackward. I'll be working here till I die, in the same job I have now—unless you'd like to take Christian Miller out behind the woodshed."

If I'm the last to hear, don't even bother saying good-bye."

Patrick leaned over and eased Sean's final transcription out from under his hand. "Staying here. Now let me see what else you have. All long trains," he said, studying the schedule. "We've been hanging out on curve number three for quite a while. I hold my breath every time a hog barrels through there. Which brings up me to the main reason I'm here: Miller said some heavy loads are coming up."

Sean nodded.

Patrick lowered his voice. "I need you to figure out a way to keep the track clear for about twenty-four hours before they come through."

"Hah!" Sean leaned forward and slapped Patrick's knee. "That's a good one."

"Do I look like I'm kidding?" Patrick said, stone faced. "We need time to rework the curve. Can't do it piecemeal. Fix this piece," he said, moving an imaginary tie, "and the next one's out of whack." He moved another tie with his left. "Got to do it all at once." He clasped his hands together. "Never seen ground so waterlogged. I've half a mind to send a search party beyond the right-of-way to look for a spring. Don't understand it."

"You know Mr. George? Carts in all that corn and stuff to ship out? Been farming for thirty years and never seen so much rain. Says he's really hurting—may lose his whole crop."

"Doesn't seem to slow down the amusement park any," Patrick said. "They've been out there every day, never mind the weather."

"Lots of money at stake. The more money gets involved, I guess the more serious you are. If *you're* really serious about delaying incoming shipments, I can ask Miller, but I doubt it'll do any good."

"Miller told me to handle whatever comes up, carte blanche. He's checking with the farm owners to get their permission to relandscape up there. "

Sean looked Patrick square in the eyes. "Well, Miller gave me different marching orders, and until I hear directly from him, Carr's freight remains top priority on the line. Zippity-zip, those trains come in, and zappity-zap, back out they go again. So no can do what you're asking."

Patrick returned the hard look. He'd had his finger on Sean's pulse since they were nippers, growing up on the same riverfront block in Philadelphia. All he had to do was keep his mouth shut and wait out the depot manager. After the indignant stare would come the furrowed brow, and before Sean gave in, a last face-saving slap of whatever Sean had in his hand, down onto the desk.

The line between Sean's two brows deepened. "Jesus H. Christ," Sean said, clicking the top back onto his fountain pen and tossing it onto the desk. "No."

"Great," Patrick said, rising. "Wait . . . *No?*" He sat back down. Sean's train of thought had obviously jumped the track somewhere.

"Damn right, *no*. I'll lose my job. Got to talk to Miller."

"How about a track delay, then—stretch out a couple of arrivals and departures? Give me *something*. The weather's been killing us and we're going under out there."

Sean shook his head. "Sorry, Pat. I can't do it."

Patrick studied Sean's earnest expression a moment, then let out a heavy sigh. "Okay, if that's the way it's gonna be. But make a note in your books I talked to you about track maintenance. Then Miller won't have *my* job when everything goes to hell out there. And can you write '*derailment*,' too?" He handed the last transcription back. "Still plenty of room in the margin on this one. Let me know if there are any drastic changes."

He got up and headed out the back door. What else could he do? With luck, Sean would decide it was safer and easier to impose a twenty-four-hour moratorium—quietly, of course—than get nailed after a load jumped the track. Otherwise, well, Patrick was in a pickle.

"Jiminy sakes, Pat, hold on! Come back. Why you always gotta dump the guilt routine on me?"

Patrick came back inside and let the door slam. Sean was sitting with his head in his hands. "'Cause it works and you end up thanking me later."

"Stuff it, you self-serving jack-ass," Sean growled. "Sit down, and don't say another word." I'm only helping you because I don't want to be out there panhandling with the rest of the layabouts." He fumbled through Patrick's message tray. "Are you worried about the expresses, too, or just the big, heavy loads?"

Patrick read the tension in Sean's posture. He would be willing to negotiate. "Well, all of 'em." Patrick could give a little, but no use starting from a weak position.

Sean rolled his eyes at the trainman. "Come on, Pat. You know I can't shut it *all* down." He found the sheet he wanted, and pulled it from the stack. "My question to you: With the rain slacking up a bit, is there a chance things will dry up by Friday when the first red ball comes through, or do we have to shuffle, delay, and finagle regardless? Give it to me straight."

"The latter. Even if the rain stops completely, we still risk the creek flooding. Whole area's saturated, including upstream."

"Okay, then. Let's assume for argument's sake that it's the fast, heavy loads you're more worried about. Could we work with that?"

"Yep."

"Good. The first red ball Friday is the heavier of the two. It's the killer—lots of fully loaded boxcars, and flatcars with lumber and steel. It'll be the biggest load of freight we have coming in for a while, so if we squeak past that one . . ."

"Here's what I can do," he said, circling a place halfway down the page. "There's no passenger service this week, and Carr has a monopoly on all trains for the week. So far, only two freights are scheduled. The four-oh-two, light freight, is headed to Solomons Wednesday morning with a maintenance layover until Thursday morning, when it comes into Nevis. If we flip-flop the four-oh-two's runs, making it come in and leave Nevis on Wednesday morning, and then go to Solomons, you'll have from Wednesday morning when it clears town, until late Thursday to get things done. I think I can switch those." He ran through the list again, tapping each entry with his pencil until he got to the last one. He shook his head. "All I've got, man."

"We'll take it, Patrick said. "That's what I needed." He got up, grinning broadly. "Oh, one more thing. Miller was in a foul mood this morning. Said not to bother him with the details, so how about we stay on his good side and keep this between friends?"

Sean gave a melodramatic sigh. "I've come to hate your 'one more thing's.' So help me, if you're sellin' me a bill of goods, I'll boot your Connacht ass all the way back to the emerald isle myself. Now, get out of here before I change my mind."

After Patrick got what he needed from Sean, he picked his way through the inner sanctum of the rail yard instead of hunting up a ride out to the crew. Being a section foreman had its benefits: a bit more in the paycheck, getting to sit out the more backbreaking tasks, and the glimmer of chance, eventually, to get off the line altogether. On the downside, Patrick found himself doing a smidge more nursemaiding of adults than he preferred. Right now he could not afford to carry any dead weight, and experience had taught him that if mischief was afoot, it tended to fester at the fringes and in the darkest corners of the yard. He passed the green corrugated-metal maintenance shed and the hump used to slow down incoming loads, and crossed over the short section of track leading to the turntable. The area was predictably deserted, and it would remain so until another Consolidation locomotive pulled in Carr's next freight shipment later in the week.

The turntable had been a compromise of sorts between Carr and the railroad. The Chesapeake Railway considered revenue from Carr's freights a temporary economic expedient in the life of the line and the station—eventually, only passenger service would generate income along the line. Instead of investing big dollars for a turntable, the company had pushed for the far cheaper alternative of a rail loop large enough to turn its locomotives around. Carr had refused to sell or grant rights to partnership land, anticipating greater profit from commercial development of land that would be wasted as right-of-way for any rail loop deal. So he pushed for a turntable design—pricier but requiring much less land. In the end, he anted up the extra money to get what he wanted. The Chesapeake agreed, and in the end nobody gave two hoots what would eventually become of it. Certainly not Patrick. He would be with the B&O by the time the turntable became superfluous and went to rust.

He passed the turntable and kept going. He was not as interested in *what* was down here as *who*: a few slackers he had spied dodging the first work crew. As he approached them, Patrick made a mental note: Moran, Butler, and Reedy, passing a smoke back and forth. They were dressed out for work in their overalls and bandannas, but apparently found it more fulfilling to sit on a stack of ties chewing the fat than earn a paycheck. He could make it a permanent arrangement.

Catching sight of him before he got there, they hopped to their feet, looking for something to appear busy doing. One of them ground out the cigarette under his boot, and the three of them waited, hands in pockets, kicking sand and talking softly among themselves.

"Morning, fellas," Patrick said. Glancing past them, his eyes lit on the nearby maintenance crew's Sheffield handcar, pulled off the rails next to their shed—five hundred pounds, and its steel tires demounted and lying close by. "Just the men I was looking for. Get the Sheffield back on the track here," he said, nodding toward the car. "Load it with enough gear for four, and pump the whole shebang out to Duckett's Mill." Not waiting for a reply, he turned and headed back up the hill. "Night crew needs a few extra men tonight," he called over his shoulder. "Plan on working late."

CHAPTER ELEVEN

Babbling Brooks and Gandy Dancers

Patrick scanned the rails ahead as the rail car clattered along at a good clip. Whatever his three deadbeats thought of him, they didn't let it interfere with getting him where he needed to be. The realization they had caught Byrne's notice seemed to have an energizing effect. When it came to section gangs, Harry Cooley had always run one of the best. Harry might be gone, but as long as Byrne had a say in it, it would remain so.

This track section still looked good: ties, rails, and joint bars aligned and tight; brush and vegetation cut back along the right-of-way; and the ballast looking solid and undisturbed. He wished he felt the same about the northern section. He squinted at the rail line ahead, past the siding coming up in a few hundred feet on the left, to the beginnings of the wide, graceful arc of curve three as it stretched out to the west before swinging back in and heading north across Ducketts Mill Bridge, over Piscataponi Creek. He could not make out the rest of his section: the

76

switch on the far side of the bridge, and the mile or so of track heading south from the switch to the first siding as the line headed down the southern leg to Solomons at the peninsula's tip. As assignments went, the section from here to Nevis was sweet. The mile of curve to the bridge, on the other hand, was hell on earth. There was more shimmying and shaking around those ties than Little Egypt at the Chicago's World's Fair.

Patrick slowed the car and hopped off. This stretch would never pass muster. He had never seen track move this much. He walked the length of the curve up to the bridge, then doubled back to the work crew.

Frank's dark blue work shirt flapped in the breeze from the pick handle he had tossed it over, and he had already sweated through the gray undershirt. Patrick beckoned him over. Frank hopped out of line and jogged over.

"What do you think?" Patrick said, looking down the line of the curve. "We tightened all this up not two weeks back. Too much vibration through here. Got a red ball this Friday and another next week. Friday's will be big and heavy."

Frank nodded. "Engineers are running way too fast—damn ballast scorchers."

Patrick grinned. Leave it to his brother not to mince words. "Didn't think I was crazy. They can get away with it on some of the other sections, but this'n won't take it." He turned to look at the straightaway behind them. "Straight shot into town." He shook his head. "Guess they like to make up time here."

He turned back around to his crew. "We need to get in here, fellas," he called out. "Clean dirt, ballast, tighten it again. Mac, finish out where you are and then get 'em in here with the lining bars. Let's get everybody dancing. All-day job." He surveyed the right-of-way down the west side. His eyes lingered on the creek, hopping and splashing as it flowed parallel to the line for several hundred yards, its surface almost level with the right-of-way and the track barely fifty feet away.

Frank followed his gaze. "Damn, that water's high! You thinking what I'm thinking?"

Patrick nodded. "One, maybe two, more of these heavy afternoon storms, and it could spill its guts right about here. Everything goes: track, freight—oh, and did I mention the bonus for beating Sandy Point? Son of a gun. I'm not sure there's a thing we can do about it, either."

They walked across the right-of-way to where the Piscataponi ran closest to the track before meandering off north, away from the line, and disappearing behind a thicket of oaks. They crossed over the creek to the far side on a wood-plank bridge wide and sturdy enough to drive a wagon across. On the far side, they could go no farther. Barbed wire separated them from a herd of brown milk cows grazing in a gently rolling farm field.

Frank looked at the fence, then back at the bridge. "Whose farm?"

"McClelland's. Sure would like to get in there and rearrange some of this dirt."

Frank put his boot against one of the crooked posts and shoved. The wood broke off at ground level with a soft, wet crunch.

The men exchanged glances. "All these rotten?" Frank asked. "Isn't this an invitation for a mess?"

Patrick kicked the next post, with the same result. He continued walking, jiggling posts and stomping the ground around them, testing his footing as he went.

"It's all spongy," he said. He stopped. "Look—natural spring bubbling up. I thought so. No wonder the herd's down here. Nice, fresh drinking water. Can't do nothing till Miller gets off his bum and gets us permission." He studied the cows a moment, shook his head, and walked back toward the bridge. "Before I forget, Frank, we need to double up on the warnings at the crossings. Miller's worried about livestock on the track slowing down the big loads coming in. I don't have time to worry about these here with a fence and a bridge to keep 'em outta the way. Come on."

Frank turned back to the bridge, scooping up a handful of pebbles as he went. He tried to skip one across the water, but it vanished in a froth of angry white foam. "Why would they put the track so close to wet ground?" he muttered. Doesn't take a Tom Edison to see high water wiping this section out."

"Water." Patrick rolled his eyes. "See a water tower around here anywhere?"

Frank turned around in a circle. "Nope. Are you telling me—"

Yep," Patrick said. "This here's part of the old Chesapeake line. It went the whole way to Solomons when that burg was a wide spot in the road, before they built up the place with all those warehouses. The line came in here and snaked all along the coast, hitting every jerkwater town they could. It took forever. They jerked water right outta this creek for the locomotive boilers. Now the water tower in Owings gets 'em out here and back, so no need to jerk." He studied the scowl on Frank's face. "What?"

Frank rolled his eyes. "You read that on a bulletin board somewhere?"

"Nope, but it's still true. Dad told me while you were off playing stickball and beating up the other kids. Chesapeake Railway Express bought out some of the locals," he said, looking west, "for more right-of-way. Ripped out the ties along here and created a faster, more direct route that switches off on the far side of the bridge and goes directly south. Didn't save 'em any money in the end, seeing as how they had to march right back out here and lay track to establish service for the park. The farm probably used the creek water, too, or met the train out here over the bridge. Dunno." He swiped his boot across the weedy patch of ground they were standing on. "Been a while since the bridge was used. It's all weeds—no discernible trail coming or going across it."

Frank snorted. "Real nice story, Mr. Know-It-All." He looked at the water again. "Would have been smarter to move the line over when they rebuilt, but when you think with your wallet, it doesn't always come out right—easier to think about the short term."

Patrick nodded and walked away. "You got that right," he said over his shoulder. "Guess during normal weather, the creek never gets this high. Let's hope their decision was a wise one. Otherwise, that creek'll be all over the rails, and Carr'll be all over Miller."

Frank tossed the fistful of rocks into the current and fell in step with his brother as they hit the right-of-way. "Pat, all we can do is watch it, I guess, and you try to talk some sense into those boneheads who always lose money by holding on to it too tight."

Patrick stopped. "Sean's giving me a day and a half with no through traffic so we can fix some of this. He's too scared to do much more. Can't blame him. Miller's leaning on him hard to keep Carr happy. With enough time, I can try to coax the creek to flood away from us. I'll get 'em to send a hopper of riprap to dump in here, build up some rock. It might divert the flow if the worst happens. We gotta make sure nothing comes through unless we're sure it'll hold. I want a check twice a day on this section, a written report on every visit, and a description of what that creek is doing. Can you handle it for me?"

"Oh, yeah," Frank said, "What are brothers for?"

"Covering each other's asses?" Patrick threw him a sidelong glance and sniggered. "But you do owe me less now. I'll holler at the front office and see if we can't get 'em to slow down through here. That ought to go over really well."

As they walked back to the rest of the crew, Patrick squinted against the sun and checked the sky—clear and blue to the east, and low gray clouds already building from the west again. The best of the day was fleeting. Lousy weather was getting ready to barrel in once more. "Come on, grab a bar, Frank," he said, pulling one off the handcar. "Help 'em out."

Frank whisked it right back out of his hand. "Thanks."

"Christ, Frank, rip my arm off," Patrick said. He grabbed the bar, but Frank held on and took another step forward, coming nose to nose. "I think we've already had this discussion," Patrick said. "Get on the line over there."

"Yep, we have. Foremen direct; everybody else lines up." Frank yanked the bar free and walked away.

Strike three for Frank Byrne. "Moran, Butler, and Reedy have volunteered to keep an eye on the line out here tonight," Patrick called after him. "You can join 'em." Brother or not, nobody challenged a track foreman. And nobody else was gonna decide when he was too sick to break a sweat. He climbed onto the rail runner to watch his crew.

———◆◆◆———

In the middle of the work group was Mac. At a glance, he would not have stood out from the mostly colored crew—sinewy build, dark brown skin, in the thick of the labor. He would never be a foreman, but he had a solid reputation spanning years, and as gang caller, he was more essential to the crew's success than any other man but the foreman. Mac would never be promoted—there was no place for coloreds in management, even as section foremen. Patrick had bounced a few whites over the years—no-goods who thought the company owed them something for showing up on time. But not the gandies, Mac's people—not a single one over the ten years he had worked for the Chesapeake. They worked hard and took pride in their labor. He did the best he could to be fair to everybody, but past that, he didn't get involved with what he couldn't change.

As the men drove their chisel-ended bars under each rail and levered up on them, using their combined weight to align the rails, Mac's baritone rose above the din, the rhythm and sound of the work swelling up into work songs that he called. All down the line, his group chanted as they heaved their bodies in unison with the leader's call, responding with the beat of their bars and the stamp of their feet, their exertion punctuated with "*bah*" and "*uh*" as, straining muscle and dripping sweat, they shifted steel rails and wooden ties. And when Mac didn't stamp, he swayed and bobbed, exhorting the boys to *line 'em right.*

After much cajoling and a chorus of hollering, Mac let go his bar and pulled out his harmonica. The first cadence began slow and passionate, and the crew matched its pace, taking a brief respite as Mac wove into sound their personal dreams and laments. Then the music slowly changed, the deep blue notes becoming energetic, motivating and pushing the men to ignore their pains and fatigue. At times, the sound became the chugging, churning of steel wheels on the rails, notes bending into the long-drawn-out call of a distant train whistle as Mac reminded them of the danger of tarrying too long in the task at hand. As he exhorted them, the workers straddled bars and yanked back as their counterparts dug in and leaned into the rails to keep them positioned.

At the end of the day, the music often sneaked back up on Patrick in his quiet moments traveling back to town, or late at night when he heard the distant click and hum of steel wheels, or a lonely whistle's moan. Some songs were improvised, but others he recognized, here and there a particular favorite that would perk his ears a bit more. He could not recite the words to a single tune, mostly getting lost in the hypnotic beat. And some lyrics were simply not repeatable in polite company. The most risqué were met with grins and the occasional laugh, but Mac never broke rhythm, and the more groans and laughter he elicited, the harder he would work and the louder he would get, the gandies all feeding off each other's energy.

There was an esprit out here that Patrick would never find in an office job—the bond between real men, who made their way by their own sweat and not family connections or politics. But if he wanted to make Dr. Bagley a liar and beat the odds of dying young, he would have to leave it all behind. It would be his deepest regret.

CHAPTER TWELVE

Fountains and Carousels

From the eighth floor of the Parker Building, Lawrence Carr gazed down at Pratt Street. It was bustling, like everything else in Baltimore this Tuesday morning except the people attending his meeting. He pulled the unlit stogie out of his mouth, ran his finger and thumb down his mustache, and looked back at his Bayside partners. One more conference room in the ongoing struggle to keep things rolling along. Carr gave up trying to keep them awake. Someone else should take on the job for a while. It may as well be Reginald Bush. He looked at the sleepy-eyed son of a steel magnate, picking lint off his gabardine jacket. Carr could not recall the last time he had heard the man's deep, somnolent monotone.

"Mr. Bush, I think it's time we shared with the rest of the group the philanthropic overture from Mrs. McClelland."

Pettigrew's head popped up. "Mrs. Camilla McClelland, as in spinster waving temperance placards and generally disrupting business?"

"None other than—the late widow of Spencer McClelland," Bush said, depositing a white fluff of something on top of the little pile he had been accumulating during the meeting. "Lots of money, dabbles in farming, has a misguided need to save people from themselves regardless of how they might feel about it."

Carr chuckled to himself as he watched the heavy-eyed men in the room push up in their chairs and look a little more alive. Apparently, threatening to take away these lazy sluggards' liquor was the best way to motivate them.

Pettigrew was bristling already. "Are we really going to put up with this woman?"

"Temperance ladies?" Carr said. "Of course not. We have the same policy we've always had: ignore them. They'll eventually get married and start a family, create a sewing circle, or find some other womanly pursuit. We'll continue to ignore them."

"I don't know, Lawrence, they seem pretty dedicated to me," Bush said, opening the buff-colored folder in front of him and adjusting his reading glasses. "Mrs. McClelland is offering to donate three fountains—created by the well-known designer Henry Cogswell—to be placed along the boardwalk. They're supposed to offer a ready supply of drinking water," he said, reciting from his paper, "with little brass cups. It sounds modern, novel. People would drink it up, so to speak."

"How do we keep them from taking the cups?" Pettigrew asked, smoothing out the front of his vest. "Sounds like a continuing expense. I don't like it."

"*I* like it," Carr said, bobbing his head in approval. "What's the catch?"

"None I'm aware of," Bush replied, avoiding Pettigrew's glare. "I think she's buttering us up. But if so, we should take it. We don't have to change our principles or tap one less keg."

"Absolutely not," Pettigrew argued. "It'll be like the monstrosity Cogswell designed for Washington: spouting water and having all kinds of temperance nonsense chiseled into it. It's an outrage. We'll be a laughingstock!"

"If there's any hope of luring the Preakness here from Gravesend, we need to keep this town wet," Carter Wallace said, his boozy eyes betraying a personal interest in the subject. "Once they dry up the liquor, the next step is gambling. New York is a prime example. Crazies are killing horse racing up there."

"Any objections to accepting *one* fountain?" Carr asked. "It'll make the ladies happy, maybe get 'em off our back until they find something else to complain about. It doesn't need to change our stance on liquor in the park. Besides, all our agreements for German beer are in place." Carr found himself staring down at Carter Wallace's bald spot as the man's large, meaty hand doodled with a gold-tipped fountain pen along the edges of his notepaper. Thurber appeared asleep, eyes closed and chin resting on his chest. Browning appeared startled and shifted in his seat but remained silent.

"Settled then," he said. "We'll take one. If, later, the gift has more strings than we anticipated, we cut them and her loose, but keep the fountain . . . perhaps sell it for scrap." Carr stared at Pettigrew a moment, waiting for an argument. *Contrary son of a gun.* He trusted him even less than he did Mrs. McClelland. *She,* at least, was firm in her convictions.

Pettigrew huffed his indignation. "Make sure it goes in an out-of-the-way corner, and be done with the hag."

"Final piece of business would be the carousels" Carr said, pushing on. "A. J.?"

A. J. put his coffee cup down and rose from his place at the side table, where the coffee urn sat. "Some news, actually. Our carousel was not in the Dentzel warehouse destroyed by fire. That is the good news. Unfortunately, because of the fire, he has too many obligations to entertain building another for us. I reached out to William Mangel, who agreed to commission artisans to build the second one. He put out notices, accepted bids from a lot of carvers, and they are at work as we speak."

"Just any old Tom, Dick, or Harry?" Pettigrew asked. "Temperance fountains and second-rate amusement rides. This is absurd." He waved him off.

"Just so long as they're not from Nevis," Carter Wallace said. "Like I said, their beer and furniture's fine. Not good for much else."

A. J.'s countenance hardened, but his voice remained steady. "I can assure you, Mr. Pettigrew, Mr. Wallace, none of this will be second-rate. Dentzel will be sucking up every decent carver he can find to replace what the fire destroyed. Mangel knows how to go about his business. He has a keen eye, and even Dentzel recommended him. We give him the latitude to get us the best, wherever that might be. In case you've forgotten, an added bonus to working with Mangel is the carousel platform he uses. For an extra fee, he'll sell us the mechanism that moves the carousel figures up and down. It's patented. No other carousel makers can boast that. That's a leg up on every other amusement park within a hundred miles of here. I've personally paid him the additional fee, and he's sending me the parts directly."

"Settled then," Carr said. "And Dentzel's grand carousel—coming when, A. J.?"

"This Friday, the thirty-first. It's already crated and ready to ship."

"Excellent. Knowing Dentzel has passed it along into the capable hands of the Chesapeake should have us all breathing easier."

CHAPTER THIRTEEN

Bowlers, Britches, and Bird Shot

C hristian Miller may have been lousy at human relationships, but where railway business was concerned, he gave it his all. By late Monday afternoon, he had hopped on Patrick's request for access to Mrs. McClelland's pasture and sent a rail rep out to negotiate.

On the north side of Nevis, two men in a small mule cart jounced along the sloppy wagon road. The wagoner, Jimmy Baker, a tall drink of water in brand-new denim coveralls, pushed an unruly lock of auburn hair off his furrowed brow and concentrated on maneuvering the animals around the deepest ruts. His passenger, Robert Lucas, employed by the Chesapeake, sat next to him, one hand clamped over the crown of his bowler hat, the other clutching the front gate of the cart. His lips moved in silent prayer as he asked God to keep his new gray suit presentable long enough to talk to Mrs. McClelland.

"We're there?" he asked with relief, pointing across acres of alternating tobacco and dark green fallow, toward the three-chimney white clapboard farmhouse and the handful of outbuildings clustered about it. Not a soul was around—no farm hands, no livestock bellowing or bleating, no chickens scurrying about. "Doesn't look like anyone lives here. You sure?"

Jimmy nodded and drove the team between the largest barn and the corncrib. He pulled up at the white picket fence separating the green grass around the house from the rest of the yard—a plantless morass except for the tall, wiry weeds and Queen Anne's lace running along the building foundations. He climbed down but stayed behind the wagon while Lucas hopped out and started for the door.

"Don't venture off. I won't be long," the rail rep said over his shoulder. "Long" lasted three good strides. Some thirty feet from the door, a shotgun blast sent him scampering and dirtied up his shiny new two-tone shoes. He scrambled back behind the wagon bed and joined Jimmy, already crouched there.

"Mrs. McClelland?" Lucas yelled into the side of the wagon. "If you'll hold on a minute, I can introduce myself. I'm Robert Lucas from the Chesapeake Railway office. I'd like to talk to you about your pasture out along the rail line."

Silence. Perhaps yelling into a board inches from his face was not the most effective way to make himself heard. He peered above the wagon's edge. "Mrs. McClelland, if you could hold on—"

A fresh spray of bird shot sent his bowler flying off in the air behind him.

"She's crazy!" he said, ducking down again.

"Yep," Jimmy said. "Husband's death pushed her 'round the bend. Nothing worse'n a crazy woman with a scattergun. Spends all her time yelling about women not getting a fair shake with men, and trying to shoot anybody sets foot on the forty. Hell, God's giving her a chance right now to act like a man and come out here, and she ain't paying him no mind. Don't never round up the herd and bring 'em in, fence posts leaning and rotting out there. And that tobacco out there? It's going nowhere."

The two men eased up far enough to take a quick peek out over the edge of the wagon. Nothing stirred across the yard or inside the house. They ducked back down anyway.

"So far, you're holding your own, Mr. Lucas, but you're fighting a losing battle. Last time I brought a stranger out here, she sent him ske-daddling back to town with a britches load of rock salt. You've gotten your only warning. Next time it won't be your bowler."

"Why didn't you tell me this before I hired you to bring me out here?"

"Five cents is five cents, sir. Man's gotta make a living somehow."

Lucas gave Jimmy a blank stare. Then, shifting tactics, he pulled the white handkerchief from his vest pocket, tied it around the end of his cane, and swished it around a couple of times to make sure it was secure.

"Mrs. McClelland!" he yelled, staying low and out of sight. "Before I go back to town, perhaps we could talk about your temperance fountain." He counted to three and slowly raised the cane above the wagon, swishing the hankie again.

"Both of you, come out slow with your hands up where I can see 'em!" she yelled back.

Jimmy looked at Mr. Lucas and motioned for him to go on ahead. "She probably coulda' shot you already if she wanted. I'll keep it right here waiting on ya."

"See that you do," Lucas said, getting up off his knees. He came out from behind the wagon with his hands raised and got the whole way to the porch without the woman unloading both barrels on him. He had a good feeling about this.

CHAPTER FOURTEEN

Birds

Her face was hidden under a maroon-and-white striped parasol as she stood outside the Wesson Building late Tuesday. A long-sleeved pink tailored blouse and off-white A-line skirt, in the latest high fashion, set off her hourglass figure. She drew many furtive glances, and several of the less furtive sort, including that of Patrick Byrne, who was heading home, dirty and beat. To say she was a vision would be no exaggeration. He also noticed the man standing next to her, in a tan suit and a boater: none other than Mr. A. J. Packard.

Mary, wife of Lawrence Carr, represented all the oppressive weight threatening to crush the life from him: moneyed entitlement that demanded immediate fulfillment of every little whim. She stood with head down, intent on something in her hands. After the gloomy lecture Dr. Bagley had just given him, he was not in the mood to engage. He glanced around, but there was no convenient doorway or alley he could duck into. He crossed to the other side of the street, set his gaze on the middle distance, and walked faster.

"Mr. Byrne? Mr. Byrne, from the railway?" Her voice—his luck. He looked up and she gave him a polite smile, beckoning him over with a flutter of gloved fingers. She turned and whispered to the third in their party: a young man holding the parasol—the same assistant she had been nattering with at the pier the first time Patrick saw her. The assistant handed the parasol to her and scuttled off toward one of the other buildings down the street. Packard touched two fingers against his temple in polite acknowledgment and sauntered off in the same general direction.

Patrick walked over. "Afternoon, Mrs. Carr," he said, sweeping off his flat cap.

"Good afternoon," she said, tucking something under the arm holding the parasol, and offering her other hand. "*Byrne.* It's an Irish name, isn't it?"

"First-generation American, born and raised in Philly."

"Where in Ireland?"

"Mayo County, south of Knock. Did you hear about the Virgin Mary appearing there a few years back? My cousins saw her." She nodded, but he could tell she had no idea what he was talking about. He glanced around. "Are you wandering around here with Mr. Carr?"

She nodded toward the water. "Down there, but he won't miss me for a while. I have an assistant tagging along—he's a little bored, but dutiful nonetheless. And it isn't 'Mrs. Carr.' It's Partridge, Mary Partridge, fiancée, but most friends call me Birdie. I was hoping I would run into you again."

He glanced at the ring on her left hand. Fancy, expensive, it said "spoken for" loud and clear, no matter what you called it. "I'm surprised you're not back in Baltimore," he said. "Not many exotic things to explore here in Nevis."

"We'll have rooms at the Bayside Hotel until Lawrence is satisfied things don't need his attention. I thought I'd venture up this way and see what Nevis is all about."

"Has anyone taken you down to see the cliffs?" He smiled at her puzzled look. "Trust me, you'd know. Buckets of fossils—sharks' teeth, that sort of thing—in the surf and sticking right out of the cliffs. Something not easily forgotten. There's talk the National Museum will be studying down there. Have someone take you out there. Ricker's Cliffs."

"Sounds like something Mr. Carr would be interested in buying," she said with a laugh. "I'll put it on my to-do list."

"And what have you decided?"

"Hmm?"

"About Nevis."

"Charming and . . . quaint," she said, producing the sketchbook she had been hugging against her. "And it inspires me, although I'd much prefer to set up a camp chair and spend a while, instead of sketching on the fly."

"Really, now." He took the offered book and leafed through it. The first sketch was a street scene bustling with activity: work wagons, laborers in denim overalls, a man in business attire escorting a striking brunette in her jade and white Sunday go-to-meeting clothes up the stairs of the First National Bank, here and there a mother and children on some typical small-town errand.

"First Street? You're very good, Miss. Partridge." He flipped to the next: a single-story yellow brick building, two full-length windows flanking a central screen door opening out onto a wide porch overhung by a red tin roof. "Dilly's," he said, starting to run his hand across the sweeping flow of precise oval-styled lettering in the restaurant's sign— lettering that bore no resemblance to the actual sign. He snatched his hand back, suddenly wondering how clean his fingers were. "Sorry. You do calligraphy, too?"

"Oh, no." She laughed. "A. J—Mr. Packard—added that. He calls it his *Spencerian* penmanship. It's a passion of his. He's an excellent artist, too. He thought it added . . . *je ne sais quoi*," she said, with a wave of her hand. "Everybody has a vice—at least the interesting ones do. Lawrence, for example. His is success."

"Can't fault that."

"I guess it depends on how you define it. For Lawrence, it is ever changing."

Patrick gave her a quick look and then returned to flipping pages: the steamboat *Chessie Belle*, billowing silvery-white clouds behind it as it churned up the bay from the south to dock; a bevy of children playing ball down by the Bayside Hotel.

"Kids a favorite, I see. Well, there are a lot around. Can't seem to keep 'em out . . ." He stopped flipping. The next sketch was of a railroad man sitting on the rear platform of a caboose, back against the cab, one foot wedged tight against the railing—eyes closed, face weary and smudged with grime. He closed the pad. "Charming or quaint?"

"Nice quiet spot on the spur—definitely charming," she said with a smile.

"How long was I asleep?"

"You're a blessed man, Mr. Byrne. To a man, not one of your crew tried to wake you. They know you'll be there if they need you. True loyalty is rare. You should treasure it."

"I hope you don't think I do this as a matter of course. We've been running full throttle, virtually nonstop—"

"You don't have to tell me how driven Mr. Carr can be, and as long as things keep running smoothly, I'm sure he doesn't care how many naps you take."

"To be honest, the 'smoothly' part is what's worrying me." He offered her the sketchbook back.

She slid it out of his hands. "Don't read too much into this. There are *other* men in here just doing their jobs. I'm interested in everything going on at the waterfront." She studied him for a moment and then laughed. Not the sort of polite, mannered laugh that they taught in finishing school, but a hearty one that crinkled the skin around her eyes—and not, Patrick thought, in an unattractive way.

"Oh, no, not at all. It's just—"

"My father was an enlightened man, Mr. Byrne. He left me financially secure and made sure I received the same excellent education my brother did, including spending time in the Catskills studying art with Candace Wheeler. To the discomfort of many, I can discuss finance, the fall of the Roman Empire, and the correct way to splint a broken arm. When called upon, I can debate with the best of them."

"You have to admit," he said, red faced, "it's an unusual talent . . . for a lady. You remind me a little of my sister Moira. She's, um, opinionated. You might find her out here somewhere waving a placard."

"I think I like her already. Of course, you'll never see me out here marching, Mr. Byrne—it wouldn't be proper. But I do support worthy causes. Someday I intend to run my own business, but it won't be a cutthroat one. I intend to help people. After all, what's the use in having money if you can't spend it wisely and compassionately?"

Buying shiny new cars, he thought to himself. "I am impressed," he said, "but not impressed or enlightened enough to let you wander around unescorted. Is your assistant or Mr. Packard coming back?"

"Mr. Abbott? Not if I can walk away fast enough and we avoid the post office," she said, looking down the street. "Do you have time to show me around?"

Patrick pulled out his watch and did his own looking around to see who might be watching. "I have a few minutes. Have you seen Mac's?"

"The butcher?"

"Pharmacy. Now, that's something worth drawing, and I think you'd really appreciate going inside. It's on Seventh. I'll make sure you get back before anyone misses you." He offered his arm, and she took it.

<hr />

"Was I right?"

"Absolutely," she said, standing before the red brick building, eyes wandering from the ornate cornices on the building's facade to the massive white granite block centered in front, with "1891" carved into its face. "Is it as beautiful inside?"

"Let's just say it'll surprise you. Come on, I'll introduce you to Hans." A bell on the back of the door jingled them in, and he followed her across the honey-colored heartwood plank floors.

The dark-haired, white-shirted man in bright gold wire-rimmed glasses looked up from behind a carved mahogany counter that ran the length of the back wall. As impressive as the counter was, the wall behind it was grander still: five dark-stained wood-paneled archways filled with shelf upon shelf of white earthenware containers, their fronts labeled in gold script and decorated with pictures of colorful botanicals.

"Can I help you?" Raymond MacIntosh, the druggist, asked. I'm closing it up for the night."

"We'll be back out in a moment, Mr. MacIntosh. Miss Partridge here is an associate of Mr. Lawrence Carr. We're going to say hi to Hans, and then we'll be off."

Raymond MacIntosh nodded and went back to his work. Patrick directed Mary to the right, toward the birdcage inside the entryway. "Miss Mary—"

"Birdie," she corrected him.

"Um, Birdie, meet Hans."

The blue macaw's dark pupil dilated, and the feathers on his head rose up in a wave from front to back before settling flat again. "*Guten tag*," he said. He fluffed again.

"He talks?" She laughed and leaned in toward the bird. "Lordy, he's talking to me! Hans, I think I love you."

"Whoa, not too close!" Patrick pulled her back a bit. "He's been known to take a chunk out of people he doesn't like. With names like Partridge and Birdie, I thought you might like him. Ever raised birds?"

Shaking her head, she handed her parasol to Patrick and reached out with a gloved index finger. Hans's head drooped forward, and he closed his eyes as Birdie stroked his feathers forward and back. "John James Audubon and his bird sketches—you've heard of him? We're connected through the Tylers."

Patrick shook his head. "Sorry, I haven't. Your sketch of me says it all: railroading and sleep. That pretty much covers it."

"Maybe." She withdrew her hand, and a small fluff of down stuck to her index finger. She studied it a moment, closed her eyes as if making a wish, and then blew the down out into the air. With a sigh, she turned to Patrick, offering him a smile he could describe only as halfhearted.

"I should probably get back, Mr. Byrne, and you surely have better things to do. I'll add Mac's to my list for a return visit. Mr. Abbott is no doubt frantic by now. He's nice enough, but he answers to Mr. Carr in the end, and Lawrence doesn't need a play-by-play of my day. Of course, our little excursion was aboveboard, but I think it should remain a secret between friends. Is that all right?"

"Of course." Patrick had his doubts about the secrecy of anything in this little backwater, but one could do worse than be friends with Miss Mary Partridge. He didn't live under any delusions that her attention was anything more than cordial, but on the other hand, he could not deny that he would do it again given the opportunity.

He escorted her back to the sidewalk where they started, where a fretting Mr. Abbott was perhaps already considering what kind of recommendation he could hope for after Mr. Carr booted him for misplacing his fiancée. Relief swept Abbott's face, and he promptly suggested a return to the hotel. Patrick excused himself and slipped away.

He was not sure what prodded him to do it, but fifty feet or so along his way again, Patrick turned and took one last look. In spite of Mr. Abbott's entreaties that they leave, she was still entrenched where Patrick had left her, and, guessing by the gesticulating and shaking of heads, was already dispatching her worried assistant on another errand.

She did not remain alone for long. As if on cue, A. J. Packard reappeared. That they appeared to be friends was not surprising, given their apparent shared interest in art, and Mr. Packard's close working relationship with her fiancé. What was interesting, however, was the way Birdie Partridge's whole countenance brightened at the sight of him, and even from here, Patrick could hear the quiet mirth in her voice. The lack of physical space between them, and the familiarity with which Mr. Packard placed his hand along her arm, should have raised the eyebrows of anyone watching closely. They spoke a moment, and he was gone again. The moment was fleeting, the conversation unheard, but their encounter spoke volumes. Mr. Lawrence Carr and Miss Birdie Partridge's relationship was one of smoke, mirrors, and societal expectations. And if the arrangement should prove unsatisfactory, one was to be discreet in establishing any new ones.

CHAPTER FIFTEEN

About That Box

A late, quiet meal with Frank was not to be. No sooner had Anna put down their plates than a gunshot rang out—not directly out front, but not too distant, either. Patrick bolted, leaving his food untouched, paperwork on the table, and Frank three steps behind him. The street looked deserted until, almost immediately, heads poked up around hogsheads and over farm wagons. A few of the bolder souls even took off at a run toward the train station and beyond, where Bayfront Road headed out of town.

Patrick vaulted the depot steps two at a time. "Get outta the way!" he said, pushing through the crowd to reach Sean's work area. To his relief, Sean was alive and talking, sprawled in his swivel chair with a bloody bandanna pressed against the side of his face.

"How bad?" Patrick asked, kneeling beside him, trying to pull the cloth away.

"Been better." Sean lowered the cloth to reveal an ugly scrape. "There was nothing I could do. Shoved a piece in my face soon as I looked up.

Didn't need to hit me, too. Two dirty-looking hobo types. They took the cash box, incoming mail sack, and a high-priority box of freight I had to sign for, then went flying down the tracks on foot. Can't be too hard to catch if they don't have horses."

"We heard gunfire."

"Mine. I got off one bad shot from the freight bay."

"Know either of 'em?"

Sean shook his head. "Not local."

The crowd surged forward with a flurry of panicked questions and brave threats, packing the small office with bodies while doing little of any real use. The throng moved again, parting down the middle with grunts and swearing as a skinny blond youth, barely shaving age, pushed his way through. "Sir," he called, "they robbed us—set the barn on fire."

"Whose barn?" Patrick asked. "What's your name, son?"

"Gus Zugel, the Zugel farm down—"

"*Michael* Zugel's barn? Patrick grabbed him by his arm and hauled him out of the crowd. "Anybody hurt?"

"No sir, but we need help."

"We'll send help, Gus," Patrick said, "but first, how many? On foot or horseback?"

"Two men . . . white, grubby—cross-tie walkers, by the look of 'em . . . Didn't see any horses." The kid started shaking, as if the enormity of his family's misfortune were just now dawning on him. "They took the till and set one of our barns on fire."

"I saw 'em earlier today," someone else yelled out. "On the road between town and Foggy Bottom, heading this way. Not stealing chickens or anything right then, but they looked plenty shifty."

"Please, we need help. All our buildings down there will burn."

The crowd moved once more as a tall redheaded fellow worked his way to the front. It was Packard, the young man Patrick had seen on the street with Miss Mary Partridge. He pointed at Sean as he came. "Call the firehouse. We have park materials stored in some of these barns. Call it in. *Now.*"

"And who exactly are you?" Sean asked, still pressing the bandanna against his head.

"Partnership. Now, they gave you a fire code. Type it, damn it, or I'll have your job."

Sean looked at Patrick, who clenched his jaw and nodded. Sean moved to the telegraph's Morse key, staring for a moment at a handwritten card impaled on a spindle. A hush fell over the crowd as they listened to the tapping rhythm of Morse code.

Gus suddenly went limp and sank toward the floor. Patrick tightened his grip on the boy. "Come on, Gus, we'll fight it," a voice in the back of the crowd yelled, and other voices joined in, offering support. Patrick let go of the boy, and the crowd sucked him back out the door with the volunteers.

"Now, sir," Packard said to Sean, "there is a high-priority package due in for me. Not the larger shipment received today, but a smaller one you would have signed for. I need that package."

"I received it, all right, but I'm afraid they took the package along with the cash box and mail. You'll have to fill out a claim form . . ."

Packard stepped closer. "You don't understand. There's something much more valuable—"

Patrick slid in front of him. "Back it up a step there, mister. Sean'll help you when I'm done here."

Packard squinted and stepped back but remained front and center in the crowd.

Patrick reached into the drawer beneath the Morse key, pulled out a tin badge that read *Police, Chesapeake Railway Express,* and pinned it to his shirt. "Frank?" His brother nodded, and he tossed him an identical badge.

Then he turned to the gathering. "I need a gun."

"Take mine," offered a man in the back. "And my horse, Joppy, if you need him."

"We'll go with you, Mr. Byrne," someone yelled from the back. "Stolen mail could be anybody's."

"Don't need anybody doing anything hasty," Patrick said. "Keep watch here in case they double back. We'll handle the rest. Come on, Frank." He made his way through the crowd, thanked the man for the loan of his Winchester carbine, and untethered the swaybacked roan Morganhorse at the hitching post out front.

Packard followed him out. "Mr. Byrne, wait," he said, grabbing the horse's reins. "You need to find that box."

Patrick leaned down. "Let's see, Mr. Packard, isn't it?"

"Right—A. J. Packard. I work for the partnership. Just between you and me, that box contains the master key and gears for the mechanical system for the carousel. They are one of a kind and control the unique motion of William Mangel's carousel platform. There are proprietary issues involved here, Mr. Byrne, and I gave Mr. Mangel my personal guarantee I would protect his business interests."

"Well, *Mr. A. J. Packard*," Patrick said, pulling his reins free, "your due diligence is a little bit late, don't you think? Now, you must excuse me, but I've got a couple of mail robbers to catch." He reined the horse past him.

Packard approached as Frank was unhitching the black quarter horse's reins from the post, but stopped when Frank flipped his stirrup up and pulled a shotgun out of the beaten leather scabbard. Frank broke open the gun, checked that both barrels were charged, and snapped it shut. Then he swung up into the saddle up and goosed the stallion after Patrick, who was already a hundred feet down the track.

"Put that thing away," Patrick said, eyeing the gun in Frank's hand. "Main thing here is, we want the loot back. If we don't need to shoot anybody . . ."

"Whatever's necessary." Frank slid the gun back into the scabbard. "Guess the uppities' carousel part is a priority?"

"It would seem so."

"God, I hate the attitude that always seems to come with those people." Frank scanned the horizon: shiny steel rails disappearing in the distance, with the Little Pomonkey River running parallel for a while before it meandered off to the right and disappeared in the woods. "What's the plan? Only two ways without getting lost: the rails or the river. Unless they know this area well, the woods would be foolish. With the ground this wet, they'll be easy to track."

"They won't be on the tracks," Patrick said, squinting into the distance. "It'd be faster, but there's nowhere to hide. More than likely, they'll stick to Pomonkey and stay inside the tree line till the river cuts under the road to the north at Shady River. They get that far, they could head any which way. We'll let the local police have it."

"Split up?" Frank leaned back in his saddle and stared at Joppy. "That nag looks like she's two steps ahead of the knackers. You won't make any time on that old thing. I take the tracks, and you take the slower river course—can't go fast through there anyway. If I get as far as the road without finding anything, I'll double back along the water."

"Agreed." As Frank turned his horse up the track, Patrick said, "We want these guys, but don't get it in your head you need to be a hero. We do our best, but we get out of here by dark, before we run into more of them and get ourselves in a situation."

Frank nodded and took off down the tracks while Patrick veered right and urged his horse across the rough-hewn oak-beamed bridge over the Pomonkey. Soon the dense thicket was tearing his shirt and leaving long, white scratches on his unprotected arms, but turning back was not in the cards. No one was going to rob the depot under his watch and get away with it.

The thicket gave way to old-growth forest, and the air hung heavy with the smell of leaf mold. Whoever owned this land had never clear-cut it. The woods were deep, and in some places, daylight filtered through canopy a hundred feet high. He crossed a sunlit glade and dismounted, forced to lead his horse around fallen oaks with trunks too thick to get over.

The terrain shifted again as the soft duff underfoot yielded to sharp strata of weathered shale that made footing treacherous. The horse moved gingerly forward.

A sudden flash of blue caught Patrick's eye. Then a crackle of wood. What color was Frank wearing? Brown?

Patrick slid the Winchester out of the saddlebag and shouldered it. Whoever it was continued moving through the trees, giving no indication they had seen or heard him. Patrick watched, controlling his breathing, tracking the movement, waiting. *There,* in his left hand, as the man in blue steadied himself against a tree trunk . . . a bright red Chesapeake Railway Express bag.

"Stop and drop the bags!" Patrick yelled. "And I'll let you go."

The guy lit out running, with no sign of his partner anywhere. Patrick tracked the retreating figure and squeezed the trigger. The report of the .30-caliber cartridge seemed astonishingly loud. A scream followed, but as far as Patrick could tell, the shot hadn't dropped him. He worked the lever, ejecting the spent brass and chambering the next round, as he moved across the broken terrain. Ahead, a ridge of fractured dark shale rose above him. Slinging the rifle over his shoulder, he stooped low to the ground and scrambled his way to the top. From the ridge top, the terrain rolled down the other side, falling away to the riverbank a hundred yards beyond. He could see the blue-shirted man clearly now, moving awkwardly and favoring his right side. Before Patrick could get off another shot, the man disappeared into thicket. There was a crack of gunfire, and Patrick stumbled, lurching forward on loose shale. He tumbled down the rocky slope, shale edges biting into his hands and knees as he tried to slow himself. He came to rest on his back in a pile of rocks at the base of the ridge.

CHAPTER SIXTEEN

Coming Up for Air

At the second report of a rifle, Frank slid to the ground, keeping the horse between him and the gunfire. Suddenly, from his right came the sound of snapping wood and thrashing vegetation as something barreled at him. No, make that *somethings*. Patrick?

Reaching up, he slid the shotgun out of the scabbard and leveled it in the general direction of the noise. He could wait some, but whoever it was, they were bearing down on him at a dead run. He steadied the shotgun, then let the muzzle sag as the racket diverged in at least two distinct directions—coming now from the deep woods and up the river path. He flexed his fingers and raised the shotgun toward the woods. A flushed-out robber would be coming from there.

He could see movement in the woods, a hundred feet out. His heart pounded as he tried to make out the clothing, the build—anything distinguishing about what was now clearly a man, charging toward him. And the man was *not* Patrick. As he was registering this, the source of all the noise coming from the river path smacked into him hard. The shotgun discharged into the air before flying out of his grip, and he tumbled down the bank and plunged into the icy cold river. A horse and two men splashed in after him.

The cold almost took his breath away. Thrashing and tumbling in the murk and bubbles, he looked for daylight, kicked his legs, and broke the surface, gasping for air. Near him bobbed a dark-haired man in a blue shirt, shouting in a panicked, strangled voice as he flailed toward the horse, which was swimming for the opposite shore. He lunged for the horse's tail and disappeared below the surface. Moments later, he bobbed up long enough to slap at the water a few times and was gone again.

Frank heaved from the exertion in the numbing cold. The current was gentle, though, and when his feet hit bottom, he realized the water was shallow enough to let him bounce along on tiptoes if he kept his chin up. He scanned the water, but there was no sign of a blue shirt. The only sound besides his own gasping breaths was a second, dark-shirted man and the horse as they reached the opposite shore and scrambled up the rocky bank.

Frank half-waded, half-swam back to the other side and pulled himself out. Though shivering already, he felt the grip of a different sort of coldness: fear. "Pat!" he yelled. "Patrick!" The woods offered nothing but silence. Where was his brother?

He looked back at the water. The blue-shirted man had never made it out.

One horse, two men, no Pat. The horse was Patrick's swaybacked Morgan. His own mount, a *proper* horse, stood nearby, picking at the sedge on the bank. He sorted through what he knew and what he only suspected. Two rifle shots. He would bet his life that Pat had fired the first one. Maybe the second one, too. It looked as though the robbers were interested only in hotfooting it out of there.

He got up and searched the area where he, the two fugitives, and the horse had gone into the water, then traced the men's path, as near as he could guess, back away from the shoreline. A railroad pouch and a mailbag—both sealed—and a small leather moneybag lay nearby. No priority parcel. Two robbers, but were there more? Frank retreated to the cover of the high brush.

He drew a mental picture of the men barging out of the woods, and the horse galloping up the river path. Pat was likely midway between the river path and the men's path as they broke for the river. He collected his horse, picked up the shotgun—lying two feet from the water and still dry—and retrieved the stolen bags. Then he headed away from the creek, following the trampled vegetation where the robbers had run for the river. A span of oxen could not have stomped an easier path to follow. At some point, it would curve back toward Nevis and, hopefully, his brother.

He pushed through the thicket and into the woods. He was wasting precious time.

"Pat!" he yelled again, but he succeeded only in quieting the birds in the creekside willows.

———◆·≻◦≺·◆———

Patrick sat up and checked himself out. Wherever the bullet had gone, it had not hit him. His pants were shredded and his knees bloodied from the fall. He looked around for the horse, but it had apparently bolted. He whistled softly. Not a whicker or any movement he could see. He whistled again, louder this time. It was useless. Joppy was a plow nag, not a battle-hardened cavalry horse.

He lowered himself back down onto the rocks and ripped open his right pant leg. The deepest wound was not serious, but it bled. He knotted a strip of trouser denim around it and leaned back against the ridge. His ankle throbbed. He left the boot on, knowing that if the foot swelled, he would never get it on again.

He looked around for something to use as a crutch, but fifty feet of loose, sharp rock lay between him and the trees. He would have to wait for Frank. Without that plow horse, he was going nowhere.

<hr />

Frank found him, lying still, at the base of the first rocky rise.

"God Almighty, Pat! Wake up!" he said.

Patrick moaned and opened his eyes. "Frank . . . I knew you'd find me."

"Yeah," Frank said. "I heard two shots, so I thought . . . Hell, if it weren't for your fancy red bandanna, I'd still be looking for you. He pulled on the shreds of Patrick's pant leg. "Where'd they get you?"

Patrick grimaced and pushed his hand aside. "They missed, but I twisted my ankle all to hell. Blue shirt—you get him?"

"No, but I think you did. I heard him yelp. Two of 'em bowled me over down at the water. Fools came right at me."

Patrick's grimace softened into a smile. "I knew I could count on you. Where'd you leave him? Nag's run off somewhere. Take the guy in and come back for me. I'll be okay."

"Didn't get him."

"Shit. Then we got nothing. Miller'll chew my endgate right off. Hell with him—*he* can foot Doc Bagley's bill. I never signed up to be sheriff. Next time, the old skinflint should invest in some Pinkertons." He tried to get up.

"Hold on," Frank said, putting a hand on Patrick's chest to keep him still. "Not everything's in the crapper. The one in blue never got across the river. He was there one second and went under the next. Drowned like a rat in a rain barrel. Second one made it out, but they dumped the loot before they tried to cross." He pointed at the bags tied to his saddle. "I didn't see Packard's box, though—just the mail and some cash pouches."

"Mr. A. J. Packard can take responsibility for that," said Patrick. "Not really our problem. Can we both make it back on your horse, or do you want to return the bags and come back for me? My ankle's not bad, but I'll never get across this rough terrain."

Frank shook his head. "Don't be crazy. I see two choices. I can send you ahead with a note pinned to your shirt, or you can ride and I'll walk. I'd hide the bags and come back for 'em before I'd leave you here by yourself. What if there's more and they double back?"

"Forget it. We're not going back without the bags, and you're not tagging me like a sack of dry goods. We don't leave anything behind." He eyed the black quarter horse. How'd you end up with the better ride, anyway?" he asked, struggling to get up.

Frank laughed and gave him a shoulder to lean on. "I took a minute to think about what I was doing, and picked the best one out front. Would be nice if we could bring him back in decent shape, seeing as how I didn't ask to borrow him. Figured I'd be out of town before the owner could object."

"And you thought you'd send *me* back to town on him? You trying to get me shot, or just hung?"

"If it makes you happy, I'll lead you back into town—that way, I'll get shot first."

"Yep. Now, shut up and let's get outta here before they come back for the bags and kill us both."

<hr/>

Patrick kept watch behind them, listening and glancing back occasionally to make sure no one followed. He was thinking less about his ankle than about his empty stomach. Another night with no supper, and where the hell had he left his paperwork?

At the moment, he felt like two separate people: the first watching Frank trudge along while the second latched on to random thoughts that flew every which way. He tried closing his eyes, but it made his head spin, so he went back to staring at the back of Frank's curly hair and thinking about the Germans in town.

Some of the Zugels were good people. The little waitress at the diner was all right. Cute, but too young to take seriously—and she was a Protestant.

Maybe he could salvage the cold supper he had left behind at Dilly's. Come to think of it, his paperwork was there. But he couldn't get at it—Anna would have locked up and gone home as soon as she heard about the robbery. His reports were locked up there, too. *Damn.*

It was bad when shifty types drifted through, saw the prosperity in town, and tried to get a piece of it the easy way. Nevis, the apple of both the partnership's and the Chesapeake Railroad's eye, had grown ripe for the picking, and its stolen innocence would not be so easily regained as the money and the mailbag. Maybe Frank was right: something better than Nevis was out there somewhere.

Patrick left off his musings to see that they were back in town, with daylight slipping away. The crowd had dispersed. The only one in sight was Connor, six feet of Irish hothead, whose loyalty was exceeded only by his sense of fairness and retribution. He sat slouched and half dozing on the slat porch bench. His head suddenly popped up, and he bounded out to meet them.

"Where's Sean?" Frank asked.

"Took him home. Last I saw, he was sprawled out in bed with his head wrapped like a sideshow mummy. Should I fetch the doc?"

"Just get me off this animal," Patrick said, already trying to dismount. "Just a scratch."

Frank rolled his eyes, then eased him down and seated him on the steps while Connor watered the quarter horse at the trough and hitched it to a post.

"You got the bags back. They ditch and run?"

Frank shook his head. "Got one. Couldn't get close enough to drop the other. Lost him across the Pomonkey. The one drowned crossing."

"You don't suppose they put Packard's stuff in there?" Patrick said, seeing the railroad bags dangling from the saddle straps.

"Sean said mail and cash," Connor said, untying the railroad bags. "He didn't know what was in Packard's box." He peeked inside the bags to make sure.

"Well?" Patrick asked.

"Just mail and cash," Connor reported.

"So they hid the box out there somewhere. I can already see the reports I'll have to write explaining that. Tomorrow, though—all my papers are at Dilly's. Packard will have to search the woods himself—we've got two red balls to contend with."

"No, your paperwork's inside," Connor said. "Anna Zugel made a special trip over with it. We had to break the news about the fire. She went flying home."

Frank nudged his brother in the side and winked at Connor. "How do I get some of that special treatment?"

Patrick groaned and shoved him away. "Spend your time getting better looking. You should have taken after Mom and not Dad."

"Zugel's girl?" Connor asked. "Better nip that in the bud, Mac. That old buzzard's crazy mean."

Patrick shook his head. "Please, I've got better things to do than chase after little girls."

"Open your eyes man," Frank said. "She's eighteen—stopped looking like a little girl a couple summers ago. If I didn't think they'd run me out of town on a rail, I'd be there myself."

Patrick pointed to the depot door. "Now, stop yammering and help me inside. I'm not looking to form any attachments—I'd just have to break 'em when I go to Baltimore." He looked at Connor. "Why are you still here?"

"Sean wanted me to tell you the red ball's been rescheduled. It's coming tomorrow, not Friday."

"Criminy. If that red ball is due in tomorrow, I'm parking it right here so it's easier to get out. Can you bring me another pair of pants when you come in tomorrow, Frank? Nobody needs to see this much ugly."

Frank put his hands on his hips. "*Pfft,* you're not staying here all night. Connor," he said, pointing out in the rail yard, "get that wagon. You and I are taking Knothead home." He turned back to his brother. "Then Doc's gonna have a look at you."

"No, I'm—"

Frank waved away any argument. "Gotta trust people, Pat. Tomorrow, I'm getting a temporary promotion to foreman, and you'll have to live with it. You're going to take it easy and let me earn my stripes. If that's not all right with you, I'll make sure there's not a horse or a wagon at the house for you to come back to work in. *Stranded,* my brother."

CHAPTER SEVENTEEN

Hogs and Turtle Brains

J ust when it seemed the afternoon storms would cease and Nevis would start drying out, nature mixed it up and delivered a booming morning deluge. The rain came in horizontal bands, driven by wind so stiff it bent saplings sideways and snapped limbs off some of the bigger trees. Across the bay, lightning blazed and crackled in long, jagged fingers. Patrick lay in bed listening to the rain pound the tin roof as evil thoughts of Christian Miller ran through his head. Carr's red ball was due in anytime now. It was the Chesapeake's top priority, and yet Miller had the stupidity to insist that the foreman report to the Wesson Building before hitting the rails—*"six o'clock or else,"* was how he'd put it. Patrick was tempted to ignore the order. *Sorry, Mr. Miller, when they moved the red ball up from Friday to Wednesday, I guess your message got lost in the shuffle.* Jiminy, Miller wasn't even *in* Nevis. The summons was probably a needless trip to pick up another of his useless to-do lists left after one of his pointless site visits. It was conceivable Miller hadn't learned of the reschedule, but Patrick didn't feel like cutting him any slack.

Thank God for Frank. He had promised two things when they learned of the rescheduled run: first, to pray for divine intercession to delay the red ball until Friday; and second, barring that miracle, to pull a second shift overnight and haunt the rails until the red ball passed through early this morning. If there were problems, Frank would alert him, no matter what Miller's instructions were. So far, not a peep. It was good, but not best. Best would be standing at the depot as the engineer powered down the red ball and hopped down from the hog.

Patrick pulled his watch off the dresser and shoved it in his pocket. Ten till six. If all was well, engine 873 right would be past the Nevis switch and steaming toward the curve. He said a silent prayer for its safe passage and the hefty bonus it would bring.

<hr />

The section house shook, and the night's skeleton crew swapped stories about when Nevis had last been pounded this hard, for this long, with this much rain. None could remember a season like this. For the superstitious, it was a bad omen, and it elicited hushed discussions of the fabled dead lineman who swung his lantern with each flash of lightning, endlessly checking the rail line. For those grounded in reality, it just meant eternally wet shoes.

Frank would have gladly paid the lineman to inspect for him while he sat perched in a wagon out on curve 3, making sure the morning red ball rolled in without a hitch. It was his second straight shift, and hot food, dry clothes, and a warm bed kept calling his name with every crash of thunder. He could hack this for a night or two, but he didn't like fatigue. With some jobs, tired was okay. But in railroading, life was always one action or hesitation away from ending badly. For now, though, he had it all covered. The track looked okay, and in another fifteen minutes everybody would be satisfied. Come sundown, he would sleep like a baby.

He took another sip of the goopy coffee he had poured into a mason jar before leaving the section house. It tasted like mud. He dumped it out over the side of the wagon and peered down the track. Despite the rain and poor visibility, the shadowy outline of the train was visible in the distance, and he could hear the engine working. He checked his watch. That would be 873, rolling in right on time. Seconds later, he heard the distinctive sound of its whistle, with the extra higher-pitched note Jake had creatively built into it—an allowable flourish in an occupation that didn't leave a lot of room for personal expression.

With a sigh of relief, he pulled his wagon far enough from the right-of-way to keep the horses calm and waited for the train to pass. Then he stared in disbelief as the Consolidated did nothing of the sort—instead, after clearing the switch, heading *away* from Nevis, toward Solomons on the southbound Chesapeake line. He wiped his face on his coat sleeve and squinted back out into the gloom. No, he was not mistaken. Sure enough, there it went, *south*.

"Dear God, where are you taking Carr's train?" he murmured as it continued puffing and chugging away from him and Nevis. The next thought sent a cold chill up his spine. What was on the track coming *north* out of Solomons? Only the depot knew.

"Hey!" he yelled, then realized he was waving frantically and idiotically with both arms over his head. He turned the wagon around and hightailed it to the section house and the closest phone.

Frank pushed through the section house door, past a dragging night crew heading for the other wagon at the end of their shift. Dashing to the far corner, near the back window, he pulled down the oak box sitting on a low shelf. He flipped up the lid on the field phone and pulled out the silver hand receiver. It felt cold in his hand. He turned the side crank and suddenly became conscious of the press of bodies behind him. The line crackled with static.

"Problem?" one of the night crew asked. "Call everybody back, Frank?"

"Good luck with that," someone else added. "The line's so wet, you won't get anything but static."

Frank ran his hand through his wet hair as the crackling continued. "Eight seventy-three missed the switch, and I have no idea what else is on the Solomons track. I need Paul at the depot." Frank dropped the receiver and plowed back through the crew, heading for the one horse still tethered outside. "Wait for the day crew," he called over his shoulder."

He took off for town as if the dead lineman's ghost itself were after him, and entered Nevis at a dead gallop. Businesses on the west end were shuttered, the streets all but deserted, and dark except for the soft yellow light inside the depot. He headed straight for it like a bug to a lantern, took the porch in a single leap, and pushed through the front door like a gale. Harmon was sprawled in the far corner, feet propped up on Sean's desk, and a blue bandanna draped over his upturned face. Paul, Sean's assistant and the night depot manager, was nowhere in sight.

"Harmon!" Frank yelled, snatching the cloth off his face. "Where the hell is Paul?"

Harmon pulled his feet down and popped up out of the chair, wiping his bleary eyes and trying to stifle a yawn. "He left an hour ago. Wife's in labor."

"You're here alone? Where's Sean?"

He nodded. "It was so close to shift change, I didn't roust him."

"Christ Almighty!" Frank said, looking around in a wild eyed-hunt for anyone at least marginally competent. Finding no one, his eyes returned to Harmon. "What's coming up north from Solomons this morning?"

Harmon responded with a series of rapid blinks—his own personal Morse code for not having a clue.

"Holy Mary, Mother of God, this is not working." Frank strong-armed him back down in the chair and knelt beside him. He took a deep breath and spoke in a quiet stream, his hand gripping the back of the chair. "The switch has failed at curve three. Eight seventy-three is headed south toward Solomons. If you don't know what's on the track, you've got to shut down the line from the switch to Solomons or pull Eight seventy-three onto the siding near Turner. It's an hour trip. If there's northbound traffic on the track, they'll meet somewhere in the middle, and it won't be pretty. Understand, Harmon?"

Harmon broke out into a smile. "Everything's under control. I switched 'em."

"Oh, thank you, God, for this miracle," Frank breathed. "They changed the schedule." He patted Harmon's shoulder. "What's the new time for the red ball? Back to Friday?"

Harmon pulled a paper from Sean's desk. "All I know is the Four-oh-two is going to Solomons today. The red ball isn't due in till Friday. Four-oh-two is to be switched south."

Frank cut his eyes at Harmon and snatched the paper. "Nope, you've got it wrong. This changed last night. Where's your update? The red ball was to come in this morning, *followed* by the four-oh-two. You sent *Eight seventy-three* to Solomons, not the Four-oh-two."

"Possibly." Harmon took the paper back with a trembling hand. He pointed to the Morse key. "Updates are over there. I figured they'd call if something changed." He offered the paper back. "Sean would know best."

"But Sean isn't here, is he? Christ, you just sent one of Mr. Carr's most important loads of freight the wrong way. Holy Jesus!" Frank thundered, springing to his feet. "You're going to send out a dispatch closing the line." He grabbed Harmon's arm and dragged him and his chair over to the Morse key. "Close down the track before someone gets killed."

Harmon turned ashen and dragged his boots along the floorboards. "I c-can't . . . Morse code . . ."

"Get on the *phone* and call Central Dispatch. *Now.*" Frank picked up the candlestick phone and shoved it at him, stretching the extension arm to its full length.

Harmon swallowed hard, tapped the cradle several times, and waited, his eyes never leaving Frank's face. Sweat trickled below his sideburns. "Nothing but static on here," he said, returning the receiver to its cradle. "What should we do now?"

"You? Nothing, Aristotle." He pointed his finger at the tip of Harmon's nose. "*Don't touch anything else* until I get back with Sean. Catch the day crew as they come in, and tell them to stand down at the depot until I get back. Otherwise, *keep your mouth shut.*" He hastened to the door, flung it open, and almost ran over his brother, who came limping up the steps.

"Christ, Frank, the train . . . Tell me it's come and gone already."

Frank grabbed him by the shirtsleeve, pulling him along as he made for the horses tethered out front. "What are you doing here?"

Patrick shook him loose. "Watch the ankle, man. Hell with Miller. What's going on?"

"Jiminy. We're in it deep. Eight seventy-three is heading for Solomons, courtesy of Harmon's goddamn missing brain. Saw it switch with my own eyes."

"Where's Paul?" Patrick asked, trying to catch a glimpse inside."

"No time. Get on a horse. Paul's baby decided, Carr be damned, he's in charge and he's making his worldly entrance today. Harmon thinks he's in charge, but he has no clue what's on the tracks. Oh, yeah, and he doesn't know Morse from ancient Hebrew. We need Sean. We're looking at a derailment, a collision, or getting fired. Maybe all three."

CHAPTER EIGHTEEN

Little Boy Blue

Four men huddled around the depot desk: Sean transcribing, Harmon wringing his hands, Frank staring at Harmon, and Patrick deep in thought. *Tap, tappity, tap-tap, tap, tappity.*

Eventually, Patrick gave up his seat, driven away by Sean's dirty looks as his nervous jittering competed with the staccato of the Morse key. They all waited, fixated on the tap-tapping.

Sean pushed back in his chair, and all eyes went to the paper in his hand.

"Oh, God," Harmon squeaked.

Frank shot him a nasty look. "Don't blame God—he's not the eejit here."

"We're okay," Sean said, relief sweeping his face. "Carr's freight is on the siding at Turner. Nothing's coming northbound, but the Four-oh-two is en route southbound to Solomons, and almost to Turner. After it clears, they'll send ours down to the roundhouse for a quick turnaround and have it back up to the Nevis trunk in less than two hours. No one should be the wiser."

"Except everyone in the rail yard down there," Patrick said. "Miller'll know by supper."

Sean shook his head. "Don't think so. Rupert Shaughnessy, remember him? Nine-fingered, gimpy beanpole, had a run-in with some couplers a few years back? He's the man down there. Right cagey fellow, and he owes me one. God knows, I've covered for him enough. He'll gin up some cock-and–bull, and we'll all be on the same page. Once the freight is back all safe and sound, who'll care?"

"All right, then," Patrick said, eyeing each of the men in turn. "We keep mum, be patient, and get by this. Sean, you got anything here besides coffee? I think we all need one."

"I won't tell if you won't." Sean opened the bottom desk drawer and pulled out a full bottle of Jameson.

Harmon politely waved his hand. "I'll pass."

Frank leaned toward him. "Nobody passes," he whispered. "It's an Irish pact. First one that squeals gets done in by the rest. Honorable men got nothing to worry about."

Harmon nodded, and took a swig when the bottle came his way. Patrick took the last and longest slug, let out a satisfied sigh, and handed it back to Sean.

"Good, then," he said, peeking out the back window. "Troops are getting restless out there, but I think we can send 'em out now. Don't need any rumors getting started."

Frank hopped off the counter and peeked out. "What'd you tell 'em?"

"They were doing such a fine job that Miller gave 'em some time off. Well, they have worked their cabooses off," he said with a laugh.

Frank walked outside.

Patrick followed but stopped in the doorway. "Call the section house phone if anything changes or"—his eyes cut to Harmon, sitting with his forearms on his knees, head drooping—"if you need another opinion."

Sean closed his eyes and let out a deep sigh. "No news is good news. Please don't call me, either."

———◆◆◆◆◆———

Patrick was too busy praying to think about calling Sean. All he needed was a simple blessing—one he would humbly and gratefully repay with more church visits, less taking of the Holy Family's names in vain, and a reining-in of the occasional lustful thought about Mr. Carr's fiancée. "Please, Lord," he prayed, "send one of your angels to watch over this train."

It was not too much to ask. They needed a little luck to swing their way and stay there. He had a full crew—healthy and, but for a few sluggards, generally self-starters. They could handle whatever came up, and they were probably in a better mood today after the unexpected morning break. The line this morning would be as solid as it was when they left it late yesterday. Eight seventy-three would be in soon, and bonuses were back on.

When they reached the section house, the storm had moved on through and the sky was brightening. The crew took its time. No use getting everything on the track only to pull it all off again when 873 came through. Patrick took Connor, Thomas, and a couple of others by wagon, along with a load of equipment, and headed up track to take a look. After the red ball, his main concern would be improving the landscaping for the soggy area he and Frank had walked earlier, encouraging any high water to run toward the farm and not the rail. Apparently, all the land running along the creek with the rotten posts and sagging fence belonged to the McClelland farm. And Miller, good to his word for once, had worked out a deal with Mrs. McClelland to improve the flow of water through her land. Scuttlebutt had it that he had played hardball with the old woman, but nobody had the details.

Except for the rumbling of the wagon, the occasional finch's warbling, or cicadas buzzing off in the distance, the ride out to mile marker 6 was quiet, all five men keeping whatever thoughts they had—the cause of the delay, their own evening plans, or how much their backs already ached—to themselves. Patrick sat up front with Thomas, who held the reins but provided little direction to the horses. For the dray horses, Billy and Isaac, following the well-worn path was as routine as the stall they slept in at night, the feed they got twice a day, and the snacks Connor slipped them every time he ate something, which was often.

Patrick looked out toward Mrs. McClelland's property. The land-holding was extensive, and its northern edge ran parallel to the track for acre after acre of green rolling pasture and fields, both fallow and planted. A number of barns and outbuildings were clustered off to the south—one painted red, and all covered by tin roofs in various states of deterioration—with large plantings, probably tobacco, close by. The cows were gone. Given the bad weather, they were likely tucked away warm and dry in a barn somewhere. On a day like this, he would con-sider trading places with them. Fond memories of his mother's garden washed over him. Crop farming appealed to him, but he could never imagine minding a bunch of dumb cattle anywhere.

Thomas yanked the team up sharply, and the wagon lurched to a stop. Patrick grabbed the side of the seat to keep from pitching forward over the front of the wagon. "Holy Christ!" Thomas murmured, con-tinuing to pull up tight on the reins. "What in God's good name . . . ?"

Patrick whipped his head around, expecting to see Carr's red ball fully engulfed in flames, in the process of derailing, or fallen prey to some other disaster. But there was no such calamity: no train barreling along belching grayish-white smoke, and not a hint of chugging steam pistons or clickety-clacking steel wheels on the rails—just a lot of small brown dots on the landscape. He squinted. The shape and fawn coloring had him thinking deer, but when he took it all in, it was cattle—lots of them. They were on the bridge he and Frank had walked across, on the right-of-way and the track—Jersey milk cows scattered in every direction.

"Holy hell." He pointed toward McClelland's. For a distance of a hundred feet or so, the fence had been pulled down and all the posts snapped like toothpicks.

Connor climbed out of the wagon. "Stampede?"

"Looks it. One big thunder boomer and an antsy cow is all it takes." Patrick looked down the rails. "Dear God." All it would take for a derailment was *one* cow and a ten-ton hog barreling along at thirty miles per hour.

He stood up. As he saw it, there were two choices, neither of them good. They could try to reach Ducketts Mill Bridge and put out a warning flag for 873, or hightail it back to the phone at the house. That phone communicated only with the depot, but Sean could change the all-clear signals at the bridge to a caution. Which of those options gave enough time to stop the train from making hamburger meat out of a dozen or more cows?

"Section house phone, or the bridge and a flag—which one?" he asked the others.

"Er, bridge," Thomas said, and one of the others agreed.

Connor looked behind them and then out along the track in the direction of the bridge, as if he could gauge the time and distance between the two locations, neither of which he could actually see. "Back," he said, jerking a thumb over his shoulder. "Never make the bridge in time."

"Agree—too far," Patrick said, shaking his head. "Turn this buggy around, Thomas, and show these animals you know more than they do. And God help us. They'll have to shut this section down now whether they like it or not."

Billy and Isaac had never worked so hard, but they seemed willing enough to give Thomas all he asked of them. God must have been looking after somebody, because the section house phone was nearly static free. As Patrick waited for a connection with Sean, Frank dispatched the crew out to mile marker six, with firm instructions from Patrick to round up, scare off, or shoot, if necessary, any bovine on or threatening to cross onto Chesapeake Rail right-of-way. A couple more men raced to the bridge switch to affix a blue flag and close down the track heading into Nevis.

"Sean," Patrick said, finally getting connected. "Damn cows are all over the track. Change the signal at the bridge to a yellow caution or we're cleaning up a derailment."

CHAPTER NINETEEN

Yippy Ti-Yi-Yo

Sean changed the signal and alerted the 873 as it approached the switch at the bridge, and it stopped within sight of the wandering cows. In a stroke of luck—or continued divine intervention—the general movement of the herd was toward town, not the bridge, although 873 found several fine specimens solidly planted in the middle of the track directly ahead. The train proceeded with caution onto the siding, to keep the main line clear. The last thing Sean needed was to juggle a series of trains backed up on the eastbound run.

With the crew chasing the herd off the track, Patrick gave a blow-by-blow to the train's engineer. Jake was a competent, patient father of six. Employed by the Chesapeake for some fifteen years now, he took the stop well. He had a clean record and good on-time numbers and seemed to grasp the situation: nailing a cow, even at slow speed, would have resulted in a derailment, loss of cargo, and personal injuries. As he sat up high in the hog with a bird's-eye view of grown men sweet-talking and tail-twisting a bunch of Jerseys, Jake appeared content.

The disposition of Patrick's crew was another story. Not a man among them knew a thing about cows except that they were the dumbest critters on four legs. Connor was for shooting them all—clean, quick, and, as Patrick pointed out, totally indefensible before a railroad review committee. So they chased them, pulled them, and herded them off the track. It was a frustrating, hellish day for everyone except Jake, who sat in the hog, playing cards with his stoker.

By sundown, they had led the last of the dairy herd back onto the McClelland property, shooing them a good distance in from the property line while other crew reinforced the posts and fence. Patrick left the boys at the creek, rinsing cow reek off themselves, and headed toward the train.

He hoisted himself up into the engine and shook hands with the engineer, nodding to the towheaded stoker affectionately known as Turnip. "What we do so you people can ride around in these things all day," Patrick said, mustering a weary grin. "How soon till you can get out of here?"

"Not long—couple hours," said Jake, jerking a thumb toward Turnip. "He's been tending a light fire. Been under light steam the whole time you were out there playing cowboys." He pulled out his watch. "So if you don't mind, I'd like to maintain some sort of schedule here. We'll be going as soon as you get off my train and let us get back to our business."

Patrick gave him a wink and hopped back out of the cab. "No objections from me. I don't want to see your face around these parts anymore. Got it?"

"You got it, Mr. Byrne."

———◆◆◆◆———

Jake was a decent man, good to his word. But two hours later, the 873 was still on the siding, without a head of steam and with no timetable for getting one.

The crew lounged near the creek, talking among themselves and careful not to be caught looking the foreman's way. And God forbid anyone should ask Patrick a question, because right now he was in a foul mood. When they stole a glance, they could see him up in the hog, yelling. Poor Jake.

Patrick hopped down and walked back to the creek. Silence descended. To Frank, he said, "Split the crew up—half checking that the track is still clear to the bridge, the rest here to the section house and back into town."

Frank hopped up. "Where you going?"

"Depot . . . to get *something* done."

Sean and Patrick stood in the middle of the depot like mirror images, each shaking his head and glaring at the other. Having it out face-to-face in the depot did not get Patrick any more traction with Sean than he got by yelling at Jake. Either his technique was slipping, or Sean had grown a backbone.

"Sean, we're going to do our damnedest to get it into station, but you need to keep a lid on it for a while."

"Listen to yourself," Sean said. "Go read the bulletin board over there, Mr. Let's Follow Regulations. If there's a new procedure saying I don't have to report an inoperable train, or cows menacing the right-of-way, I'll jump right on it." He sat down at the telegraph.

Patrick leaned on the counter beside him. "You want me out of your hair because you know I'm being reasonable. Just because they give you a big old pocket watch doesn't mean you have to use it all the time. I'm not asking you *not* to report it, just not *right away*. The track out there is clear, and it won't hurt anybody to wait. With a little time, we'll have

Eight seventy-three in and nobody'll be upset. Water under the bridge. You know Carr will go bananas. We won't have to worry about Miller on our back, no sir. Carr will go straight to the *top* man. No bonus, and we all get a pink slip."

Sean muttered some choice expletives. "Only fella gonna get upset is me when they don't promote me, or, worse still, they send me to the bread line. Can't hide this, Patrick. They'll be wondering where Eight seventy-three is."

"Wait—promote?" Patrick drew back to take a close look at Sean. "What's that about?"

Sean avoided eye contact. "Charlie Broderick's job," he mumbled. "Nobody's supposed to know. Miller told me if I did a good job, he'd promote me into Charlie's position. You can't repeat that, Pat."

Patrick's mouth dropped open. "Fat chance, seeing as how he promised me the same thing. "Conniving son of a . . ."

"Dirty, low-down . . ."

"No wonder we've been arguing so much—we've been at cross-purposes. I'll bet you a quarter Miller gets what he needs and neither of us gets it. It'll be Harmon or some other moron. That settles it. We're definitely not telling him. Payback starts right now."

Sean sighed and walked over to the depot ticket window, where he could see the Wesson Building. He shook his head. "I should have known it was too good to be true. But we can't get around telling him. We need to send a maintenance crew out and that can't be done without authorization. If they can't get the hog going, we need to send in another one and pull it, or push it into Nevis."

"*That's* an idea. Now we're talking, Sean." Patrick took him by the arm and directed him back to the telegraph. "Who's got a free hog sitting for the night that we can bring in and pull the train off the siding and get it into Nevis? Nevis—a much better place to fix it, by the way. Talk to Rupert. What's he got in Solomons?"

"Christ, you're crazy. I can't go shopping around for another engine."

"Just Rupert. Can you just ask him? Then whatever falls out, I'll shut my mouth. I promise. Just try Rupert."

Sean pulled his watch out, and Patrick rolled his eyes but managed to refrain from making a comment. They had stopped competing and shouting at each other and started listening. Now they were getting somewhere.

"If there's one laying over in Solomons, I'll get it for you. If there isn't, you're out of luck because there won't be another freight to Solomons until midday tomorrow. That's the best I can get you, Mac. But before I call Rupert, we give Maintenance a try. Okay?"

Patrick nodded and patted him on the back. "I can ride back out with Maintenance," he said, walking toward the door. "See what Rupert has. Call the section house and let me know."

Sean nodded and lifted the phone receiver from the cradle. "Mac?"

Patrick let go of the doorknob. "Yeah?"

"I'm all in on that retribution thing."

CHAPTER TWENTY
A Little Bump and Grind

The maintenance workers threw in the towel on the stroke of midnight and pronounced the 873 dead on the siding—victim of a blown regulator valve and an array of other possible afflictions. The fix would be routine work, they declared, but only if the locomotive was in the depot. Maintenance on the line, especially at this time of night, required approval by the head of the maintenance section—current whereabouts unknown. They cleared out fast and headed back to Nevis and bed.

None of this was surprising to anyone. There was an uneasy relationship between the maintenance crew and, well, everyone else, including Sean, who normally considered himself everybody's friend. Jake, the engineer, who probably considered throwing in with the maintenance crew better for his long-range prospects, stayed in the cab and kept his mouth shut until he and Patrick had a quick conference and threw the whole wretched mess back into Sean's lap.

Sean contacted Rupert in Solomons right after midnight, calling him on a line reserved for emergencies—the phone in Rupert's house. The two worked well together in an almost magical partnership of give-and-take. Engine 322 was arriving as they spoke. It was scheduled to lie over at Rupert's end—a quiet arrangement between Rupert and the engineer, Wilson, who was godfather to Rupert's nephew. After all, family was family. The only one truly put out by the whole process would be Sean—by precisely twenty bucks for the favor—but he, in turn, would probably squeeze it out of Byrne somehow. Then it would be Byrne's problem. Right now, it was a good investment in everybody's future with the Chesapeake Railway.

The day crew, with the exception of Patrick, Connor, and Frank, had been swapped out for the night watchman and his small skeleton crew, although this crew was larger than most—another accommodation for Lawrence Carr, the perennial worrywart. They were scattered about, lounging in one of the work wagons or leaning against the poplars on the far side of the tracks opposite McClelland's land. Night work was generally quiet and slow, reactive as opposed to proactive, and its crews were a peculiar breed, much like a family's middle child. They were mainly loners and outsiders, given to feeling invisible out in the pitch black of night, and resentful of the day crew, whom they considered, rightly or not, privileged in praise, salary, and promotions. But tonight was proving different. Suddenly, the nighters felt energized, renewed, with a story to tell at dinner tomorrow. Patrick didn't much like it; flapping lips were the last thing he needed.

A thought suddenly popped in his head and gave him a worse feeling. He picked up a lantern and walked toward the end of the train, raising the light to each of the cars as he passed, as if memorizing the call numbers on the side. When he got to the caboose, he lowered the lantern and strode back to the rest of the workers."

"Problem?" Frank asked, getting up and walking over.

"Where's the livestock car?" Patrick asked. "Miller said the shipment had ponies—dancing, farting ponies. Where'd the livestock go?"

"No livestock cars, Pat. Been sitting here all night staring at 'em. If he wants livestock, we can go rustle a few milk cows, though. Lots to choose from. Don't know about dancing ones, but they're all farters. Ask Connor. He had one—"

Patrick chuckled. "Maybe later, Frank, when I can enjoy it. Must not have scheduled 'em. Sure don't hear any animals."

"Who's driving and how long, Byrne?" one of the crew shouted at his back as he stood staring down the dark track.

"Wilson. Two hours," he said, not turning around. "Three twenty-two never powered down. Time in the roundhouse, and they're out again." It was nothing short of providence. A cold engine would have taken hours to stoke and bring around. It gave him hope they might pull this off and, amazing as it might seem, move past it with nary a management ripple.

Patrick climbed up into the caboose bird's nest. Nothing fancy about this car. All it had in common with the quaint caboose connected to the Nevis passenger train was a coat of red paint. It was essentially a no-nonsense modified boxcar with a history of bouncing from train to train over the past dozen years. Downstairs housed a desk stacked and stuffed with various papers and manuals, a small kerosene stove, and a hanging bunk bolted to one of the long sides of the box. A steel ladder mounted to the front wall led to a punch-out on top, guaranteed to be sweltering hot in the summer and frostbite cold in the dead of winter. Up there was a smaller makeshift desk—wide enough for writing paper and a cup of coffee and not much else. Strictly utilitarian, the punch-out allowed one to scrutinize any trouble spots along the length of the train—provided it was during daylight.

Patrick sat down on top of the makeshift desk and propped himself against one of the metal sides so he could see 322's lamps as it approached. Then he promptly drifted off into a shallow sleep.

He had been dreaming for a while when he jerked awake, disengaging from a confusing vignette of disjointed images, people, and train whistles. His mouth was moving, gibberish spilling out and directed at no one in particular. The rails were humming faintly. *Wooo-wooo.* There it went again and, clearer now, the chugging of 322 as it powered down in response to the warning signals posted at the bridge. Down the track, still far in the distance, he could make out a speck of light as her headlamps burned away the darkness.

"Flag, Turnip," Patrick yelled, jumping down off the car. "Get some lanterns in here. Connor, O'Connell, climb aboard and get him in close so he doesn't bang the crap out of the rear end."

Everybody bolted. Some grabbed kerosene lanterns from the wagon while others made sure the line stayed clear. Their eyes strained in the darkness to see the train that promised to send the day crew to their beds, and the night crew back to the newly appreciated comforts of the maintenance house.

Connor and O'Connell moved up beside 873's last car and, in a dance of lights, waved lanterns to bring Wilson in. The final approach seemed to take forever as the train slowed to a crawl, its brakes screeching, and metal grinding against metal.

Patrick walked alongside the hog, watching as his heart pounded a hard rhythm. Sweat ran down the back of his neck, and his chest constricted. He ignored the increasing pain as the distance between the two trains shrank from yards to feet. There would be a bounce when they made contact, and nobody was under any illusions that the caboose would look the same afterward, but they didn't have to start out the process by banging the crap out of it.

"Steady," he yelled right before Wilson pushed his hog up against 873. There was some bouncing and the sound of groaning metal, though not as much as Patrick had anticipated. He blew out a sigh of relief and turned to grin at the 322's engineer and his light touch. Cheering broke out.

"Don't come out of there," Patrick said to the fireman, who was starting to dismount. "And don't get comfortable. Connor, O'Connell, great job. All crew clear," he yelled. He waited a moment and then gave 322 the thumbs-up. "Now, get her out of here before something else goes wrong."

And damned if it didn't all go right for a change. Patrick and crew stood mesmerized as the 322 inched forward, nudging along the broken-down 873. Off the siding, toward Nevis, the two engines crept back out onto the main line. It was exhilarating, like watching the ponies hit the home stretch at Gravesend.

CHAPTER TWENTY-ONE
Patience Is a Virtue

There was never question of a runaway. The trains crept at a turtle's pace for the interminable seven miles back to town. After a rough start, Wilson developed "the touch," and things went relatively well. They might not even need to explain why the caboose frame was bent. Things sometimes just *happened* in a rail yard.

A hair past four in the morning, and not more than two hours from when 322 came to their rescue at the siding, they reached the depot. Patrick cringed as the trains ground to a stop at the loading dock. Nevis was dead, but even if there had been an audience, the locals would not have questioned the nighttime activities of the rail yard. Neither were there worries about someone running off to tattle to big boss Miller. He had returned to Baltimore yesterday to bootlick some bigwigs passing through.

The hog's stacks bellowed their final clouds of smoke, and Patrick closed his eyes and savored the deathlike hiss as the train shut down.

Frank joined him as he mooned over the blue and silver engine sitting motionless at the dock.

"Loveliest sight I ever saw," Frank said with a deep sigh."

"Ain't it, though? I don't know how we did it, but thank you, God. It's done. As far as I'm concerned, when it's all unloaded and 873 transfers to maintenance, this never happened. The yard crane's fired up and bellowing steam. Get it all done before daylight, and we're home free."

"Look at this." Frank pointed to the small crowd of gawkers attending the arrival. "Everybody's beat, but they're still sticking around to see it all on the dock. Know it's off the rails and out of their hands before they walk away."

They watched as yard workers, prepped and sworn to secrecy—knitted together by their Irishness and a shared dislike for Miller and just about any other form of authority—swarmed the train and attached winch cable hooks to crates, hoists, and pulleys and started swinging crates to the loading dock in a flurry of activity.

The gawkers were a patient group, sitting there with glazed eyes and weary bones. So Patrick should not have been caught off guard when, in their haste to finish putting one over on management, catastrophe struck.

As the last crate rose from the train and swung out toward the dock, there was a loud pop, as if something under great tension had suddenly snapped. The crate sailed out past several yardmen, clipped one on the periphery, and sent him tumbling across the dock. As it swung back in again, it arced low, spinning and wobbling before careening into the crate offloaded before it. Then connecting cables sprang loose completely from the winch, and the crate dropped down into a third, crushing the top. Silence fell as crafty plans shattered and splintered against the dock like waves against a rocky shore. All eyes went to Patrick.

Patrick's hands went to his face, and his legs nearly buckled. In an instant, he was pushing his way through the throng of workers crowding around Peter who lay sprawled flat on the decking. "Broken shoulder," they were already whispering. If so, he was a lucky man. Someone took off to fetch the doctor.

"Stay still, Peter," another cautioned, holding the yardman's enormous, callused hand. "Doc's coming." Peter opened his eyes and nodded with a grimace, tightening his grip on the other man's hand.

Somebody produced a flask. With the gentleness and care usually reserved for newborns and lovers, one of the bigger men, with arms muscled from years of hoisting and hauling, tipped Peter's head up just enough for a swig or two. Whiskey may not have quelled all the pain, but Peter and everyone around him were no doubt calmer by the time Doc got to him.

Everyone except Harmon. He had been a quiet nonpresence at the depot, taking it all in while offering nothing in exchange. He took the latest setback with the silence of the introverted, intellectual sideliner that he was. He watched a moment more, then disappeared from the rear of the crowd. Frank had been open about his distrust of the man, and if he had been watching tonight, he would have insisted that Harmon insert himself into at least one damning activity.

Doc Bagley's house was a four-minute sprint from the loading dock, and the runner they sent had him out of bed and at the accident scene within fifteen. Doc was a good man, and Peter O'Malley a lucky one. Doc taped him up and told him his shoulder would heal given time and patience. Still, with a wife and four kids to feed and clothe, it was a rough blow.

While Doc worked on Peter, friends kept a steady stream of liquor coming his way, and by the time they loaded him in a wagon and took him home, he was fighting not the pain, but unconsciousness.

Perhaps he rested easier knowing that the railroad men handled the day-to-day perils of a dangerous occupation with individual wit and community support and affection, but also with a certain Irish fatalism. Things happened; they got handled; life moved on. And the lot of them would do what it took to support Peter O'Malley's family during his recuperation.

Patrick did not subscribe to fatalism, since doing so would have tied him to a sickbed long ago. He would have none of it. Even in the face of irrefutable facts and insurmountable odds—as Doc never tired of reminding him at each appointment—he simply was not one to give in without fighting the good fight. Those who knew him never expected anything less, and it was why his crewmates now stood wide-eyed and slack-jawed, eyes on him, waiting for an answer.

Only this time, he had no answer. He beckoned Sean to follow him inside.

CHAPTER TWENTY-TWO

Worth a Thousand Words

Sean flopped into his desk chair and shoved the other one toward Patrick with his foot. He opened his mouth as if to speak, then closed it again.

"Send the crews home," Patrick said, sitting down. "Lock it all up. We'll figure it out, Sean. Miller doesn't win."

Sean groaned and stared at the ceiling.

"Look at me." Patrick rolled his chair closer and jostled Sean's arm until he did. "*Miller doesn't win.* We're all tired, and we're panicking. It seems bad, but we need to stay calm. There's a way out of this."

"Jiminy, you know it's all busted to hell."

"Hold up, Sean. It was equipment failure. This wasn't our fault."

"All those unauthorized things we've been doing . . . I'm done for." He had a hunted look in his eyes. "*You're* done, too. You recognize that, right? And neither one of us has a snowball in a steam boiler's chance at Broderick's job. First Packard's missing package, and now this."

"Packard has searchers all over the woods. They'll find his precious carousel thingamabob. But if you think this'll ruin my chances for that bonus and getting off the rails, you don't know the first thing about me, Sean Michael Murphy. You're letting Miller get to you. We're better than he gives us credit for, so don't go jumping the tracks. Until we know what's in those crates, the two of us are missing something that should be obvious. What's the inventory say?"

Sean ran his finger down the shipping list. "Stuff? No idea."

Patrick pulled the list away from Sean, studied it a moment, and dropped it on the desk. "Doesn't really matter at this point. We'll open the boxes, assess the damage, and if we can't salvage it, we'll reorder. Yeah, of course!" he said, warming to the idea. "We thank everybody for their participation and send 'em home. Then we go in with a few trustworthy lads, open the crates and see what's what, then reorder, fix—whatever."

Sean looked pale. He arched an eyebrow and waited, looking too drained to fight him.

"Uh-huh, now you're tracking with me," Patrick said, his enthusiasm continuing to build. "Everything that's still in one piece gets sent merrily along like nothing happened. Anything we can't fix becomes a crate lost in the transit system somewhere. When they find the order incomplete, they'll send out a tracker, am I right? When they can't account for the cargo, Chesapeake and company will suck it up, make it good with Carr, and pony up their own dime to replace it. Chesapeake can afford it; they'll soon be raking in the dough. Not our problem. Everybody keeps their job, gets a bonus, and I'm out of here in a few months. We can live with this. If you can't, do it anyway and then go to confession."

While Sean continued staring at him in horrified wonder, Patrick pressed on, a little faster now to keep him off balance. "All is forgiven of those who repent, right? God will understand. He understands *everything*.

He wouldn't want us to go hungry and homeless, Sean. Think of our families. Do it for your family."

Sean blinked twice, which Patrick took as Morse code for *yeah, sure.* He plowed on.

"Here's what you do. Move the damaged crates into the shed. Then clear out the audience. We'll see what's what and then we'll deal with it. Right now, stay calm and don't report anything yet. After we see what the mess is, I'll come up with something, I promise. No use agonizing till then. Okay?"

Sean latched on to his arm. "I have to tell them *something.*"

"No-o-o," Patrick said, peeling his arm free. "Our first priority is to duck 'em. If that doesn't work, *lie.* You've been around Frank long enough to know how it's done. Stay calm and pretend you're Frank." He nodded. "Yeah, that'll work."

Sean pulled out the silver medal dangling on a chain inside his shirt. "Blessed Mary, pray for me now and at the hour of my death," he murmured. "Otherwise, I am in so much trouble." He put the medal to his lips and kissed it.

Patrick stepped away. He hated leaving Sean like this, but he needed to get alone and think. If the Virgin Mary failed to calm Sean, what could he possibly do?

An hour later, Patrick and his usual accomplices—Frank, Connor, Thomas, and Sean—crossed the deserted yard and slipped inside the maintenance building closest to the loading dock. They squeezed past the damaged crates piled on dollies inside the door. Beyond stood a series of long tables, set up parallel and stacked with piles of metal parts, rags, tools, and whatnot. Routine and emergency maintenance went on here, but as a rule, no train laid over in the Nevis yard unless it couldn't leave under its own steam. Outside, 873 sat alone in the dark.

Sean wedged a two-by-four against the inside of the door. The men stood silently, crowbars in hand, their motivation ebbing away like water dribbling from a leaky bucket. After wrangling balky cows yesterday and spending all night bringing in the hog, they were spent. Only Patrick seemed unwilling to give up and go home.

He looked at them with guilty eyes. He had led his friends into a precarious position, and they had already given more than he had a right to ask of any crew. Breathing deeply, as if sucking in enough air would relieve the tightness in his chest, he slung his cap over a nail on one of the support beams and laid his bar on the end of the nearest table. Then he turned and looked at them.

"I've asked you to do things in the last twenty-four hours that weren't exactly according to the rules," he said. "And now I've got you here, exhausted, hating life—maybe even hating *me*. But the fact remains, if we can't salvage these crates, everything will unravel. You can kiss your bonus good-bye, maybe even your job along with it. What do you say?"

"Not saying nothing," Frank said, giddy in his fatigue. He shambled over to the least damaged crate, nudging his brother out of the way. "You look a little pale. Let the master show you how it's done." He pushed up his sleeves. "I say we shake a leg so we can get this done and get outta here." Nails squeaked as he pried up a loose board.

Connor grumbled something and moved down to the next crate.

Thomas took the third crate, and soon the warehouse was filled with the squeaking of pried nails, and the occasional muttered oath. Patrick took a seat on a table with Sean and watched them work, amazed that they had any energy left at all.

Frank put down his crowbar. "Last chance to strike a match and walk away," he said, looking at Patrick and Sean.

Patrick hopped down and watched as he cleared away the straw and paper packing inside the crate.

Patrick uttered a string of profanities. "Sweet Jesus, you are our saving grace," he murmured. "Now please come be our carpenter."

"Wow. What's this?" Connor said, pulling away the excelsior packing and peering inside the crate.

"Screwed, that's what," Sean said, peering in. "No way we can reorder this. What do we do now?"

Patrick walked over to see what Connor had. "We knew they were gonna be a mess. Don't give up yet." He leaned past Connor for a look and burst out laughing. "*Ponies.* Damned if it isn't!"

"What the hell's wrong with you?" Frank asked, moving in to see.

"I'm worried to death about a lost livestock car, and here's your ponies—*carousel* ponies." Patrick wiped the tears from his eyes.

Sean snorted. "That's the saddest pony I've ever seen. In fact, I'd say that's one dead carousel pony."

Each crate held the same cargo. Some of the legs were broken off, and sections of the bodies split and mangled beyond the conspirators' ability to repair with glue or hide with sleight of hand.

It would have been an injustice to call the horse in Connor's crate a mere *pony*. It would have been a grand stallion, and the colored bits and pieces in the crate hinted at intricate details: an elaborate saddle studded with red and blue glass jewels, a gold and green dragon's head peering out from between the back edge of the broken saddle and the jet-black saddle pad. Bits of carved red flower garland still clung in jagged pieces around the scraped and gouged white neck.

Thomas's animal was in the best shape of the three, although not by much. He stood quietly beholding a defiant, stalking tawny lion, the shape and details of its mane now anybody's guess from the handful of puzzle pieces lying in the bottom of the crate.

The saddest figure, the one that looked the most in pain, if that were possible, was the third carved animal: a cottontail rabbit painted in tones of mottled gray and brown, both ears broken off at the head, which seemed to huddle in fear at the bottom of the crate.

Connor tossed aside his crowbar. "Boss, maybe Frank's right: torch it all, mislabel 'em, or shove 'em in the back where no one'll notice. This is bad. I think we're licked here."

"Oh, like a bonfire's not going to draw any attention," Sean said.

"What about talking it over with one of the German woodworkers in town?" Frank said. "Someone could build us new ones. We could have him in and out, see what he needs, and still nobody the wiser. Can't be any tougher than carving cuckoo clocks."

Patrick shook his head. "Can't go talking this around. And somebody will guess we're up to something soon as we start sneaking Germans in and out of here."

"Well, ain't nobody gonna rebuild what he can't see," Sean said, checking for nails before sitting down on a pile of lumber scraps. "We've accomplished nothing. The faster we buck up and admit defeat, the better off we'll be. We should give the company time to make good with Carr on this."

"Absolutely not," Patrick said, rubbing the sore muscles in the back of his neck. "After all this, I'm not walking away without my bonus. Let's think, people."

"If we can't burn this mess, I say we bury it out there somewhere," Connor said, waving a hand toward the most cluttered corner of the yard.

"What about a photo?" Thomas asked, grimacing as he got a look at the pony. "That photographer that passed through and took Harry's picture after he passed—he could do it. A carver could work from that."

"Naw, long gone," Patrick said. He sat down next to Frank. "Probably all the way to Boston by now. Don't know of any others."

Frank dug a small divot with his heel into the dirt floor. "So we're sunk for lack of a picture."

"Yeah, one measly picture . . ." Patrick stared at Frank a moment, and his face lit up. "Or a very good *drawing*."

"Yeah, well, look around," Frank said. "So unless it's gonna get painted with a lining bar, you can drop that idea down the two-seater out back."

"Frank, see if you can clear a path through all this mess," Patrick said, looking around at the detritus from their efforts. "And sweep it good, too. We all go to work today like nothing happened. Then go home and get a little shut-eye. I have a plan." He lifted his cap off the nail and put it on. "I know just who can help us."

CHAPTER TWENTY-THREE

Note to an Angel

As much as he would have liked to, Patrick did not believe that God would send his only son, the carpenter, to help put the figures back together. But he did believe that God was more apt to help him if he tried to solve his own problems. He had not spent his *entire* time in catechism daydreaming and dodging ruler-wielding nuns. In fact, God had already helped him, and he had almost missed it. Meeting Birdie Partridge was not happenstance. Even before he needed her, she had appeared—the answer to his prayer. She could draw like an angel, and his gut told him she could be trusted like one, too.

Getting to her would be dicey, though. He was not one to court trouble, and asking about town, even discreetly, after the betrothed of the most powerful man in Nevis could easily go wrong. Since their impromptu walking tour of Nevis, Patrick had seen her here and there, but always at a distance—the inaccessible showpiece of a proud, possessive man. He was torn between giving Main Street a once-over and heading toward the wharf. His gut told him to start at the water. If she was out anywhere late this Thursday, she would be with King Carr where he usually held court, at the water's edge, either in his temporary office near the boardwalk, or at the Bayside Hotel.

After a short walk, he spied her unforgettable figure, mixing with the uppities around the newly constructed stables by the almost-finished racetrack. She was the only woman in the crowd, and her flamboyant broad-brimmed, peacock-feathered hat bobbed in a sea of staid brown bowlers.

It made sense Carr would be here. In a stroke of genius, the partnership had decided to tap into the long-standing Maryland horse-racing tradition. This was the last big area of construction, as well as the showiest. With an air of confidence, the partners had dismissed outright the competition posed by the successful, century-old track and grandstand in Upper Marlboro, a mere dozen miles away.

Gazing out across the track, Patrick inhaled the smell of freshly broken soil. It brought back memories of a lovelier, less complicated time, in his mother's garden, where she had taught him to eat sweet green peas popped right out of the pod. Gone two years now, he still missed her. He studied the oval track. He would have liked a crack at planting something there. What a waste to dedicate it all to gambling. The previous landowners had no doubt gotten more money selling it than they would ever see from a lifetime of corn or tobacco crops. Still . . .

His father's property down in the foggy bottom was too wet to farm easily. He had pride of ownership, but precious little income from it. It was a disadvantage for all the Irish there. They would remain manual laborers, not farmers, and completely beholden to the railroad. He envied the Germans and their sunny, well-drained farms.

He tried to look at the images before him with a business eye, although the closest he ever got to high finance was adding columns of numbers in his log. Certainly, the track would be profitable for the developers. Bored people with excess money loved to fritter it away on the horses.

He checked the crowd again. Finding the high-society woman had been easy enough, but approaching her in that crowd of uppities wouldn't be. In his twenty-six years, he had seen his fill of "*No Dogs or Irish*" signs, and he had to consider his reception. Irish *and* a railroader—not exactly the pedigree to let him mix easily with this crowd. What would the dangerously confident, always opinionated Connor do? Not even Connor knew the answer to that one, but he would at least be direct. Patrick pulled out his foreman log, scribbled across the first blank page, ripped it from its binding, and crumpled it into a ball. And off he went.

As Patrick approached, Carr seemed totally engrossed in his conversation, but Birdie appeared bored, her hand bouncing like a metronome against the side of her dark-blue skirt. No longer engaged in the conversation, she looked around. A fleeting smile lit up her face when she spied Patrick walking toward them. She did not engage him, but instead turned back to Carr, stopped her bouncing, and appeared suddenly intent on the conversation.

Patrick approached but did not intrude, stopping a few paces short and waiting, eyes cast down as he studied the dirt on his work boots. Eventually, Carr wound up his conversation and turned to him.

"Why, good day, Mr. Byrne. What can I do for you?" he asked, all cordial affability in front of his peers.

Patrick played along and tipped his hat. "Yes, sir. I saw you standing down here. Track is looking swell—puts Upper Marlboro to shame, yes sir. I thought to give you some good news. Don't know if you've spoken to Mr. Miller recently, but we are right on the money with the freight coming in. Everything is on schedule. Thought I'd check and see if there are any concerns or problems I can take care of personally or bring to Mr. Miller's attention."

Carr nodded, puffing his chest out a little just as Patrick had anticipated he would. "Mr. Byrne, on the whole I've been very impressed with the Chesapeake. Barring any kind of mishap, we have a chance to finish ahead of schedule. I know I don't need to tell you how happy and grateful I'll be. No," he said. "Everything is shaping up just fine. Keep it up, son."

"What we want to hear," Patrick said. "I'll pass it along to Mr. Miller. Now if, you'll excuse me, I'll get out of you good folks' way." He tipped his hat once more, and as he turned away, he stooped suddenly as if to pick something up from the ground. "Excuse me, ma'am," he said to Birdie. "I believe you dropped this." He handed her the crumpled page he had ripped from his logbook.

"Oh," Birdie said. Looking a little puzzled at first, she took the paper and smiled, sliding it into her skirt pocket. "Thank you. Dressmaker's list," she said to Carr, bowing her head as the color rose in her cheeks.

Patrick smiled and walked off. The crew's fate was now in her pocket.

CHAPTER TWENTY-FOUR
Everybody Wants Something

F or a late Friday morning, the wharf was extraordinarily busy. The well-heeled lingered about in fine suits and best dresses while workers hurried by in worn work shirts and coveralls, doing the jobs that had to be done whatever the day of the week. Arriving by foot, bicycle, horse, or automobile, all were with a common purpose: to greet the arrival of the Baltimore steamer *Chessie Belle.* Some were here to take delivery of offloaded goods, some to gawk at the steamship's size and marvel at the efficiency of modern transport. And no doubt some, like Mr. Patrick Byrne, were here to conduct carefully arranged liaisons that would appear to the casual observer as pure happenstance.

Patrick and Frank stood outside the throng, as close to the road and beach as they could get without leaving the wharf. They had been waiting a while, and Frank, having the shorter attention span of the two, had pulled out his pocketknife and was discreetly carving his initials in the handrail.

"Sure she's coming?"

"Gotta hope so," Patrick said, continuing to stare at the entrance to the Bayside. "She's the only idea—"

"*Chessie!*" Frank said, pointing his knife at a dot on the southern horizon. They had seen it come in dozens of times, and still he stood agog, taking it in as if for the first time. "Do you know how big the wheel is? Criminy, I can't get over how much water that thing can spin!"

"You have saltwater running in your veins," Patrick said, jostling him with his elbow. "You should have gone to sea."

Frank continued staring. "Maybe I will someday. Can't be any worse than washing cinders out of your eyes every night."

"*Chessie, Chessie,*" a young boy chanted, and the throng on the pier pushed forward, shuffling toward the spot where the gangplank would soon be lowered. Frank and Patrick hugged the railing to withstand the surge.

Patrick shook his head. "I never did get this part of the show. If the merchandise doesn't change hands here, it'll be carted off to any of half a dozen warehouses, or sent to Tanner's."

Just about everything Patrick needed, he bought at C. W. Tanner's Mercantile and Post Office, the little white-framed store right down the road. George Dilly and Carter Tanner were close friends and cut from the same cloth. About fifteen years before Dilly cornered the market on meals for the working class, Tanner had had the foresight to grease a few palms and become the town postmaster—and put up the only Post Office and dry-goods store for ten miles around. Aided by his wife, Nancy, the biggest purveyor of personal information in town, Tanner seemed to have an uncanny ability to predict weddings, births, funerals, and all manner of indiscretions, and stock his shelves accordingly. The only competition he need worry about was the occasional peddler. But being on cozy terms with the local constabulary, he could rest easy knowing that any drummer or tinker nervy enough to wander into Nevis would be booted back out with his wares bouncing along right behind him.

"Pat . . . *Pat.*" Frank elbowed his sibling and cocked his head toward a group of matrons descending on a man in faded black overalls as he moseyed along puffing on the remnant of a stogie, shouldering bolts of colorful fabric likely destined for Tanner's.

Patrick chuckled. The women clucked and fluttered as they fanned away tobacco stench with their lacy white handkerchiefs and scurried along as decorously as they could manage, in the workman's wake. Patrick would give Tanner's a wide berth until the bolts sold out an hour from now.

"You, ho! Outta the way, Mac—barrels coming through." A broad-shouldered bull of a man dressed in a wrinkled work shirt and grimy, baggy pants waved them to the right as he directed two farmers unloading tobacco hogsheads from their oxcart. Patrick bristled at the contemptuous way "Mac" rolled off the dockworker's tongue. Another time, he might have followed up on the perceived slight, but today he would let the insult pass.

He and Frank jumped off the pier and hunkered down on the sand to wait and watch. Birdie should be about soon, if she was coming. He didn't expect her to be out here early, for she had no need to barter or battle with the cluckers for things being sold at dockside. Anything she truly needed, she would likely order through a personal representative in Baltimore, or farther north, and have shipped directly. There were other options, too. With an automobile at her disposal, and premium service from the rail company, she didn't have to stalk a dock man.

"Is that you?" Frank asked, elbowing his brother in the ribs.

"What?"

"You're grinding your teeth down to nubbins. You don't think she's coming."

"Criminy, I don't know. Do you see her out here anywhere?" He surveyed the beach. "I don't think she's going to come waltzing right up to us." Patrick stretched his legs out and wiped away the sweat collecting under his hatband. "I didn't think about how hot it was going to be out here."

He couldn't shake the nagging sense that things were not going to pan out. He took out his watch—ten past noon.

He was ready to call it a bust when she came out the side door of the Bayside Hotel, his angel in white, opening her maroon and white parasol as she floated down the beachside stairs. Most importantly, she was alone.

He left Frank and walked at a pace measured to cross her path. In her flouncy cotton dress and wide-brimmed straw hat, she seemed more appropriately outfitted for a city boulevard stroll than a walk along the bay. She made eye contact for an instant, then looked past him and proceeded along as if on some errand. It was not until he almost collided with her that she paid any obvious outward attention.

"Miss Partridge, so sorry," he said, reaching for her.

She took a step back, waving off his attempt to steady her. "Mr. Byrne. How much?" she whispered.

"What?"

"The amount that would allow you to live with your conscience. Name it."

Patrick gave her a confused look.

"In town the other day," she said, giving him a hard look. "I don't know what you think you saw, but Mr. Packard and I are friends through Mr. Carr. There's nothing remotely—"

Patrick put a hand up. "Now, hold on. I don't know how we got headed down this path, but you're way off base."

"Please. Do you think you're the first to try to squeeze a buck out of Lawrence? Passing notes to me in front of him like a schoolyard bully."

"*Bully?* Hey, wait. I'm not trying to do anything to anybody, and I don't want your money. What did I do to rile you up like this? I thought I conducted myself with the utmost respect." He checked around to make sure no one was within earshot. "We've run into a problem and I need your help."

She glanced back toward the hotel, then eyed him cautiously. "What kind of help?"

Patrick followed her gaze and took a step closer. "Can I count on your discretion? This affects a lot of good, hardworking people."

She looked hesitant. "Tell me and then I'll decide."

"There's been an accident at the depot. Some of the park's cargo got damaged: carved animals for the showpiece carousel. If Mr. Miller finds out, he'll fire me to save face with Carr, and the rest of my men will lose out on a bonus they badly need."

"Mr. Miller of the wandering eye?"

"Excuse me?" he asked, frowning. "Well, yeah, probably," he added, his cheeks coloring.

She shook her head. "If you think I'm going to approach *that* man—"

"No! Oh, God, no. My advice would be to trust your instincts and steer clear of the man." He paused as two women strolled past them. "No, I was hoping, *really* hoping, you might help us out artistically. I may find someone who has the skill to repair them, but when we move them, we're going to damage them even more. Repairing them on-site would invite too many questions. But if I had pictures before we move them, I could give them to a woodworker here in town and maybe get detailed replacements made. Nobody would need to be the wiser. I hate involving you, but I can't think of any other way. It's not for me so much . . ."

"You want me to *draw*?" She tightened her grip on the parasol. "I don't know. Mr. Carr generally supports my pursuits, but he's not too happy with me right now. I made a mistake when I went into town last week. Mr. Abbott—he's a bit insecure about his position—told Lawrence I had wandered off alone and returned with you. Then it was Lawrence's turn to feel insecure. I told him you saw me walking alone and insisted on accompanying me back, and he accepted my excuse with the broadest of smiles and the sweetest words. What that really means is, he didn't believe a word I said. If he thinks I've gone behind his back again . . ."

"He doesn't need to find out. Keeping this nice and quiet is to everybody's benefit. If you can get out, we can do it at night. And I'll make sure you get back and forth safely." Patrick stopped to let her consider and looked around to make sure they weren't drawing attention. Only Frank appeared interested in their conversation. "The cargo is at the depot. With a little juggling of paperwork, the cargo has been, um, *misplaced*. We might have a few days before we have to report it as lost. No one but Frank and I will ever know you helped. I give you my word."

Her eyes darted back toward the hotel. "Just my standing here with you looks inappropriate, but I won't give you a rushed decision. If I decide to help, expect me at eight thirty where we met the other day. That's my best offer. Make sure you're on time."

He offered a silent prayer of thanks. "You have no idea how much we appreciate the help, and you can be sure I'll be waiting for you. No one is more punctual than a track foreman. Oh, one more thing you should know: they aren't all horses. There's a lion, a rabbit—"

"They all have four legs and ears, sir," she said, suddenly stiff and formal. "Now, if you will excuse me."

She sidestepped him and continued on her walk, parasol spinning slowly as she strolled toward a cluster of equally well-dressed women she apparently knew, coming from the opposite direction.

CHAPTER TWENTY-FIVE

Drawing Room

Patrick melted into the shadows of the alleyway between the white framed cobbler's shack and the newer brick building of the weekly *Nevis Evening Star* newspaper. No need to hide—Nevis was deserted—but it just felt like the thing to do when trying not to be noticed. Gravel crunched underfoot. He paced, turned, and retraced his steps until something else caught his ear. He eased back toward the storefronts and peeked around the corner. It was Birdie, but she was not alone. He watched as she had quiet words with a male companion, but she either bade him stay some distance back or go away entirely, because the man's silhouette quickly became indistinguishable from the shadows, and she was alone as she drew close.

"Birdie." Patrick stepped into the street and uncovered his lantern. She hesitated, then walked quickly toward him. "Did you want to include him?" he asked, gesturing toward the shadows.

"Sorry, but surely you didn't think I'd be wandering around the town by myself."

"No, I thought you'd come with someone you trusted. Mr. Packard is welcome to tag along." He heard her catch her breath.

"Mr. Packard is a good man," she said. "Lawrence likes buying people, but Mr. Packard will never be one of them. I trust him completely, and you can, too. Now, take me wherever we need to go."

Even in the dim lantern light, Patrick could see the tightness in her face, and he heard the same clipped coldness she had directed at him today at the wharf.

"I'm sorry," he said. "Maybe this is a bad idea. I'll walk you back out to Mr. Packard. We'll find another way."

"It's done now. I sneaked out through a side door and left Lawrence and his pals to enjoy the haze of wretched Cuban cigar smoke and insincere banter. He may not be standing by the end of the night, depending on how lucky he gets. Drunks make lousy company, Mr. Byrne, regardless of whether they win or lose. Hopefully, he'll sleep it off at the gaming table, and our little rendezvous will go unnoticed.

"I said I'd help, and I'll try, but no one else can ever know. After tonight, please don't contact me anymore, for any reason. Bring me back here when we're done, and A. J. will see that I get back safely."

"It may be a while."

"He'll wait."

Patrick could have made it around the yard without the lantern, perhaps even with his eyes closed, but he paused to sniff the air. It was crisp and clean. Michael, the night watchman, was a creature of habit and a heavy smoker, and right now it was a good bet that he was puffing away on the far side of the yard. Patrick would run him down later and feed him some line about stealing a few private moments in the maintenance shed with some nameless wench. Michael would buy right into it and stay out of their way.

Patrick popped the shed lock and hung the lantern on a hook inside the door. She stepped in behind him, seeming somehow small and meek, unlike the force of nature he had met on her first day in town. He took in what she was wearing, and chuckled. It was another frilly dress of gauzy material, and green like her eyes. A white shawl draped her shoulders.

"I hadn't anticipated you coming formal and all."

"I don't dig ditches for a living, Mr. Byrne."

There was that edge again. Digging ditches was honorable enough work. If anything, being a kept woman, whose life revolved around society events, was the livelihood more deserving of scorn. She was obviously nervous and apparently unused to rendezvousing with men in dark, shadowy places about town. But she got a pass right now because he needed her.

"Fair enough, but I wish you'd call me Patrick. Then I won't feel like someone your Lawrence bought." He turned away and lit another lantern. "We'll try to keep you looking that way, but I can't promise. Come, let's see what you think about the mess in here." He took her elbow and guided her to the carousel figures. Most of the crating had been pulled away, so that they reminded him of corpses laid out for the undertaker.

"Here," he said. "Three figures, or what's left of them."

"Dear me, that doesn't look good," she said, walking down the row, bending and peering at each. "Golden . . . lion, is it? I might need to guess a little on him. White horse. Brown rabbit. I'll do them one, two, three, hardest to easiest." She pulled a pad and pencil from the rose-and-green brocade bag slung over her shoulder. "Something to sit on?" she asked, looking about.

"Oh, sorry. I brought a tarp." He pulled a bundle from one of the tables and spread it out for her. "It's a little rough, but clean. Such a shame about the animals. I hope the carver got to see them on the carousel before they shipped. They were probably beautiful. Even if we find someone to fix them, I doubt they'll ever look the same."

"Hmm," she said as she sat down near the first pile and set right to work.

"I've never ridden one myself," he said. "You?"

"A carousel? Oh, my, yes. My father used to take us to Coney Island every summer. Last visit, there were probably a dozen of them operating in the park. I didn't ride them often, though. To my young eyes, the horses always looked sad, trapped forever going round and round, with their frozen expressions. Even as a little girl, Mr. Byrne, I recognized that freedom is a precious thing. I've never been one for carousels."

"And yet, here you are."

"Yes, here I am, trying to save beautiful art. Isn't life strange?" She looked back down and began drawing again.

Patrick sat down by the door, propped himself against it, and closed his eyes. Small talk was over.

<hr>

Hours passed. In the beginning, they were up and down, sorting among the pieces of each crate, and early on, she had occasionally walked the shed's length to stretch her legs. Despite the frosty edge that came and went, Patrick found her banter engaging as she commented on the inner workings of an active railroad station. She noticed everything: dented lanterns with broken red glass globes; rusty iron bars and fittings; tools; oily gears strewn haphazardly on shelves; iron hooks screwed into walls, hand-hewn support beams, doors, and any other free vertical surface—none of which made an especially hospitable suitable environment for gauzy dresses.

Now, as she tried to work out the carver's original design for the wood, the going was slow, with little movement beyond the motion of her drawing hand.

As Patrick had surmised early on, the best place he could be was out of her way. The ground proved hard, so he found a fairly clean plank on one of the tables and stretched out on it for a while. Despite his best attempts, he kept dozing, perking up now and then to check on noises in the rail yard outside, and once for a short chat with Michael.

"You can talk if you want," she said as he absently screwed and unscrewed a nut on a bolt the size of his thumb. "I can do two things at once."

"Right. Sorry. Didn't want to interfere. I suspected that if I started talking, I'd be asking too many questions, so it's probably best I keep my trap shut."

"Go ahead and ask. If I don't like the question, you won't get an answer. If I answer it," she said, turning to look at him, "I get to ask one of you. And just so you know, I'm very frank."

"You speaking your mind? I never would have guessed." He laughed. "Fair enough. Honestly, I don't get how you can stay with a man like Carr."

"That's a comment, not a question." She turned back to the animal she was drawing.

"All right, then. My first question is, how does an independent woman like you end up with a controlling man like Carr?"

"Don't mince words," she said, laughing. "Just come right out and ask." He waited.

"Because he's what I need right now."

"To get ahead, you mean."

She shrugged. "Seems that you already have an opinion. We could get judgmental about it, but if do you have a problem with that, you have no concept of the challenges facing a woman. I am intellectually equal to any of these men, and have absolutely no power or social standing to rise above what I am now: one more well-bred pretty woman. Being with Lawrence at least allows me to experience more than I would otherwise. You have a better chance of improving your station in life than I ever will, Mr. Byrne. The only thing I have to look forward to, for a good many years, is to become richer and more socially accepted—not exactly satisfying for someone like me. You have a sister?"

"That's my question?"

"Too hard?"

"One. And what—"

"Wait, wait. My question has two parts." She set her sketchpad aside on the pallet beside her. "Given a choice, would she be content to stand quietly in the background, or does she believe women can—and should—be more?"

He roared with laughter. "You've obviously heard about my sister, Moira, the loudmouthed redheaded Irish firebrand, always front and center of these crazy women marching in Nevis. What's your point?"

"That Moira and I want the same thing. I admire her for getting out there. If I tried that, I would never survive the wave of condemnation that would come crashing down on me. Unbelievably, it can get a little boring going around with a pleasant expression plastered on your face all day long. It's like being one of those carousel ponies. Just once, I'd like to try . . . to try going the other way." Smiling, she stretched out her left hand and rubbed her right thumb across the knuckles. "Do you ever feel trapped, Patrick?" she asked, looking up at him.

"Don't think I'm not onto you—the way you snuck that third question in there so smoothly." He chuckled, then grew serious and recentered the support beam more comfortably against his spine. "Every day, but never out on the line. When you're out there, surrounded by men you're trusting with your life, in the flow of the work, time disappears. It's backbreaking labor, but at the same time, there's a sense of belonging and satisfaction. Then there's the other side. Doc Bagley says I need a desk job. *I* say I need a desk job." He shook his head. "No desk job."

"I'm sorry," she said, picking up the sketchpad again and flipping the page. "I wish I had the pull to do that for you. Unfortunately . . ." She began drawing again.

"I didn't say that to get sympathy. It's never '*oh, so this is how it's going to end.*' It's more '*this is how it's going to go.*' I'll ride it out, and if a train gets me on a Monday when the old ticker would have lasted till Friday . . ." He tossed the bolt in his hand back onto a pile with the others. It sounded so heroic.

"In all fairness," he said, watching her reconstruct the horse's shattered mane, "I think I'm allowed two more questions, but I'll let you off the hook and limit it to one. So I should make it a good one. Let me think. Okay, last one. How does A. J. Packard fit into all this?"

Birdie's hand stopped in the middle of her sketchpad. With an arch of an eyebrow, she turned to him. "Wherever Mr. Carr wants him to be, of course. You were right: that was your last question." She turned back to her sketch and tore out the page, laying it on the stack with the others. "If you don't mind, I can finish this up in a few more quiet moments."

———

A short while later, when it was pushing daylight, she stood up, back popping as she stretched. Instead of heading for the pallets as she had on previous walkabouts, she came toward Patrick, sketchbook and pages in hand.

"I hope these are close enough," she said, her voice thick with exhaustion. She handed him the sketches, and then her hand found the back of her neck and began kneading.

He wanted to hug her. "I can't repay you for this," he said, shuffling through the drawings.

She shook her head. "I don't buy friends. See if it works out for you. I hope so. Now, if you'll get me out of here before it gets light, this might work out for everybody."

He extinguished one lantern, and they got as far as the door when she suddenly halted. Patrick could sense her struggling with something.

"There is something," she said, looking up at him. "A way for you to repay me."

"Name it. I'm really in your debt."

"It could have consequences if things were to get out of hand."

Patrick closed the door. "You have no idea how much you've helped us by being here, in spite of your own personal risk. What?"

"I may need to go somewhere soon. I'll need assistance getting tickets. But not a word to anyone."

"Just let me know when and where," he said.

"Tickets for two."

He escorted her back out into the darkness. They had gone but a short distance when A. J. Packard stepped out of the shadows and, without a word, whisked Birdie off into the night.

Back at the yard, Patrick climbed aboard 873's caboose, sat down, and wedged his boots up against the railing. He dropped his head back against the rear door and looked up into the clear, dark sky. He found the twins and made a silent wish on the two brightest stars, as his mother used to do. He needed all the help he could get.

Birdie's sketches looked as good as any work he had ever seen. She was beautiful, talented, and a shrewd businesswoman. No wonder men felt threatened by the suffrage movement.

The sketches were the easiest part of the plan. Now all they had to do was hunt down a fine wood carver. A friendly, local German artisan willing to go out of his way to help an Irishman—what could be easier?

CHAPTER TWENTY-SIX

Mutual Benefit

"She never showed?" Frank asked, dropping into the chair next to Patrick. "I need a drink." He motioned to Anna, the waitress. "So what do we do now?"

Patrick shook his head. "She showed." He shoved the drawings at him and Connor. "Draws like a pro. I've been up all night long, and for the life of me, I can't figure out what to do with them."

Connor shrugged. "They're wooden horses. The town's crawling with carpenters. We fix 'em, and Carr never needs to know."

"Yeah, I don't get the problem," Frank said, shuffling through the drawings. "Nevis has got more carpenters than you can shake a stick at. Surely someone has a good enough eye to carve something like this."

Without moving his head, Patrick rolled his eyes over to look at his brother. "And how am I going to get one of 'em? Stand in the street with a big sign reading 'Irishman wishes to hire skilled, open-minded Kraut to repair Mr. Carr's carousel figures damaged by Chesapeake Railway Company'?" Patrick ran a hand across his three-day beard. "They'll bust a gut laughing. What's the logistics? And how many of 'em do I have to approach before we get the right one: a fine craftsman who can do it and keep his mouth shut?"

"Only one," Connor said, sliding a fried potato off the foreman's plate. "Michod Zugel. He brings furniture into Nevis on his wagons. Good stuff. Carted a whole bunch of it up to the hotel the other day."

Frank sneaked a potato from the other side of the plate. "He's right, Pat. I've seen it, too. All those Krauts are crafty. But Zugel? Don't know about him. Looks like a shifty, mean old bastard."

Anna set down Frank's cup of coffee. "Mr. Byrne?" She reached in to warm up his coffee.

He shook his head and shielded the cup with his hand.

She nodded but stayed where she was. "Mr. Byrne," she repeated, "let me right off apologize. I know I shouldn't have been eavesdropping, but I overheard your conversation about the broken crates."

Patrick's eyes darted around, doing a quick check of who else was around. "*Shh!* Not so loud."

"Sorry," she said, glancing about the nearly empty diner. "I think I can help. You mentioned Michod Zugel. That's my father."

"Oh, boy." Frank slid down in his chair.

"There isn't a man in Nevis who can work wood the way he can. He's the best around, and I know they can repair your horse. His workers are good, too."

"I didn't ask," Patrick grumped. He saw the hurt in her eyes. "Sorry, Miss Zugel. It's kind of you to offer, but I don't think he'd be interested in helping me."

"Hm-m," she said, cocking her head. "You might be surprised. It's not my place to discuss his business, but I think the two of you could benefit each other. In the end, if he can help you, I suspect you might not really care what his business is. Am I right?"

Patrick turned around in his chair to face her. "I look that desperate, do I?"

She lowered the coffeepot. "Mr. Byrne, you come in all the time, and I've never seen you look so . . . defeated. I really prefer the smiling man who comes in and gets the best of his brother."

"Why, Miss Zugel, I didn't realize you noticed."

Anna's cheeks colored. "Every day, Mr. Byrne. And when you don't come in, I wonder if you're okay." Frank and Connor were staring at her now. "Like I do for all my customers," she blurted. "Now, if you'll excuse me . . ." She darted toward the kitchen.

Patrick sat dumbstruck. All this time, he had thought cocky, mouthy Frank was the one who embarrassed her. Son of a gun. He'd never live it down. He turned to the boys.

Frank was uncharacteristically quiet, but his eyes were full of mischief. "*I love you as I lov'd you,*" he purred, swaying and snapping his fingers in his best vaudeville imitation.

Connor took a swipe at him.

"*When you were sweet—*"

"Shut up, moron," Patrick hissed.

"*. . . when you were sweet sixteen.* She would do anything for you, Pat. At least see her father and make her happy."

"Sure," Patrick said, his eyes narrowing to slits as he moved closer. "Right after I beat the tar out of you."

Frank beat a path out the door instead, but Patrick could still see him through the window, a swaying and snapping in a credible imitation of George Gaskin in his best Irish tenor.

Patrick sent Connor out to drag the fool out of sight and waited until Anna peeked back out the kitchen door. She was still red faced, but she came back over to the table.

"Talk to him, at least, Mr. Byrne. You're not going to find anyone better. He's the best. Trust me."

"I do trust you, Miss Zugel, and that's a very good thing, because right now I am desperate. If we can work something out, it will benefit many people, and I will be the happiest man in Nevis. I'll never be able to repay you."

"Seeing that smile back on your face will more than suffice," she said, her face glowing. She took a hurried look over her shoulder. "Sorry, but I've got baking to do before Mr. Dilly comes in. I'll let you know what my father says."

Watching her disappear through the kitchen's double doors, Patrick realized that Anna Zugel was no longer the little girl she once was. Somehow, while he wasn't paying attention, she had blossomed into a lovely young woman.

CHAPTER TWENTY-SEVEN

Devil's Deal

Anna was right about one thing at least: whatever his motivation, Michod Zugel was amenable to talking. But any firm commitment to help them would come only after a face-to-face meeting on his home turf, that very evening. It was not negotiable. And Patrick had his suspicions that nothing in this deal would be negotiable, but what could he do?

Even though Anna had promised she would be waiting for him when he arrived, Patrick did not intend to head into the middle of the German enclave alone. He took Frank and Connor. Two additional skinny Irishmen by his side wouldn't necessarily keep him any safer, but they might serve as a deterrent. If you expected trouble, a witness or two in your corner was never a bad idea.

The Zugel homestead was prime property surrounded by fertile fields. The new immigrant family had done well for itself. In the old world, they had been artisans, but here in their new home, they had worked the land until they were financially secure. Then, it seemed, their efforts had returned to where their true talents lay and their hearts had stayed: working in wood.

"What do you think they're doing over here at Zugel's?" Frank asked, riding beside him in the front of the wagon. "It's busy as can be. Sean thinks it's the Klan—swears somebody or other saw 'em meeting in the woods one night, wearing sheets."

"*Pffft.* Says who? And what night? This is how it always starts: *he saw this; she heard that.* They may not like us, but there's no Klan around here."

"Farther north or south, though," Connor said from the back of the wagon.

"Sean didn't think they'd be planning anything, did he?" Frank asked.

"Stop it," Patrick said. "The Germans got no bone to pick with us. They keep north; we keep south. It's a reasonable arrangement. You stay Main Street and south, and there'll be nothing to worry about. Don't go thinking up trouble."

Frank turned to Connor, sprawled out in the back and checking for trouble behind every tree they passed. "You just going to sit there? Conversation means listening *and* talking. What do you think?"

"It's probably beer," he said. "I overheard a couple Krauts at the butcher. They've started a partnership with Carr to supply brew in the park."

"Hey, we need to get in on some of this," Frank said. "Maybe we could supply the park with corned-beef hash or Irish stew."

"As long as it doesn't involve stirring up the Germans, I'll back you on anything you want, Frank. Should I let Carr know you want to talk to him?"

"Naw, but you can have Zugel's daughter ask if they need a beer taster."

"Now, why would I do that?"

"Because she misses you when you're not at Dilly's. Do you miss her when you can't be there?" Frank fluttered his eyes.

"You're a regular Uncle Josh comedy routine," Patrick muttered. "Hold it. What's this?" Two wagons bore down on them from the opposite direction, rumbling and jouncing along at a good clip behind double spans of white oxen. Patrick directed his Morgans to the right to make some room, and each party nodded solemnly to the other as the wagons passed within feet of each other.

The flatbed wagons, loaded with freshly milled logs, carried a couple of workers up front on the plank seat and another riding high on the load. The resemblance between them all was strong: blond and blue eyed, eyes filled with mistrust and questions.

The two log wagons were scarcely out of earshot when a house and other buildings came into view. If the largest outbuilding—a massive tin-roofed barn on a foundation of mortared limestone blocks—was any indication of Zugel's carpentry skills, they may have found their man. The building was accessible at ground level from this approach, with access to an upper level from the hillside it was built into—a style common in the German enclave.

The three men hopped out, and a dozen barred rock chickens scuttled off behind the corncrib, while a sociable black cat approached from barn. It appeared that no one else was especially concerned about their presence.

They walked into the barn without salutation. The air smelled of damp earth and sawdust.

"If you open your mouth, I'll kill you slowly," Patrick muttered, throwing both Frank and Connor a stern look. "Stay here at the door."

Just inside the huge doors, in the right front corner, a business office had been walled off with rough-sawn planks. Through the open door-way, Patrick could see mathematical calculations and geometric figures scrawled in thick pencil markings on the wall above the desk.

He was a few steps inside the barn before a human being finally reacted to their presence. A middle-aged man eased the end of a freshly sawn board down onto a sawhorse and shouted to the workers at the other end of the barn. The sounds of sawing and pounding ceased as the workers jerked tarps over what lay before them.

All eyes were on the Irishman as he walked toward the man he presumed to be Zugel. Only the barn swallows, swooping in and out of their nests high in the rafters, seemed to ignore them. Patrick felt as if he was being sized up like cattle. Where was Anna? He tried to see what he could without looking impolite or snoopy. Anna was right. Whatever they had under the tarps could stay their business.

"Mr. Byrne." Relieved to hear a friendly voice, Patrick watched Anna slide down off a bale of straw near the doors. He had almost walked past her. She pulled on Patrick's sleeve and, with a schoolgirl's excitement, walked with him to Zugel.

"Father?" she said to the middle-aged man. "There's someone here I want you to meet."

Patrick offered his hand. "Patrick Byrne, track foreman betwee—"

"I know who you are," Zugel said, ignoring the offered hand. "You're Irish."

"Yes, sir." Patrick dropped his hand.

Anna wrapped her arm around her father's big shoulders and gave him a gentle squeeze. "Mr. Byrne needs your help."

"What do you want?" he asked.

"I have damaged resort cargo—carousel figures. We need to fix or replace them, and your name came up. Your daughter says you're a gifted woodworker."

Zugel let out a grunt. "Mr. Carr is good at getting things accomplished. He drives one of those brand-new expensive automobiles. Have him bring someone in. I'm busy fixing wagons."

Patrick glanced at the tarps. Mighty small wagons, and well-hidden ones at that. "Mr. Carr doesn't want to be bothered with things like this."

"What you really mean is, Mr. Carr doesn't want to be bothered with incompetence. What happened?"

Patrick hesitated, but the old man seemed too wily to lie to. "I made a mistake. I helped promote someone who can't do his job, and a train was misrouted. I'm lucky that cargo was the only thing we lost. My men have been counting on a bonus from Mr. Carr. If word gets back to him, he'll take it out of their pockets. I can't let that happen."

"So, you're gonna pay for my time and materials?"

"Yes, sir . . . but it may take me a while."

Zugel traced a circle in the dirt with the toe of his boot, and Patrick began to sweat through the front of his shirt.

"You're the one who tracked the men who robbed the depot, aren't you?"

"Yes, sir. Same ones who robbed your mill."

"You saved a month's worth of till. Without it, things would have been bad around here. The men who work for me—I'd never let them go without."

"Yes, sir. My men are counting on this money."

"I don't like Irish. My wife ran away with an Irishman. I never saw it coming. This man Carr—I can see him coming, and I do not like his type. What kind of animals?"

"A horse? He's white, and then there's a lion, and a bunn—a rabbit. Mr. Zugel, I'll be honest with you. They're broken up pretty bad, but that's what we have." Patrick swallowed hard. Zugel was going to turn them down. He could see it in the narrowing eyes, the tight way he held himself. The man already hated every Irishman he was ever going to meet.

"Okay, railroad man—"

"It's *Byrne,* Father"

"Okay, *railroad man,* there are things I'll need to know. Standing? Running? How high, wide, long? He threw his hands up. "*Verdammt.* Bring it here," he said, pointing outside the door.

Patrick smiled in relief. "Yes sir, but only when it's dark. You see, we're trying to keep it quiet-like."

"*Sneaking,* you mean."

"Exactly, sir."

"Bring it here and leave it for me. I can't promise to look at it tonight, but I'll get to it. Now, about what you are going to pay me. "I want only one thing in return."

"Name it." Patrick swallowed hard and met the old man's hard stare. "I always pay my way, and you'll be pulling my rear end out of the fire here."

The old man studied him for an uncomfortably long time. "Actually, *two* things. Out here past Padgett's Corners," he said, pointing west, "near where the creek comes in close to the rail line—next to McClelland's property—there's a stand of trees I have the rights to. Elm trees."

"I know the grove you mean," Patrick said, nodding. "Near curve number three."

"The big curve," Zugel said impatiently. "I lost a lot of timber when the robbers torched my smaller barn. Working on your animals will set me back on materials for other things. To do what you are asking, I need to get the seasoned lumber I've milled there and bring it back here. I could do it by wagon, but a train would be quicker."

Patrick studied the old man as he made his demand. The cagey old buzzard made it seem so simple. It was no small request—unauthorized cargo, unauthorized stop, unauthorized loading and unloading. He looked at Anna, her lips puckered in the slightest hint of a smile, and a shine in her eyes that she could not mask. Evidently, something more than his gratitude was motivating her. As she had said, a deal between him and her father would benefit everyone.

He looked at her father again. Sure, Zugel was pulling him out of a jam, but he had already walked a fine line between moving freight and manipulating the bosses and the books. Eventually, it was going to be hello to hard knocks, and good-bye to employment. He could feel the older man's eyes as the seconds ticked by. They both knew that Zugel had him over a barrel—one that Patrick had picked out and all but spread-eagled himself on.

"Done," Patrick said, offering his hand again. This time, Zugel took it. "I'm grateful to you for helping us out. You understand I have to come at this from several angles to make it work. I need a few days. What's your second request?" Patrick looked deep into the old man's eyes and saw a defiant spark burning there.

Anna gave a comfortable sigh as Zugel released Patrick's hand and dismissed him with a flick of his callused hand. "Later—nothing you can't handle. The timetable is up to you. Sooner you get me what I need, sooner I can start." It sounded to Patrick a great deal like *take it or leave it.* Having gotten a deal to his liking, Zugel was finished with him and turned back to his wood.

Again the barn filled with sawing, pounding, rasping, and humming as the workers resumed their tasks. Anna walked Patrick back to Frank and Connor at the double doors, but he didn't feel like chitchat. It felt as if spiders were scampering across his sweaty back.

The ride back to Nevis was even quieter. The Irishmen were all in apparent agreement. They had made a deal with the devil and didn't even know the full terms.

Still, Patrick felt better coming out than he had going in. He had run into Zugel's kind before and even had a kind of admiration for them—masters of their craft who wanted only to be left alone to ply their trade in an often hostile environment. With the pictures and some of the larger damaged pieces, Zugel had plenty to work from, and not having to hover over the old German would be a blessing.

Then there were the elm trees. What was one little extra train stop? Nobody that mattered would ever need to know. Except Sean Murphy, who hated Michod Zugel and anyone like him. He was the only one of the bunch who had regular contact with the group he referred to collectively as "the Krauts," and he nursed a thinly veiled distaste for them that was one note short of a hate song. Sean was the linchpin in getting Zugel his lumber. Patrick could already see the shake of the head and hear the venomous refusal, but he knew his friend well. He would spring it on Sean when his back was against the wall and he would have no choice.

————◆◆◆◆◆————

After work the next day, the conspirators loaded up a wagon with the broken carousel animals, and Patrick and Frank headed out of town, once again bouncing and squeaking along the rutted dirt lane toward Zugel's. Nerves were on edge. What Irishman with a lick of sense would venture into the German side of town in the dark of night? *"A soon-to-be-dead one,"* Sean had warned.

They jounced down Zugel's lane, Frank clutching the side of the wagon as Patrick leaned forward, peering into the black velvet night, searching for the barn. Off in the distance somewhere, an old cock was warming up his pipes even though it was still hours from daybreak. Frank twisted and fidgeted as if his underwear had hitched up.

"Stop jigging," Patrick whispered. "It's driving me 'round the bend."

"Dad's great, great-grandmum, Lizzy—wasn't she the English one?"

"Half-English, I think. Why?"

"Close enough. Smart Irish, dumb English—reckon she's the reason for the stupid part of our brain we're using right now, riding up to Zugel's barn in the black of night, just asking some German to ventilate our carcasses with double-aught."

"I'm sure they'll figure us out before they start blasting." Patrick squinted at dark shapes suddenly looming ahead. "Look like barns?"

"Mm-hm. Let's dump and go, brother." Frank jumped as the cock crowed again, and remained standing the last hundred feet as Patrick pulled the team up close to the broad doors of the massive barn. He was off the wagon and securing the pair of Morgans before Patrick could join him. He yanked the tarp off the biggest piece: the shattered white horse. "Zugel have any dogs?"

"That big one over there?"

"Christ, jiminy!" Frank growled, scrambling into the wagon bed and pulling a stick as thick as a man's wrist out from under the seat.

Patrick exploded in laughter. "Peeing your britches would make this all complete," he said.

Frank lowered the shillelagh and glared. "You're goin' to hell, brother; you know that."

"*Sh-h.* Now, quit cutting up and grab the tarp so we can scram. It's such a relief to get rid of this." It was as quiet as a country night could get: chirping crickets, katydids, and the occasional bullfrog chugging, and, of course, Frank. Nevertheless, Patrick didn't think Frank's antics mattered much. Although they had come in slow and quiet, Patrick was sure they had announced themselves the moment they started down the unpaved road. But as long as they only unloaded and didn't take any untoward interest in barn doors or equipment, Zugel's people were not going to mess with them. And this was exactly what they did: they unloaded the cargo, left Birdie's pictures on top, and got the hell back to the Irish side of town.

CHAPTER TWENTY-EIGHT

More than Just Beer and Sausage

The cock finally got his timing right and announced the break of day. Zugel went straight out to check on his barn and property. Thankfully, the Irishmen had come and gone without disturbing anything. He mistrusted townies mucking about on his property and failed to understand their need to vandalize fences and run his livestock.

This railroad man had seemed honest and industrious enough. He recalled evenings when he had seen the railroaders' drawn and cinder-smudged faces as they dragged their exhausted bodies back to Nevis at the end of a day on the track. Still, if Anna had not vouched for Byrne, Zugel would never have suffered him to set a boot on his farm.

He turned to the two pallets stacked neatly by the double doors. *This* was all they brought? Puzzled, he leaned over and picked up the papers placed on top and weighted with a rock. He flipped through the sketches of the horse, lion, and rabbit. No battered and beaten railroad hands had made these meticulously detailed, finely shaded drawings.

They were helpful—maybe better than the actual pieces, he thought, looking at the battered remains of the figures.

The sketch artist had taken liberties and guessed at details in order to draw complete animals. That helped. Subtle detailing on the figures would also come from the feel of the basswood under the carver's hand. Only the original carver would recognize the difference. Was he worried? Hardly. Good carvers did a good job, sold their work, and moved on to the next project. If the Irish kept their mouths shut, no one would be the wiser. Certainly, *he* would have no need to discuss it further.

He walked to the back of the barn and stopped near several craftsmen in dark twill bib dungarees and felt caps, already hunched over and engrossed in chiseling the wood before them. It was barely daybreak, and they worked from the light of several lanterns. Eventually, they would work by the natural light that streamed through the windows set high on either end of the structure. And if that was inadequate, they would move outside.

"Jakob, what do you think?" Zugel asked the nearest worker, holding up the sketches.

The man looked up, but his shoulders remained stooped, his posture hunched. His face was carved with lines of age that grew deeper when he frowned. He brushed the wood shavings out of his woolly gray hair and stepped away from his work, shoving his chisel into a loop on his overalls and wiping his big, gnarled hands on the seat of his pants. He took the drawings in his hands and shuffled through them once, then returned to the sketch of the white horse, stroking his long gray-flecked beard as he studied it.

"Red specks here, here, along the neck and chest," Zugel said, tapping the top picture. "A large garland. King horse?"

Jakob nodded. "King horse. Such a shame. This was beautiful, but the carving . . ." Jakob tapped the picture and shook his head. "We can do as well. This is done by an artisan? It is hurried and sloppy. *Artisan,*" he said with a snort, pointing toward the wood he had been chiseling—a horse head with finely curled lips, flared nostrils, and half-completed detailing along the bridle. "I can do much better. All of us can. I know Gustav Dentzel is your cousin, but if this is the best his carvers can do . . ." He shook his head again. "This is from the Irishman? Anna told him, and now our secret is out?"

Zugel clapped him on the shoulder and shook it gently. "The secret is safe, Jakob. She promised me she told them nothing."

"To see what the Dentzel carousel looks like . . . this inside knowledge is too good to be true," Jakob said. "But the Irishman's coming to us cannot be a coincidence. If someone finds out we are negotiating with Mr. Mangel to build the second carousel, we will have competition—or, worse still, someone comes and torches your lovely barn again and all our work goes up in cinders."

Zugel shook his head. "I think this is a sign. We know exactly how much better we have to be." He stopped and studied Jakob's deep-set frown. "But maybe I should have talked to you first. I have insulted you, yes? Can we fix these and still meet Mr. Mangel's deadline for the carousel figures?"

"I am not insulted. Such a shame," Jakob repeated. He lowered the drawing of the king horse and swept his gaze across the length of the barn and the handful of craftsmen engrossed in their work, heads down as they stood amid stacks of varying lengths and shapes of wood. He passed the sketches to Zugel, walked over to a tarp-covered bundle, and carefully drew the cover away. Beneath lay two exquisitely carved and painted carousel horses, an appaloosa and a bay, caught in mid gallop with their legs tucked up toward their chests. "Twelve done, three more to do, to win Mangel's admiration and his confidence that we can finish and deliver a full set of fifteen."

"And pay us," Zugel added.

"Yes, and pay us. The additional work—it will not be easy," Jakob said, easing the tarp back over the finished carvings, "but if you promised, we will do it. If we cannot easily fix, we will substitute what we have already carved, and discard the damaged. Who is to know?" He studied the drawings. "How do we know these are for the Dentzel carousel Carr has already bought? They look inferior. Perhaps, Mangel is not dealing with us in good faith. Perhaps, he has already bought the second carousel from someone else. If so, fixing their broken animals will be hurting us. Do we know this? Yes? No?"

Zugel bit his lower lip. "I did not ask, but I will find out if they are Dentzel's. If these are someone else's," he said glancing at the papers, "we are working against ourselves."

"Inferior," Jakob repeated. "Even if we repair them, they will not be as good as the ones we make for Mangel. We will fix them exactly as we find them, maybe a little better." He looked back at the carvers. "When he compares the two, ours will win him over, hands down."

"Then, it is settled: even if they are for the contest, we will honor my commitment and fix them. And," Zugel said, "we will get the Irishman to deliver new wood to replace what we use, and then some."

"Agreed." I will do the lion, you can have the horse, and I think Matthias has enough skill to help with them. I will work with him." He eyed the two covered wooden pallets sitting outside the door. "What else did they bring you? More?"

"Pieces." Zugel lifted back the tarp and showed him the remains of the three hollow-bodied figures. He stooped and ran his hand down the flowers and stars carved on the horse's bridle, and flicked peeling paint off the headstall, where the grain had raised up. "Too much moisture. And the rabbit is not much better. We will substitute pieces—we can't save this."

"Agreed. We will use what we have, and carve something new only when we cannot salvage or substitute." Jakob looked at the third damaged figure. "The king of the jungle—he is not so bad."

Jakob leaned inside the barn door. "Matthias, come here, please."

A lanky youth in the corner stopped his sorting and stacking and strode over. At over six feet, he towered above both his elders.

Jakob nodded at the lion. "Judge what these colors are, so we can repaint them at the end. Then get turpentine and strip the paint down to the bare wood. Fill in all this pitting and the gouges with putty, and sand it smooth again. Do not get discouraged; this will take you a while. When you are done, come find me, and I will decide if it is ready for primer. Are you agreeable?"

"Yes, I am, and I understand," Matthias said. He hurried off to fetch the turpentine.

Zugel left Jakob to his carving and took the drawings to his office. He relaxed a bit. They would get their lumber, and Anna would stop talking about the railroader now. His decision to help Patrick Byrne had been a wise one.

CHAPTER TWENTY-NINE

Honus

Patrick met up with Frank and Sean at the depot and joined the steady stream of humanity heading for the partnership's scheduled exhibition baseball game on Bayland's new ball diamond.

"I can think of many other places I'd rather be on my first day off in ages," Patrick said, eying a bench at the entrance. "Maybe I'll just sit over there and watch the world go by. You two can run along and get your fill of all the National League all-stars and local talent you want. Wake me up on your way out."

"Nope, we're sticking together," Frank said, tipping his cap to a young blonde beauty on the arm of a young man. "I don't see any problems brewing around here. Think they know what we're up to?"

"If you can leave the women alone," Patrick said, following his brother's gaze, "and act norm—er, casual—everything will be fine. Zugel isn't going to blab, and neither are you. Just keep your trap shut and enjoy the game."

It was close to game time, and dozens of baseball fans queued up outside the newly constructed masonry archway, awaiting admittance. The entrance was an imposing Corinthian-columned construction in the style of the Arc de Triomphe du Carrousel in Paris, its central arch rising some sixty feet high and spanning seventy, topped by three prancing carousel horses. It was ostentatious, but excited families marveled at its grandeur. Young newsies cruised up and down the queue, handing out programs—one per family—stirring up excitement and generating fear of being denied admittance to so grand an experience.

Patrick took a program while they waited to get in. It contained a pompous and effusive welcome from the owners of Bayland, with a nod of thanks to the businesses and individuals whose generous donations of time and capital made it all possible. The program also included a short history on each and player, and his ball club affiliation.

The line moved forward and they followed the crowd through the archway and down a broad promenade. "You know, Frank," Patrick said, waving the paper at him, "you've got an arm on you, and two good eyes. Forget joining the merchant marine. This here's your future—outfielder for the Boston Beaneaters. Good Irish town."

Frank stopped to read. "Maybe. Does it say anything about the women they attract?"

"Better. You can be buddies with this fellow, Hamelin Russell, their catcher. Program says he 'plays like Marty Bergen . . . good arm and quick.' Considering Bergen died a few months ago, I'd say anyone could play as well as him, but what do I know?" He grabbed Frank's arm and pointed to Honus Wagner's name. "Or maybe *he'd* let you into his inner circle." He ducked away as Frank grabbed for him.

"You'd *better* run. The day I leave and don't come back, you'll miss me."

Patrick grinned and kept walking. "Sean, you're awful quiet."

"I'm here for Honus."

"Yeah, me, too." Frank pulled a card out of his shirt pocket. "I'm getting him to sign this, and then I'll hang it in a little frame next to my bed."

"Where'd you get that?" Sean asked, gazing at the lithograph of Honus Wagner. It was a colored picture on white stock, with a narrow black border.

Frank flipped it over and showed him a checklist of player cards. "Michael Fahey, night watchman. Pays to work the nightshift once in a while. He pulled it out of a pack of Allen and Ginters. Smokes like a chimney, but had no use for this."

"Dang," Sean muttered. "But don't forget Cupid Childs. Someday, he'll have a card like that."

"Cupid?" Patrick asked, the smell of peanuts distracting him. "I seriously doubt the women here are looking for romance." He noticed the vendor near the bleachers and promised himself a trip over there.

Frank's mouth dropped open and his eyebrows shot up. "You been living in a hole? Nevis hasn't been talking about anything else all week. Cupid Childs plays second base for the Chicago Orphans—at least, he did until a few weeks ago. He's like a folk hero around here. Grew up down the road in Sunderlandville. South of Friendship, north of Huntingtown? Anyways, he throws righty but bats left-handed. Good fielder and hitter."

Patrick shook his head. As much as he loved baseball, putting out one crisis fire after another didn't leave a lot of room for leisure pursuits.

Frank put his hands on his hips. "Jiminy, now who's looking stupid? Just because I don't read the depot bulletin board doesn't mean I don't know anything. I know lots of useless information. Like that guy over there," he said, pointing to an all-star player warming up. He was tall, lean, with bulging biceps and thick black wavy hair that disappeared and reappeared as he adjusted his hat. "That's Hamelin Russell, catcher.

Come on, and I'll teach you a thing or two more." He climbed up into the bleachers.

———◆◆◆———

In the first inning, the home team batted first and was a quick three up, three down. As they took the field, a low murmur in the crowd began near the visiting team's side and moved like a wave across the crowd, rising to a roar by the time it reached the other end. The all-stars were up, with Honus to bat cleanup.

"It doesn't get any better than this," Frank said, rubbing his palms down the side of his pants. "Honus, Honus, Honus!" he yelled with the crowd, thrusting his fist into the air. He elbowed Patrick, who belted out a loud *"Honus!"*

"Something you can tell your grandchildren," Sean said, going up on his toes to see over the crowd. "Son of a bitch!" He grabbed Patrick by the sleeve and yanked him sideways. "Son of a bitch, it's him! There." He pointed into the crowd of people. "Dark-brown shirt, black cap—the man who robbed the depot."

Patrick dropped his bag of peanuts. "Next to the lady carrying the baby? You sure? See the second guy anywhere?"

Sean looked around. "Nope, just him. I never forget a pistol-whipping."

"Cops are only around when you don't want 'em," Patrick said, scanning the crowd for a blue uniform. "Maybe he's come back for Packard's box. We'd be gold if we could . . ."

Sean ignored him, jostled past the couple next to him, and began pushing past everyone between him and the man. "He's here watching Honus on Carr's dime. Wait'll I—"

"Slow down, man," Patrick said, following right behind him. He grabbed Sean's arm and stopped him. "What if he has a gun and starts shooting with all these people around?"

Sean jerked his arm free. "He can go ahead and shoot, but he's not watching Honus." Startled women cried out and men cursed as he plowed toward the man, motioning Patrick and Frank to swing around behind and cut him off.

The brown-shirted man glanced over at the hubbub, looked about him, and bolted in the opposite direction, sweeping aside the woman and her baby along with a half-dozen others in his path. Getting through the back of the crowd, he broke into a sprint. He had a clear field to the park entrance and town, but with the Byrnes close on his heels.

Fifty yards later, Patrick pulled up short. He bent over double, his hands on his knees, his chest tight, and pain radiating down his arm as he wheezed and tried to regain his breath.

Frank lengthened his stride and closed the gap, bearing down at an angle and catching up with the runner. He grabbed a fistful of shirt and sent them both tumbling into the dirt. Frank came out on top and pinned the man facedown in a move honed by years of tussling with a much stronger older brother. He put his knee in the guy's back and twisted both arms up behind him.

"Lay still or I break 'em!" he snarled.

At that moment, above all the background noise, Patrick heard the distinct crack of a bat connecting with a pitched ball. A roar erupted from the crowd. From one end of the field to the other, a chant arose: *"Ho-nus! Ho-nus! Ho-nus!"*

Frank yanked the man to his feet and dragged him toward the field, peeking through a space in the crowd just as Honus Wagner rounded third and headed for home. "Son of a bitch! Home run? *Damn!*" He looked at the robber and bent his arm farther up his back, causing the man to cry out. "Honus Wagner hits a home run and I miss it because of you? I hope they hang you!"

"Give me that son of a bitch!" Sean said, knocking Frank off balance as he grabbed the man. His punch landed at the base of the jaw, sending the captive careening into a well-dressed elderly man. The people behind staggered backward, all struggling to regain their footing. When they did, the crowd surged back in Frank and Sean's direction, engulfing them in a tide of curses and flying fists.

"Let's get him out of here before we lose him," Sean said. He and Frank dragged the robber free of the melee that was now well under way without them. They stood clear as two Nevis police officers entered the fray, cracking heads and poking bellies with their nightsticks.

"*Now* he shows up," Sean said, seeing Patrick approach with Brian McCall, the burly beat cop for the beach, park, and depot areas.

"You all right, Patrick?" Frank called out.

Patrick nodded. "He started all this craziness," he said, pointing to the robber, who was not resisting Frank's hold on him, but looked wild eyed and desperate. "Mr. Murphy seems to think he's one of the scoundrels who robbed the depot and the Zugel homestead. There might be a reward for him, too," Patrick continued, trying to divert the officer's attention from the brawl. "Wanted posters up all over town. If you can get him to talk about the parcel they stole, I'll bet A. J. Packard will make sure you're well taken care of. Mr. Murphy can tell you everything you need to know. He's the depot manager they slugged."

"Reward, huh?" The officer looked the man up and down and started handcuffing him. "You're coming with me. Mr. Murphy, if you'll come along and give a statement, we can make short work of this."

Sean looked up at the scoreboard: all-stars leading one to nothing. Several fistfights had broken out between all-stars and local players in the middle of the field. The bleachers had emptied, and many families

Louise Gorday

with crying children were heading for the park entrance. The shine went out in his eyes, and his shoulders drooped. Honus Wagner's appearance was over. There would be no more baseball in Nevis today.

"Yeah, sure," Sean said, and started toward the arch.

Patrick fell in line with him as they left the park. "If they lean on him a bit, I'll bet we find out where that box is hidden. It should keep the front office busy and out of our business for a while."

"I'll make sure they do. This should put us back in the running for a promotion, don't you think?"

"Honus Wagner hits a home run in Nevis," Frank said, coming up behind them, "you miss it, and all you dimwits can talk about is getting promoted. Get your priorities straight. Carr's carousel is in shambles, and when he finds out, neither one of you is getting promoted."

"*Sh-h-h!*" Patrick hissed. "What'd I tell you about keeping quiet? Cops all over the place. Don't go giving them a new mystery to solve and new questions to ask. If you were using your brain, you'd be running down Honus to sign your card. Now, scram while Sean and I take care of business with Officer McCall and get Packard out of our hair."

Frank brightened, turned, and disappeared into the crowd.

CHAPTER THIRTY

On to Us

Sean and Frank stood over Sean's desk, heads together as they pored over the early morning dispatches. In typical Chesapeake Railway fashion, there was no congratulatory mention of their apprehending the depot robber.

"Okay, so there's no pat on the back," Patrick said. "What else is new?" He heard the shrill whistle blast of incoming engine 829 as it passed mile marker three.

Sean shrugged. "Until they get that louse to tell 'em where Packard's stuff is, I bet they'll keep it real quiet. Don't want to tip off anybody else who might be lurking out there."

"Yeah, I guess so," Patrick said. "The less we hear about the park until Zugel finishes his end of the bargain, the better. Quiet is good. Our secret's still safe, so I'll stop complaining. Unless there's another baseball game and brawl today, where we can get Frank a matching shiner for the one he's got, we're outta here, Sean."

"I gave as good as I got," Frank muttered. "Nobody else in town can boast a baseball card autographed by Honus Wagner, neither. As soon as Moira frames it for me, I'll show you."

"Sure is a beauty," Patrick said of Frank's puffy, discolored eye. He was about to pull open the freight door when he stopped and looked about. "Where's Harmon?" he asked, addressing no one in particular. "He's dropped off the earth since we unloaded those crates."

"Miller has him in the other building," Sean said.

"Why? Oh, God, he'd better not be spilling his guts."

"Don't know. I just know he's there," Sean said. "Who knows what that moron is up to."

"If he utters a word, I'll kill him," Patrick said.

Frank made a fist and cracked his knuckles. "Get in line, bro. Everybody else on the crew's ahead of you."

"We can share," Patrick said. "Let's get out of here before the 829 pulls in."

Alas, they were too late. They watched through the side window as the train pulled in, bell clanging as the billowing steam obscured the front of the train. No passengers—this one was freight. At least, "freight" was how the manifest read, so they were intrigued when two men in matching dark suits and dark gray felt bowlers disembarked from the caboose.

Frank grinned. "Police?"

"Railway cops," Sean said, drawing close enough to the window to peek without being seen. "It's the unauthorized track movement—gotta be." He gripped his religious medal. "Dear Holy Mother . . ."

Frank swallowed. "The 'misplaced' carousel pieces, maybe?"

Patrick took his hand off the freight door pulley. "Pinkertons," he said, eyeing the six-pointed stars on their lapels. "Maybe they're taking custody of the robber. Nevis jail won't hold him if his accomplices decide to bust him out."

"Who's saying there are more accomplices?" Frank asked. "The second one drowned."

"Never found a body," Patrick said.

Sean cleared his throat. "Er, I was gonna tell ya, Pat. They found a body floating out at the mouth of the Little Pomonkey. Bullet in his bum. Not clear if he died of the wound or passed out and drowned in the water."

"The guy I shot in the woods?" Patrick asked, whirling around.

"Probably. They didn't elaborate." Sean found the dispatch and handed it to him.

"Maybe they're here about the carousel, then." Patrick scanned the report.

"Can't be," Sean said. "Not a single inquiry about cargo. I'd stake my life we're still good there."

Frank walked up to the front ticket window. "Settle down, Pat. You shot him in the line of duty. Besides, we'd be seeing the local police before the Pinkertons. A body in the Little Pomonkey's a local problem. What else do you suppose they'd want? Something routine, maybe?" He turned and looked at them both. "It could be routine, right? Somebody's been shaking down the free-riding hobos. Sam—wasn't he making a dollar a head before you booted him? There's no problem here, right?"

"Jeez, Frank, get a grip. It's probably the body, most likely a formality." Patrick folded the report in half, then in half again, and shoved it in his pants pocket. Then he thought better of it, smoothed it out, and put it behind him on the counter. He stayed where he was. Getting caught gawking out the ticket window might make him look guilty of whatever it was they were investigating. "Which way did they go?"

Frank turned again to the window and flattened his face against the glass, craning his neck for a better view. "Dunno. Around the other side somewhere."

The sound of heavy steps on the rear porch sent Frank jumping away from the window. Pulling the ticket log off the desk as he flailed about for a handhold, he thumped to the floor, sat upright, and flipped the log to a random page as the back door opened.

It was the Pinkertons—Tweedle Dee and Tweedle Dum, indistinguishable right down to their short stature, cherublike cheeks, thick dark eyebrows, and bushy brown soup-strainer mustaches.

"Morning," the one on the right said, tipping his bowler. "Officer Wakefield. Officer Smyth," he said, nodding to his left. "Would Mr. Sean Murphy be about?"

"That's me," Sean said. He got up and offered his hand. "What can I do for you?"

They shook hands, and Wakefield flashed his lapel badge. "Pinkerton National Detective Agency. We'd like to ask you a few questions about the depot robbery."

"Certainly." Sean pulled the top papers out of his box and handed them to Patrick. "We can look at these later."

Wakefield turned to Patrick. "Are you a Chesapeake Railway Express employee?"

Patrick nodded. "Patrick Byrne, track foreman," he said, offering his hand.

Wakefield ignored it. "*Byrne*," he repeated to Smyth. "Note it. This is Byrne."

Smyth scribbled in a black notebook.

Frank scrambled up off the floor. "So am I. Frank Byrne, at your service." He nodded but kept his hands in his pockets.

"We may need to talk to you later, so hang around," Wakefield said. "Excuse us now. We need a word with Mr. Murphy."

Patrick and Frank retreated to the back porch of the caboose parked on the siding, ducking a crew member or two as they reported for work.

"At your service?" Jeepers, Frank," Patrick said, rolling his eyes, "you sounded like a damn waiter! Relax. They'll poke around a while, write a report, and be gone before you know it. They aren't after the small stuff."

Of course, what constituted "small stuff" was open to interpretation. Patrick parked himself on the caboose railing so he could see clearer. Everybody needed to settle down, or small things would soon loom large. Like the man across the street from the Wesson Building right now, his face obscured by hands adjusting his black bowler. He cut a dapper though portly figure in his black four-button sack suit. Fidgeting with his collar and cuffs, he descended the brick building steps and crossed the street to the depot in a rush. Only deeply concerned people rushed. It was not a trait of Nevisites in general.

Frank looked at his brother for a moment, stuck his hands back in his pockets, and began to pace back and forth across the porch.

"Relax," Patrick said. "Their authority is limited to railroad activities." The crease between his eyes suddenly turned into a crevice. He stepped in front of his brother, blocking his way. Frank did not make eye contact, staring down at his own shoes instead.

"We're not sweating big stuff here, right, Frank?" Patrick asked. He punched Frank in the shoulder to make sure he had his attention. "Damn it, Frankie, is there something you're not telling me? Are they coming to arrest me, or something? What have you heard?"

"Noth—nothing." He cleared his throat. "You're fine. I'm wondering if they might start poking around and find things maybe . . . well . . . things that might seem different than what they are."

"Jeez, oh, Pete, what have you done?"

"Nothing, exactly." Frank dug deeper into his pockets. "It's more like what I *didn't* do."

Patrick grabbed him by the collar, yanking him off the caboose and away from curious eyes, hauling him across the yard until they were well past the main trunk line.

"Leave off," Frank said, "or I'm gonna—"

"Gonna what?" Patrick asked, inches from his face. "Take a swing at me, and then I beat the crap out of you and we both regret it when we cool off? I am so tired of this big-brother routine with you. Start talking. *Now.* Just what is it that you *haven't* done?"

Frank straightened his shirt. "Couple weeks ago, I borrowed some money from the till. Not a lot," he said, backing up to fend off an anticipated quick right hook. "Enough to get me to payday. I was gonna put it back today when we got paid . . . when there was no one in the office."

"Just this *once,* is what you're telling me. Right, Frank? Jesus, Mary, and Joseph! You've been stealing from—"

"No, *borrowing.* I always return it. I just . . . I just didn't get a chance to return it yet." Patrick saw desperation in his eyes. "You got to help me put it back."

Patrick reached out, flipped Frank's cap up and off his head, and turned away, muttering under his breath. "Christ, Frankie, you're a real pip. You've lost your mind. I'm not going anywhere near the depot. Possible murder charge here," he said, pointing at himself.

"I don't want to do time, Pat. Jails are for crazy people."

"And just what part of that doesn't apply to you? It would kill Dad. How much? Ten bucks? Twenty?"

"Hundred."

"A *hundred?* Holy Mother o' God!" Patrick wrapped his arms around his head. "Who the hell needs that kind of money to tide them over?"

He came at his brother, fist raised. Frank flinched but didn't try to defend himself.

Patrick dropped his hand. "No Byrne has ever served time, no matter how deserving they might have been. Do you have the money on you?"

"Well, not exactly."

"Which story are you going with, Frankie?"

"As soon as I get paid today, I'll have most of it." He turned away from Patrick's withering gaze. "Forty short."

"God Almighty . . ." Patrick wiped the sweat off his brow and put some distance between them. Beating the imbecile to a pulp would solve nothing. He picked up a piece of track ballast and flung it at nothing in particular. His hand went to his chest. It was tight and burning. He slowed his breathing—Doc Bagley would have called it *wheezing*—and shook his tingling hand out.

He called his brother over. "Here's what we're gonna do," he said when Frank approached. "I'll bail you out. I have money saved for moving to Baltimore."

"I don't want to be the one who ruined your chance at the B and O. Can't take that money, Pat."

"The problem isn't the money. I *am* going to get the money back from you, starting with your next check. Even when you pay it all back, you're still going to owe me—forever. The problem . . ." He took a side-long glance at the depot. ". . . is how to get them outta there to put it back—or whether we've missed the opportunity to do anything at all. We snag Sean as soon as we can, and find out why they're here. If it's not you, we wait. If it's me, you're on your own and you'll have to trust Sean and work something out. I need to circle around to the house and get what you owe."

Frank let out a sigh and slapped him on the back. "Thanks, Pat."

"Try to stay out of trouble until I get back. You're going to be the death of me yet."

"Maybe I already have—you do look a little pale. Want me to run home? Tell me where."

"And risk having you make future unauthorized withdrawals? Not a chance. Hang around back here and try to stay inconspicuous until I get back. If they come looking for me, tell 'em I'm due back in half an hour."

<hr />

He was back in under a half hour and had barely got his foot out of the stirrup before Connor was all over him.

"Pinks," Connor murmured. "Holed up in the Wesson."

Patrick's eyes made a wide sweep of the yard. Frank was nowhere in sight, and everywhere he glanced, men seemed to be skulking about, watching, waiting. How many others were sweating over past crimes and contemplating jail time?

"Hey." Frank's voice called softly from the direction of the maintenance shed.

Patrick tethered his horse to the handle of one of the Sheffield railcars and headed for the shed, Connor following at a distance. They found Frank crouched under the far eaves, drawing on the ground with a stick.

"Still hiding?" Patrick asked. "What's happened?"

Frank stood up, dusting himself off. "I'm playing it low-key, is all. The whole time you've been gone, Porky in the bowler has been scooting back and forth between the Wesson and the depot, ferrying armloads of what looks like Sean's ledgers. Don't look like anybody else has been called into the main office, which is good. On the other hand, nobody's set foot out of there, either."

"A thorough once-over," Patrick said, nodding. "Something or somebody. This is definitely big stuff. You talked to Sean?"

"Nope. I'm not going in there. Haven't seen hide nor hair of him, either. The crew is all here, Pat, but nobody's headed out. When I told them the Pinkertons were in town, all movement out onto the rails ceased. What do you want to do with 'em?"

"Jiminy, Frank, why do you run your trap?" Creates all kinds of problems."

Frank shrugged.

"Thought they had a right to know," Connor said in rare defense of the younger Byrne. "Can't work safely when a man's worrying about his job. They're all scared."

Patrick looked around. Most of the bystanders were crew members. They hung out in front and around the depot like the biddies down on the wharf, waiting for the *Chessie Belle,* although in this case, they had no clear idea what they should be expecting. Mac and the gandies seemed particularly ill at ease. Patrick didn't think any had served jail time, but given the law's penchant for automatically accusing coloreds of most local petty crimes, they wisely kept as far back in the yard as possible, keeping a profile almost as low as Frank's.

"You'll have to run things out there for me, Frank," he said, side-eyeing Connor, who was busy watching the Wesson. "I still need Sean to arrange an extra train stop, if you'll recall." He needed to hear directly from Sean about the Pinkertons, too. Someone had gotten himself into deep trouble. If they were pulling ledgers, it probably didn't involve the robbery, but Frank might be a prime person of interest.

Patrick took off for the largest group of workers. "If we've fallen behind somewhere," he said to Frank, "stay out till things are right." He was going to give it to them straight, and then let them linger a while until they decided on their own that there was no immediate threat to their own well-being. When their talk turned to other topics, he would make assignments as best he could and send them up the line.

•••••

Officers Wakefield and Smyth departed on the noon run back to Baltimore, and as nearly as anyone could tell, the fidgety, rotund ledger-bearer was still in the Wesson. Speculation swept through the yard like leaves in an autumn gust: Christian Miller had been arrested for embezzlement; the Chesapeake had gone belly-up; it was all legwork for someone important coming to town. The visit seemed to be all of that and none of that, and in the end, nobody, including Patrick, had a bead on what had happened, was happening, or was going to happen—only that Pinkertons were onto something, and that, in itself, was surely bad.

In the hours spent waiting, Patrick had racked his brain trying to work out what it all meant. He was convinced it was not the robbery. No one had complained about any missing cargo, so it was probably not related to the carousel fiasco, either. Frank, for all his dumbassedness, was spot-on about the foolhardiness of entering the depot right now. It was the epicenter of the morning's proceedings so Sean was currently off-limits to all of them.

Patrick went in search of his horse. He would hit the rails and do his job, but at the end of his shift, he would be back when nobody gave a damn about anything except food and bed. Under other circumstances, he and Frank would have been at the top of that list seeking creature comforts. Right now, it was best to be on nobody's list.

CHAPTER THIRTY-ONE

Imposing Accountants

I t seemed as if the day would last forever, but when quitting time came, Patrick beelined back to the depot. As he had expected, Sean was still at his desk. Head down, slumped in his chair, he wore the grueling day like a rumpled suit. The foreman walked in and locked the door behind him.

Sean waved him off. "Tomorrow. Three more pen strokes, and I'm outta here."

Patrick poured two cups of cold coffee. Putting one at the depot manager's elbow, he claimed the second desk chair and put his feet up on some boxes. He sipped the coffee. "First time I've ever been in here and had to settle for it cold," he said, grimacing."

Sean pushed away the ledger in front of him and took a long draw, drained the cup, and thumped it back down on the desk with a weary grin. "Been waiting all day for that."

Patrick nodded. "Wanted to see how you were faring and what in tarnation is going on."

Sean put his head down on his papers and groaned. "And in that order, right? No more, please. It'll still be here tomorrow."

"Are *we* all gonna be here tomorrow?"

"Debatable. You know how witch hunts go."

"Bad, huh?"

"Worse," Sean said, sitting up and shaking his head. "So much crap going on here, Pat. Half of it, I can't even talk about. The other half, they won't tell me. I don't know anything." He closed his eyes and let his head drop back.

"Did they discuss the dead body? I would have thought they'd send in the local police."

"Can't say no more."

Patrick's eyes flitted to Sean and then back down to the coffee dregs in his cup. He swirled them around. This was going to take a while. "Let me know if I can help any. Hate to see you all wound up like this. Mum's the word with me." He waited a beat.

"Carousel?"

Sean rolled his head back and forth.

"Is it—"

"For God's sake, Patrick!" Sean said, fixing him with a cold, hard look. "It's fraud, okay? The numbers are coming up funny."

"*Whew!* We're okay, then, right? We don't handle money. It's up the line . . . head-office stuff."

"Nobody screws with a company's money and gets away with it."

"Whoever it is, I'm sure they won't. I have a pressing issue, Sean, which needs fixed now."

"Doesn't everybody." Sean's eyes narrowed. "What?"

Patrick pulled his feet down and leaned forward in his chair. I never told you what Zugel wanted in return for helping us. "We've hit a kink in our, uh, *project*."

"I don't want to hear it. I told you those Krauts were trouble."

"I need you to authorize a train stop," Patrick said, ignoring him. "Zugel agreed to help us, but in return he wants to haul in a load of elm he has rights to. I need one empty flatcar and a little time. Nothing you can't handle."

"No, I can't." Sean took his cup over to the coffeepot and filled it up again. He looked back over at Patrick and shook his head.

Patrick watched his body language: resistant but not resolute. He pushed on. "Sean, it's one stop," he said, keeping his voice low. "We can do it on Wednesday, when the rail's light. You're good with words. All ya gotta do is write something fancy and hide it for me. Without more lumber, Zugel says he can't help us. When the robbers torched his barn—"

"Can't? Or won't?" Sean said, sneering.

"Can't, won't—what's the difference? You have to consider the bottom line. If we don't get him some wood, we're not getting the carousel fixed. Come on, Sean. At some point, somebody's going to miss the cargo. Then our goose is really cooked."

Sean sat back down and swiveled his chair away. "Absolutely not. You have no idea how far out on a limb I've already gone for you. The Pinkertons? Paid back or not, you better hope they haven't been tracking the shortages caused by your brother using this place as his personal bank."

Patrick's cup stopped midway to his mouth. "Wait—you know about that?"

"Hell, yeah, I know. Anybody else but your brother would have been out of here the first time I saw what was going on. I cut him some slack. Byrne boy, and all. I figured he had a reason and would pay it back. Only it was more, more, more. Now *I'm* getting sucked into it."

"Will the Pinks arrest him?"

"I haven't given him up yet. But I could," he said with a belligerent look. "Anybody looking good in this mess has a leg up on Broderick's position."

"You'd sell out Frank for a damn *promotion?*"

"Oh, Christ, Patrick. They'd never call in the Pinks for petty theft. Chesapeake would have fired his Irish ass and let the civil authorities handle it."

"It's not all fitting together in here," Sean said, tapping his head. "This is lots of money. Big money, much bigger than Frank's nickel-and-dime shenanigans. Over in the Wesson, the tension's as thick as oatmeal. I don't like what I'm feeling. Don't like what I'm seeing. Bertram Wesson—as in Wesson, Pepper and Smith—took all the depot records related to finance, and he's doing an audit of the money coming in and going out of here. I'm guessing the partnership caught wind of someone playing fast and loose with Carr's money, and when he finds out who, their hide'll be nailed to the yard fence with a railroad spike. If I can solve this and get ahead, why not? Whoever is ripping off the company gets no slack from me."

"The nervous round fella in the bowler hat—*he's* Wesson? Somehow I expected someone more imposing."

"Accountants are never imposing. Don't mean they aren't dangerous." Sean pulled the ledger he had been working in closer and opened it to where he had left a pencil and a sheet of paper. "None of these documents are matching up. I've got an itch, but I can't find the place to scratch it."

"Cut the crap, Sean. If everyone near and dear is out of the line of fire, much as I love shooting the bull with you, I'm dead tired and starving. Stop talking in generalities. You've found something. What is it?"

Sean sailed a sheet of paper at him. It was correspondence from the freight office in Baltimore to Christian Miller, questioning an invoice from the previous month.

Patrick shrugged. "Still not following. Did you figure out the problem?"

"Sure. Easy fix. The problem is what I found when I backtracked through our historical files. The invoice mistakenly went to Smith Protection Incorporated. They've provided protective services for the Nevis Bank a few times. The invoice should have gone to Smith *Processing* Incorporated, out of Baltimore. Simple enough mistake, right? Problem is, while I may not be able to remember the number and contents of every freight car coming through here like you can, I do have a handle on which company is sending what freight on which day, and I ain't ever heard of Smith Processing Incorporated. I've been all through these bills of lading for the past few months, and I'll be a monkey's uncle if there aren't a half-dozen bills of lading showing transport of freight for them. I might forget something here or there, but *six* cargo shipments to Carr? And look," he said, pointing to the left of the signature block. "No one initialed off. I initial everything coming through. Furthermore, I can't even find a *listing* for Smith Processing. The address we have matches the Baltimore City directory listing for the Little Sisters of Mercy mission. Payments for the cargo are sent to a post office box. It's all a front, Pat. These shipments never happened."

Patrick sat forward in his seat. "Someone's cooking the books?"

Sean gave him a pained look. "I don't know how else to explain it."

"These bills of lading," Patrick said, pointing at the ledger. "How are they routed?" You get them first, and then where do they go?"

"I'm responsible for matching up the freight coming in with what's listed in the bill of lading. If everything matches up, it goes directly to Miller across the street. He has final say on what gets paid, and then he forwards it to the billing office in Baltimore. Then I get the original back for my ledgers. He has the opportunity to submit paper for all kinds of services—including *fraudulent* ones. Who's to know? Miller's a thoroughgoing scoundrel, always has been. I wouldn't put anything past him."

Patrick handed the paper back to Sean. "Nobody else up the line could submit these claims?"

"Uh-uh. Without Miller's signature, it doesn't get paid. I've seen 'em sit in his box over there for days, waiting for him to either come into Nevis or run a courier out to get 'em and run 'em back to the corporate office. Someone would need to forge his signature and be damn good at it. Honestly, these *all* look like his signature. Think about it. Miller has respect, and carte blanche to bill Chesapeake Railway. Who would question what he submits?"

"Hm-m." Patrick slumped back in his chair, contemplating the ceiling, thoughtfully tapping his cup. "Harmon's an accountant."

"See? Not imposing."

"Why didn't he question anything? 'Cause he's in on it, is why!"

Sean shook his head. "Harmon's got no motive. He's rich as sin, isn't he?"

"His *daddy's* rich as sin," Patrick said. "Who would know better than an accountant how to steal money?"

"Exactly, but what's the motive? Thrill seeking? Getting in good with management? When he found out he'd be working in here, the color drained out of his face like someone had opened an artery." Sean closed the ledger and turned to face Patrick. "I will admit, he's done some questionable things. In fact, there are things you probably should know about, but don't. You need to remain calm if I tell you, okay? And it doesn't leave the depot."

Patrick ran his finger and thumb across his closed lips.

"If I had put two and two together at the time and told you, you would have killed somebody," Sean said, reeling it out slowly. "Being a college man and all, it didn't seem unusual for him to be interested in these." He cocked his chin at the ledger. "I chalked it up to being smart, but in hindsight, I think he was already familiar with what he would find. He took to it too quick. Somebody coached him."

Patrick looked at the ledgers and then back at Sean. "Son of a . . ." He stood up. "Miller played me. He knew I'd never leave Harmon out on the line. I'm gonna . . ."

Sean grabbed Patrick's arm and pulled him back down. "Do not do anything rash," he said. "We think he's stupid, but I've had to pull him out of these ledgers a couple of times and put him back on task. I figured his attention span was short. But nobody could be as stupid as Harmon appears.

"Yesterday, on a gut feeling, I got hold of Eddie McVeigh in the billing office and asked him to look up the most recent itinerary for engine Eight seventy-three. It was the day Harmon screwed up and sent Carr's carousel toward Solomons instead of Nevis. The thing is, when we finally unloaded here, I verified every crate. Nothing but Carr's stuff, and everything accounted for. McVeigh's paperwork said the train was carrying fifteen crates of cargo from guess who? Smith Processing! Miller made a mistake. He jumped the gun and forwarded a dummy bill to corporate without knowing we would double-check everything in that particular load. To him, it was just one more falsified cargo delivery."

Sean reached into his shirt and pulled out a wad of folded paper. "The six bogus bills of lading?" he said, unfolding the papers. "Half coincided with the time Harmon spent in the depot. It got me wondering whether the fair-haired nephew could somehow be involved, so I started matching up dates. I agree: he could be involved."

Patrick took the stack and leafed through. "So Harmon's not the fool we pegged him for. All along, he's been playing *us* for fools."

"Exactly. Harmon cuts the bill, sends it to Miller, and somewhere between Miller and the corporate office," he said, gesturing to the invoice on the top of the stack, "it gets stamped as paid. Carr's paying for stuff he never ordered and never got. If it hadn't been for the damaged crates, no telling how long their little charade might have gone on undetected."

Patrick eased forward in his chair. "You're drifting into dangerous territory, my friend. You're not thinking of taking Miller on alone, are you? You know how I'd love it to see his hide out on that fence, but you'd better make sure. I wouldn't put anything past him, but if you're wrong, your ass is his. Miller or Harmon—do we really care who goes to jail? Let the Pinkertons figure it out."

Patrick stopped and studied the look in Sean's eyes. There was a distracting emotion there, an uncommon shiftiness about the look. Sean-of-no-backbone was chomping a little too hard at the bit. Then it hit him like a freight train.

"If Broderick's job is your sole motivation, is it worth it?"

Sean glared. "I don't know, Patrick. How motivating is it? You tell me. Is all this pain with the carousel worth it?"

Patrick glared in turn, put the papers down on the table, and pushed the stack until they butted up against the ledger. "That was low. You know the carousel is all about the bonuses."

"If you say so." Sean snatched the papers back and stuffed them back in his shirt.

"I don't know what to say, quite frankly." Patrick glanced out the freight window, tapping his finger on the desk. "What risk do we run if they look too closely at the carousel manifest and bill of lading?"

"Not likely. It's one of hundreds, and it was all paid right. Hiding it from Carr is a whole other issue. We're probably okay until somebody misses the figures. Carr or Miller finding out? I don't want to think about it."

"Thanks for the info," Patrick murmured. "On more thing, and I'll be outta your hair. Authorize me a stop so I can get Zugel his lumber.

No lumber, no repaired figures. If you can't, I'll make a sweet deal with one of the engineers to make an *unauthorized* stop. The usuals hauling loads next week—Wasserman, Jake Nance? I'll make it worth their while. Because if you're going to play all the angles for Broderick's job, so am I."

Sean jumped to his feet. "You wouldn't. I'll report you."

"Try me." Patrick got up, coolly unlocked the door, and went home.

CHAPTER THIRTY-TWO

About That King Horse

Lawrence Carr warmed to the sight of the Stars and Stripes flying from the facade of every business on First Street. Rippling in the soft breeze coming off the bay, they reminded him of the enormous flag he had seen flying over Fort McHenry in Baltimore. Beyond, where the older Nevis homes began, red, white, and blue bunting festooned front porches and white picket fences. Decoration Day, May 30, 1901. He liked the spirit of the holiday honoring the Nation's fallen military: a solemn memorial to their commitment and sacrifice. He basked in memories of childhood days in Central Park, wicker baskets tucked full of picnic fare . . . But this year's holiday promised to be warmer, clearer, sweeter than any Decoration Day before it.

Yet he was on no casual walk. Today marked the installation of the park's fifty-foot grand Dentzel carousel. Of all the additions to the park, the carousels were the most widely anticipated. Truth be told, Carr hadn't seen either of them, but no matter. The grand one was a *Dentzel.* It would rival those in all the other parks for many miles around. Moreover, with the Mangel, how many parks could boast *two* carousels? He stopped at the park entrance.

"And?" Carr's assistant, Mr. Abbott, asked. Looking a little wilted in the early morning humidity, he ran a long, elegant index finger around the inside of his high shirt collar, pulled a crisp white handkerchief from his breast pocket, and mopped his brow. "We could probably see more if we stood under those red awnings," he said, pointing to the shaded area closer to the construction.

"Of course, we won't get the full effect until it's complete," Carr said, waving his walking stick in the direction of the carousel. "But the placement? Flawless. Awe inspiring how it draws you right in." He sighed, apparently satisfied, and took off at an even brisker pace to cross under the entrance arch. Mr. Abbott scurried after him. "I want to watch all this. Keep up, Abbott."

The dark, polished wood flooring was already in place around the central pole. Dentzel employees had arrived at first light and gone right to work sorting and unpacking wooden crates relocated from storage in the rail yard. Like choreographed dancers, a handful of workers were nestled in the upper reaches of the carousel's rising top, connecting the sweeping metal arms the canvas awning would lie on. Another group followed close behind, attaching the sweeps to rods that supported it all above the platform, while a third group connected the rods from which each carousel animal would hang.

Carr walked past them all and approached the apparent foreman of the work crew—a tall, thin man in black linen pants and a white button-down shirt. He cast a sideways glance at Carr's approach, but if he knew the man's importance, he did not acknowledge it. Instead, he continued to direct the activities of two other groups, pointing and calling out instructions. The first group worked to erect a series of ornamental wood panels designed to hide the steam boiler, engine, and organ, while the second group installed the great curved and mirrored expanses of the rounding boards that would adorn the base of the canvas top.

"Are you Mr. Dentzel's representative?" Carr asked, putting out his hand. I'm Lawrence Carr."

"William Dentzel, his son," the man said, returning Carr's hearty handshake. "I'll be here all day until everything is up and running correctly."

"Magnificent," Carr murmured, gazing at one of the panels. He walked closer. A teardrop-shaped painting in the center was decorated with a molded jester in red and blue harlequin. At his neck, he sported a tall white Elizabethan ruff collar, and on his head, a red three-pointed cap with a yellow bell painted at the end of each point. To the jester's right and left, large, ornately carved oval gilt-framed mirrors rested on their long sides. Carr noted with satisfaction that this motif repeated on all the ornamental panels. His gaze ran along the carved sprays of red, blue, and yellow flowers, some tied together in flowing black ribbon while others adorned the space in one exquisite bouquet. Everywhere were green scrolling vines and leaves, lilac fleurs-de-lis, and other plant carvings he could not begin to name. The names were not important, though. They were simply exquisite, and they were *Dentzel*.

"It takes my breath away," he said, turning back to Dentzel. "Tell your father he has my greatest admiration."

William Dentzel broke out into a broad smile and nodded. "Wait until evening, when it's completed," he said, gesturing around the work site. "Eight hundred lightbulbs." He pulled his watch from his pocket and checked his workers. "Come back at six o'clock. You have never seen the like. Like the first time you made love," he said, winking. "I can guarantee it'll be an experience you never forget. Come back then."

Carr flushed with embarrassment. "Six it is."

"Once the structure is up, it won't take long to hang the menagerie." Dentzel looked at the assistant who had been dogging his every step. "Since you seem determined to remain at my elbow, make yourself useful and give Mr. Carr a peek at the figures. Show him the king horse."

"Well, sir, I've been trying to . . . er, following so closely . . . not to interrupt, sir, but there does not seem to *be* a king horse. Or the lion, or the rabbit. We are missing three crates. They're on the inventory sheet, and we shipped them, but they aren't *here . . .* sir."

"Good God!" Carr gasped. "The railroad lost part of my carousel?"

"I, uh, really couldn't say, sir." The assistant pulled out a crisp white handkerchief and dabbed his neck. "Isn't this heat dreadful?"

"Stop everything!" Carr yelled, pointing his walking stick at the half-finished carousel. "Not one piece more. I am not paying for a carousel missing . . ." He turned on Dentzel's assistant. "What was it you said? Its *king* horse? Someone go get Christian Miller. I want to get to the bottom of this. *Now.*"

Lawrence A. Carr hung like a storm cloud over Christian Miller's desk. "Damn it, man, *find my carousel!*"

Miller leaned away from the shaking index finger. He tried to smile pleasantly as the usually composed millionaire raved on like a lunatic. It had been going on like this for several minutes, from the moment Carr barged into his office without knocking. Miller's eyes darted about. Carr had him pinned behind his desk, with no graceful means of escape. Undoubtedly, every other occupant of the building could hear the racket. Surely, a Chesapeake Railway office worker would soon come to calm the man and extract their boss from this verbal abuse.

Carr's face contorted in rage. "Don't patronize me! Do something *now!*" he bellowed. He smacked his walking stick across Miller's desk,

213

breaking off the bottom third of the stick. The piece bounced off the desk, and the ragged end of wood hit Miller squarely in the forehead.

Miller clasped his hands to the wound and doubled over in pain, dripping bright red blood across the papers on the desk. In the next moment, he sprang up, toppling his chair to the floor behind him. "I'll have your damn carousel for you!" he said through bloodied hands. "Now, get out of my office before I have you for assault, sir!"

Carr looked from the end of his walking stick to Miller's face, and back again. "Oh, dear. I, uh, er . . . He fumbled with the white handkerchief in his vest pocket, finally pulling it free and offering it to Miller, who snatched it up. Carr backed up away from the desk. "Well, things like this don't happen to people who do their jobs," he said, shaking his head. Then the finger started to wag again.

"By the end of the day, Mr. Miller, or I'll make sure you're sitting on the curb tomorrow—that is, if you can find one in this ragtag railroad shantytown. Good day." He slammed the door behind him.

Miller righted his chair and collapsed into it. He pulled the blood-soaked handkerchief away, refolded it, and reapplied the monogram directly to the wound.

The door squeaked open, and a new face peered in. "Anything I can get you?" the young man asked, a hand materializing from behind the door to push a lock of stringy brown hair out of his eyes.

"Get me Sean Murphy. *Now.*"

The young, thin railway office secretary, Norman, descended the Wesson steps and darted across the street. He bolted through the depot door and into Sean's office—another Nevis resident, rushing!

Sean kept a poker face as Norman explained his mission, but his blood was coursing like ice through his veins.

"Norman, I realize that Mr. Miller's my boss, but I can't leave the depot right now," he said in the most collegial tone. "There's nobody here to back me up. So either sit down in the chair and wait a spell, or go find something else to do for half an hour. I would suggest the latter. I won't tell if you won't."

Sean picked up the phone receiver as soon as Norman departed. "Trudy, connect me with the section house. Patrick Byrne—it's an emergency . . . Right, as in life or death." Sean checked to see where Norman was. The stringy-haired lad had taken up residence on the porch. Some young girls were on the street, and he seemed to have quite forgotten his mission.

"Hullo, Sean? What's wrong? Is it Dad? Moira?"

"It's Miller, Patrick. He and Carr had a big blowout. Norman said you could hear it all over the Wesson—an argument about certain missing carousel parts. Miller sent Norman to find me. I'm dragging my feet, but I can't do it for much longer. I don't think we all need to hang separately here. You can have your stop. Jake Nance is bringing Eight seventy-Three in at nine tomorrow morning. Make sure Zugel's lumber is loaded on it, so we can get those figures back. Otherwise, we are dead meat. I can give you a half-hour stop."

"Thanks, pal. "I'll hop right on it. Are the Pinkertons involved?"

"Norman didn't say, but Carr was alone. And one more thing, Pat," he said before hanging up, "get me the exact stopping point. We have one shot. Got it?"

"Of course. One stop."

CHAPTER THIRTY-THREE

All Aboard

Patrick rubbed his eyes, but the weariness was still there. The stop would be quick: a half hour and not a minute more—all Sean could allow in the exact scheduling of arriving and departing trains. It was a tiny window of time in a massive schedule affecting not only Nevis and Solomons, but a half-dozen other routes, switches, and depots up the Chesapeake line. Nobody needed another Casey Jones incident. How was he going to swing this? He hung up the phone and called Frank over.

"Zugel stop is set up," he whispered in his ear. "Half hour tomorrow at nine. Take over out here? I need to hit town."

It was midmorning, and Dilly's was deserted—no customers, no one behind the counter. Even the jingling bell on the back of the door failed to elicit a response.

"Yo," Patrick called, heading for the kitchen's double doors. As he approached, Anna burst through from the other direction, plowing right into him. He caught her in a bear hug.

"Sorry," he said, immediately letting go and backing up. He put his hands behind his back. "Did I hurt you?"

Anna blushed and shook her head. Her apron was dusted in a fine coating of white, and the spatula in her hand dripped white batter. "If you'll wait a minute, I can get you something, but it'll take a minute. I'm the only one here."

He shook his head. "No, but thank you. I need you to take another message to your father, about our business."

She broke out into a dazzling smile. "Of course."

Her look was so irresistible, he couldn't help but smile back. "Tell him nine tomorrow morning for the elm. He has half an hour to load whatever he has. That's all I can give him."

"It's enough. It's all stacked and ready to go. They've been working out there all week."

Patrick laughed. "Have they? Glad somebody was sure."

"Beg pardon?"

"It's nothing. I would love a meal right now, but I've got to hunt down someone at the Bayside Hotel."

"How soon? I'm going there myself later, for Father's business. I could deliver a message, if you like."

Patrick brightened. "You're a lifesaver, Anna."

"My pleasure," she said, walking off to find something to write on. "What are friends for?"

She gave him paper and another smile. It melted him even more than the first. He scribbled something, folded and addressed the note, and gave it back to her.

He left Dilly's and swung by the depot to tip off Sean, then returned to the rails. He felt good about this. It all felt so right, with no premonitions that anything bad was about to happen. They were going to pull this off. If Zugel was cutting wood, he was fixing carousel figures. Life was good, like Anna Zugel's smile.

———◆◦◆◦◆———

When Sean could no longer put off the inevitable, he followed Norman back over to face the full wrath of Christian Miller. He swore on the grave of his mother that the missing crates were out in the maintenance shed and he would personally deliver them to town by morning. It was a harmless enough half-truth. His mother was alive and living comfortably on Second Street in Chester, Pennsylvania, and Zugel appeared to be ready to fulfill his end of the agreement. Patrick seemed confident they could count on Zugel, but the man was a German, and Sean still had his doubts.

CHAPTER THIRTY-FOUR

Going Against the Grain

Zugel had not seen this many wagons since they raised his son's barn the spring before last. It made him happy, not only because there were so many helping hands, but also because he knew these men so well—their wives, their sons and daughters, even to whom each wagon belonged. He hummed a comforting old Bavarian folk song his father had taught him. The Irishman had kept his part of the bargain, and now he would keep his.

He sent a few of the younger workers into the barn to bring out the repaired carousel animals and load them. They were eager and had not yet learned to pace themselves. By day's end, they would be dragging as the older, more experienced men worked rings around them

"Do you want me to lock up?" Matthias called as he followed the last figure out the massive barn doors.

Zugel waved him away. "*Nein*. No more secrets. Mangel takes delivery of the second carousel tomorrow. Soon, all Nevis will realize there is more to being German than lager and bratwurst. Am I right, Jakob?"

Jakob laughed. "Hopefully. You will take the figures to the depot?"

Zugel shook his head. "To the siding, where others are preparing to load the elm when the train arrives. When we are done, we will return to the depot to off-load the wood. It will be an all-day job. Celebrating will have to come tonight. Am I allowed to look at them now?" Zugel asked, a teasing light in his old blue eyes.

Jakob tilted his head toward the wagon.

Zugel walked over to the youth tying down the back corner of a protective tarp. "Draw it back, Karl," he said to his sister-in-law's nephew. He waited as youthful hands, still unblemished by slipping chisels and errant mallet swings, did as he asked.

Zugel leaned over the wagon. "Now, *this* is worthy of a carousel," he said, reaching out to caress the muzzle of the white horse that lay on its right side in the wagon bed. The precise carving on the horse's head was a thing of beauty, and the gleaming reds, blues, and greens running down the heavy gold bridle like fiery gems coaxed him into a broad smile. It was a warhorse with shining brown glass eyes, flaring nostrils, and flying mane, its head tilted back as if answering the call to charge into battle. Zugel eyed the orange tassels along the edge of the bridle. "Couldn't resist the urge to add your own touch, Jakob? Perhaps we should keep this one."

"It is *all* my touch. The neck and head were pulled from our practice pile."

Zugel ran his hand down the arched neck and around the side hidden from view. He frowned and glanced at Jakob. The old man was suddenly engrossed in cleaning the dirt from under his nails with his pocketknife. Zugel motioned to Karl, who uncovered another figure. The lion, also lying on its right side, was majestic in shades of golden tan, darkening to chocolate brown at the mane and tail tuft. He bore a high-pommeled Asian saddle of periwinkle blue resting on a tangerine saddle blanket adorned with stars and sunbursts of green and red.

Zugel ran his hand along the underside of the figure, then moved to the rabbit, its long ears now firmly attached. He felt along the underside as he had done with the other two. Frowning, he looked from the head of the lion back into Jakob's face, where he noticed a similar strength and determination.

"Here's the problem, Jakob," Zugel said, pinching his chin between forefinger and thumb, the side of his finger scratching at his gray stubble. "When they mount these on the carousel platform, your beautiful heavy carving will face inward, not outward where it could be admired by all. Why is the heavier decorative carving on the wrong side?"

Jakob joined him at the wagon. He made a circular motion with his finger. "The English carousels, they go clockwise." "Here in America, counterclockwise." He moved the finger in the opposite direction. "I thought it good to have something different, not American." He reached out and patted Jakob's arm. "And anyway, they are much better now on both sides than when the Irishman brought them." He met Zugel's gaze and held it.

Zugel's halfhearted smile drooped into a frown. "But you are not English. You knew this was incorrect. Why did you do this?" he asked, voice rising.

A sly smile spread across Jakob's face. "How is this wrong?" he asked. "Germans have made carousels for many years. There is no rule saying the detailed carving goes on the right side and the platform must turn counterclockwise. Clockwise motion and heavy carving on the left side are okay."

"It's wrong because it's not done here. We are in America, and we do it the American way. Inside our homes, on our farms, we honor our traditions and are free to do as we please. But when we step outside, we must attend to American traditions. We do what is expected. Dentzel builds counterclockwise, carves heavily on the right. Am I not correct in this?"

Jakob shook his finger at Zugel. "Carousels can go any way they want. It is done. End of discussion."

"Jakob, dear friend." Zugel wrapped his arm around the old carver's shoulder. "It serves no point to be stubborn, except to lose us business for the next carousel. You are swimming against a current that will not change. We must assimilate and do what is expected. As a carver, you know very well that you do not go against the grain. You can still be Bavarian and have them traveling counterclockwise. Your German-ness shows in your exquisite carvings. Wouldn't it be a shame for children never to see your work, only because no one wants to buy something turning in the wrong direction?"

The older man's eyes misted up, and his gaze shifted to the darkest corner of the barn, away from the door, up to the high-set windows. "We are German. Clockwise is acceptable. No more carousels," he said, shaking his head as he hobbled off toward the darkness.

Zugel climbed up in the wagon. He could not bear to consider the direction of the second carousel. Would Mangel even *consider* a clockwise carousel?

CHAPTER THIRTY-FIVE

Wiping the Slate

E ven if he never liked another thing about them, Patrick had to give the Germans credit for their efficiency. He and Frank were the first linemen out this morning, and Zugel's men were already working hard at the rendezvous point. The elm lumber was neatly stacked along the right-of-way—most of it on the ground, the rest in a series of wagons pulled up end to end—as twenty men clustered about in small groups, waiting for the train. Patrick waved a half-salute at them and began his daily line inspection.

"Frank, take a quick peek over there. See Zugel anywhere?"

Frank stopped and stretched his arms over his head as he ran his eyes over the Germans. "Nope, not that I can find. Sure about him?"

"Anna said he'd be here."

"You don't suppose they'll load their lumber and then poop out on us?"

"Naw. Jake can enter and leave Nevis without unloading any of the cargo. The Germans know that. Reckon that elm would fetch a pretty penny in Baltimore."

"Enough to pay off quite a bit of debt," Frank said wistfully.

"And maybe pay your living expenses when Miller gives you your walking papers."

Patrick watched one of the Sheffields roll up. Linemen jumped off it and began removing equipment, preparing to lift the rail runner off the track before the train came through. He caught one of the linemen's eye. "Hey, Mike, got something for ya," he said as the man approached. "Sean's already remotely switched the color-light signal to cautionary yellow," he said, pointing toward the bridge. "Eight seventy-three will slow down, anticipating a full stop. Go up there a quarter mile or so and flag 'em in here."

"Sure, boss." Mike grabbed a red flag off the Sheffield and hustled away.

Patrick glanced back across the track, eyes flitting from one blond head to the next as he studied each wagon. So much for efficiency. Where was Zugel? "Come on, Frank. If those carousel figures are a no-show, I'll nip this in the bud. We'll wave Jake through, no stop."

They crossed the tracks and approached the head wagon. A stocky dark-haired man in overalls came forward to meet them. They all shook hands.

"Zugel?" Patrick asked.

"Coming," the man said. He turned back to a group of his men. "Karl?"

Karl joined them and gave a cordial nod, but his eyes were wary. It was the youngster Patrick and Frank had caught climbing the yard fence months before.

"Zugel?" asked the older German.

"They broke a wheel, sir, and had to load a new wagon. Mr. Zugel sent me ahead to tell you he is coming and will be here soon."

The wagon's driver nodded, and Karl disappeared back into the comfort of the bigger group. "Soon. Karl forgot to add that Mr. Zugel was apologetic." He studied the rail men a moment and then added,

"Michod Zugel is an honorable man. He keeps his promises." With that, he tipped his brimmed hat and walked back to the wagons.

"Well, there you have it," Frank said as they crossed back over the track. The railroad right-of-way had become a kind of no-man's land between forces that, though not overtly hostile, kept a watchful eye on each other. "Still think he'll show?"

"I *want* to think that," Patrick said. As his foot touched the far rail, he felt a vibration. The rails were singing. A mile out, he could see 873 chugging along, trailing a plume of smoke. He checked his watch. Unlike Zugel, she was right on time. But he couldn't fault Jake Nance for being punctual.

"Here she comes. Do or die. Stop or flag her through—what's it gonna be, Pat?

The train whistle blared, the blast magnifying as it hit the tree line.

In a quick sweep, Patrick took in Frank, the train, and a parting of the crowd around the lead wagon on the German side. God, he hoped it was who he thought it was.

"Pat," Frank said. "Now or never. Call it, man."

Patrick's eyes lingered a moment more. "Stop her, Frank," he said, sighing with relief. He waved back at Zugel, who was stepping down from his wagon, and crossed back over no-man's land once more.

Zugel ignored him, instead directing a few of the workers to untie the tarps in the bed of his wagon. "Did you get my message?" he asked.

Patrick nodded.

"I am sorry," Zugel said. He pulled the tarps back, revealing the carousel horse. "Okay?" he asked. The expression in his eyes was dark and guarded.

Patrick ran his hand down the muzzle of the white horse. "Splendid!" It was better than he had hoped. He would have hugged the man, but Zugel sidestepped the embrace, smiling broadly, unable to hide his pleasure and pride.

Engine 873 came to a shrieking, hissing halt behind them. At a nod from Zugel, his workers swarmed over the lumber and onto the bulkhead flatcar, loading the rough-hewn wood.

"Where do you want these?" Zugel asked, gesturing to the carousel figures.

Patrick pointed to the boxcar behind the flatcar. "We have a separate car and crates, too. Draw the wagon up closer." He climbed up front with Zugel, a few men climbed in back, and Patrick directed the wagon as close to the train as the horses would comfortably go. Together with several of the burlier linemen, they transferred the cargo to crates and nailed the lids shut.

Patrick left them to oversee the loading of the lumber. Within twenty-five minutes, it was done—lumber transferred, figures safely stowed, and most of the wagons gone. Having seen the Germans raise an entire barn in a single day, Patrick was not surprised at how well it all went. There was a beauty to the Germans' work-gang approach—the lifters, the carriers, those who lined the flatcar bed and the ones up top who pulled the heavy bull ropes across the load at the various tie-down points and cinched them tight. If Mac had been out there calling, they might have rivaled the gandies for smooth teamwork.

In the end, only Zugel remained, his wagon pulled beyond the right-of-way as the crew secured the boxcar doors and moved off the track. Patrick checked his watch. Thirty minutes exactly. He climbed up into the cab, had a brief word with Jake, and retreated to a safe distance on the German side of the track.

With much hissing and creaking, engine 873 stirred from its rest, and a progression of loud bangs ran down the length of the train as the couplers drew taut. Jake gave his familiar three short whistle blasts, and the beast began its crawl toward Nevis, rumbling and clacking and gathering speed until it disappeared from view.

Patrick walked over to Zugel's wagon. "I think this worked out well. Thank you," he said, reaching up to shake his collaborator's hand.

Zugel offered his biggest smile yet. He was done talking. He had obviously gotten what he wanted. "You seem a man of your word, Mr. Byrne. There is one more thing—a simple request, actually."

Patrick arched an eyebrow and waited for the second condition to their agreement.

"Stay away from my daughter."

"Pardon?"

Zugel fixed him with his wise old eyes for a moment, then flicked the reins, and the team started away. "I'd say we're even, Mr. Byrne," he said over his shoulder.

Patrick stood speechless.

"Wow, never saw that coming," Frank said, watching the wagon rumble away. "The deal with the devil wasn't as bad as we thought. Guess we'll have to find a new place to eat, though, huh?"

"Nobody tells me where to eat." Patrick pointed toward the rest of the crew. "Go, and not another word, Frank Byrne, until the train doubles back and stops again."

"*What?* Sean said a half-hour stop. What's going on?"

"One stop, *two times.*"

"Sean okayed no such thing. What are you up to, Pat?"

Patrick started walking away. "Leave me. I have to think."

Engine 873's second stop, bought with a bottle of fine Irish whiskey, took less than five minutes—just long enough to board two additional passengers, who had timed their arrival almost as closely as Zugel's.

Frank, who had been shadowing his brother since being commanded to silence, walked up next to Patrick and verbalized what everyone else was silently asking. "Delivery, boarding, what?"

Patrick ignored him and went out to meet the wagon as two men disembarked. It looked as though money may have exchanged hands, and the wagoner made a wide turn and left his passengers.

"Everything all right?" Patrick asked.

"It's good," said the shorter of the two, who proved to be not a man at all, but Birdie Partridge, dressed in blue coveralls, her hair stuffed beneath a dark leather flat cap. A. J. Packard, in railroad-striped denim overalls and long-sleeved blue work shirt, stood beside her.

Patrick handed Birdie a packet. "Here are the coach tickets to central Baltimore, then, with a short delay and change of train, up to Pittsburgh. Sorry I can't do any more than that."

She took them and smiled. "No, you've done plenty."

"It's not my affair, but considering we're only weeks away from the grand opening, and the amount of stress Mr. Carr is under, are you sure you've thought this all through?"

"No more *thinking* things through, Patrick," Birdie said. Her eyes were calm, her gaze steady. "I'm getting off this carousel I've been on, and I don't care what other people's expectations are. Let the condemnation flow. I'm going with what I feel—what *we* feel," she said, looking at A. J.

A. J. nodded. "Whatever the repercussions may be." He drew a gold S-shaped money clip from his pocket. "How much do we owe you for the tickets, Mr. Byrne?"

Patrick put his hands up. "We're more than even. Glad I could help you. As far as I'm concerned, you were never here. Where are your bags, by the way?"

"We're empty handed," she said. "Lawrence can have it all. We'll get along fine once we get to Pittsburgh."

"Then you'd best get aboard before tongues start wagging." He led them to the caboose. "It's been a pleasure," he said as he shook hands with A. J.

"Good luck to you," Birdie whispered as she stepped up into the car. "You'd best watch your back, Mr. Byrne. Steer clear of Lawrence. I wouldn't trust his capacity to forgive. I hope your bonuses make a big fat dent in his wallet and that someday you find that desk job you need."

"Not a problem. With that bonus, I'm heading straight for the B and O." He stepped away and watched as they settled into the car.

Patrick signaled the all clear to Jake, and as the train rumbled away, he returned to his men and their work. For the first time in a very long while, his slate was clean. It felt good.

Except the Anna Zugel piece.

CHAPTER THIRTY-SIX

Signatures

A s soon as Sean drove Billy and Isaac under the massive Bayland entrance arch, he had an unobstructed view of the carousel pavilion. The rectangular gray board-and-batten structure stood dead center in the main square, rising two stories to a clerestoried octagonal roof of red terra-cotta. The Dentzel carousel was indeed the crown jewel in Bayland Park, and all the promenades fed into the grand courtyard where it stood.

Sean slid down off the wagon and went inside, passing a carpenter, who was on his knees and painting pricing information on the side of a ticket booth. Two other workers were hunched over something in the center of the huge platform—working on the motor or the barrel organ, he supposed. Horses, a kangaroo, and other menagerie figures were already hanging on the platform. The carousel looked finished. Perhaps the repaired figures were extras. Where would they go?

He had sent word ahead to Miller that he was delivering the elusive "misplaced" crates, so he was not surprised when an excitable, bald man with an attitude and a notebook hailed him right away.

"Our crates?" asked the man, bypassing him and heading straight for his wagon. He directed a khaki-clad laborer up to inspect.

"Yes sir," Sean said. He followed him back outside. "Three of 'em." He watched as three more laborers joined the first and began maneuvering the crates off the wagon and prying the lids off.

Sean shoved a paper at the man. "Just sign here."

"Hold on," the assistant said. "We don't know where these have been, or the condition. Mr. Dentzel will want to inspect them. William!" he yelled, although it was unnecessary, for a man, apparently Dentzel, was already striding in their direction.

"Do they match our inventory sheet?" he asked the assistant.

"Yes sir: white horse, tawny lion, brown rabbit."

"Go ahead and pull 'em out," Dentzel said.

When the laborers had the crates pried open, he walked around the three figures, stopping in front of the white horse. He placed a hand on either side of the head and leaned the figure from side to side.

Sean watched him trace the outline of the orange tassels. "I really need to get back to the depot," he said to Dentzel. "Will you sign for this, please?"

Dentzel ignored the paper. "Is this the only white horse?"

"Yes sir," Sean and the assistant said in unison.

"Do we have a problem?" the assistant asked.

Dentzel fixed his eyes on Sean. "Superb craftsmanship," he said. "All's well. Install them." As the laborers carted the figures away, he took the paper from Sean.

"Orange tassels—an unusual flourish," he said, signing his name. "Heavier carving on the inside. European. My father and I are practical

231

men, and right now we have more business than we can handle. I don't want the story. I will just say you chose well. Give my regards to Jakob Koenig. They don't come any better." He handed the paper back and retraced his steps to the carousel platform, where the laborers already busy hanging the final figures on the Dentzel masterpiece.

Sean jumped back up in the wagon and urged the team to a trot. The carved figures were no longer the railroad's problem, and Miller's secretary, Norman, could pick up the receipt from him at the depot.

CHAPTER THIRTY-SEVEN

A Week Later

Sean stopped on the steps and said, "Since you're so confident, you go first."

Patrick took the Wesson Building's stairs two at a time. "Everything's fine. If it weren't, we would have heard by now. Mr. Dentzel would have nailed you then and there. He didn't care, and nobody else is ever going to know Jakob Koenig carved those figures."

"Sneaky Kraut, putting those tassels on there," Sean muttered, following him up the stairs. "He might as well have just gone ahead and carved his initials in the neck. You should have seen Dentzel's face. Burned a hole right through me."

"Yeah, well, it's over now. Nobody's lost their job, and it looks like Bayland is opening before Sandy Point. Haven't you been paying attention to the scuttlebutt? This meeting is about the bonuses. Hopefully, enough to float me after I quit the Chesapeake and until I get picked up by the B and O."

"I listen to scuttlebutt, like the rumor about you jumping to Baltimore. You know, the one you swore wasn't true. Do you remember what I said I'd do if I found out last? The door could hit you in the ass on the way out."

"They were all just rumors before, Sean. You and Frank are the first to get the straight story. I swear it." Patrick pulled open the oak door and took the next flight of stairs just as fast, pausing only when he arrived at Miller's closed office door. Sean made no effort to keep up.

"Come in," Christian Miller replied to Patrick's knock.

They went, but Patrick put no stock in the smug grin on his boss's face. When he had the bonus money in his hand, he would believe it.

"Yes sir, you asked us to be here . . ."

"Guess what day it is?"

Sean and Patrick exchanged looks. "Tuesday?" Patrick offered.

Miller laughed—a genuine, heartfelt belly laugh. It almost made him likeable. "Well, that, but more importantly," he said, sliding his desk drawer open and pulling out an envelope, "it's *bonus* day. "It's official. Bayland will open at the end of the month—weeks ahead of Sandy Point. A representative of the First National Bank dropped this off earlier today with specific instructions on distribution to Chesapeake Railway Express employees. Having paid myself, guess who's next?"

Patrick shook his head. He hated Miller's games. "If we're working our way down a list, Sean Murphy and me . . . maybe?"

Miller pulled a folded paper out of the envelope. "Precisely. According to the partnership, each of you—"

The office door burst open with a loud bang and slammed against the wall, and three Pinkertons, led by Nevis's own Officer McCall, barged into the office.

Miller stood up.

"Out," McCall said to Patrick and Sean. "Our business is with Mr. Miller. Christian Bartholomew Miller, you are under arrest. Please step from behind the desk and come peacefully."

"Don't be absurd! On what charge?" Miller reached for the telephone.

"Steady there, Miller. By the authority vested in me by the local authorities, you are under arrest for embezzlement."

Pinkerton Officer Wakefield walked over and snatched the envelope out of Miller's hand. "*Evidence*," he said to Officer Smyth. "Make a note."

"Dear God," Patrick murmured. "Not the bonus." He tried to step forward, but Sean blocked his path. "I believe that's the bonus—"

At that moment, Albert Harmon walked in, decked out in a Pinkerton uniform with a star-shaped captain's badge pinned to the lapel. "Embezzlement *and* fraud against the Bayside Partnership and the Chesapeake Railway Express," he said, moving past Wakefield.

"Oh, you son of a bitch," Miller muttered.

Sean stepped forward. "That envelope is bonus money for the Chesapeake crew!"

"Put them outside, Edgar," Harmon said to the burliest of the Pinkertons. "They're not involved. Then come back and help turn this place over."

Sean walked out under his own power, but Patrick dodged Edgar's advance, obliging the Pinkerton to grab him by the arm and drag him out the door and down the steps, where he shoved him out on the porch and locked the door behind him.

⬥━◆━⬥

From the stifling confines of the depot, Patrick stared out at the Wesson. He had no real idea how he might track the movement of his bonus money, but he couldn't let it go. After all the problems they had solved, there had to be an answer: reasoning, wheedling, begging, stealing. He was not above any of it. Behind him, Sean, Frank, and Connor sat silent and despondent.

"Miller arrested, and the dandy turns out to be a Pinkerton. Good Lord, what's this world coming to?" Sean asked as he watched a shiny black spider creep across the ceiling directly above him. "Harmon. How the hell did he . . . ?"

"End up with our bonus?" Patrick said. He took up the chair near the teletype. "There is no God, there is no B and O, and I reckon there is no Broderick job, either. Just shoot me, right here and now." He put his forehead down on the countertop.

"It's bad, but it ain't *that* bad, Pat." Frank propped his boots up on a mail crate. "We've never gotten extra money before, and we're still scraping by. Truth be told, I would almost trade that bonus to see Miller in prison stripes. The look on his face when Harmon walked in must have been priceless. Who would've thought that behind all that prissy was an accountant who had found his manly side. Bet Miller was ready to wet his britches."

"Let me tell you, there was murder in his eyes." Sean said, watching Connor whittle on a chunk of wood. "Anything, Connor?"

"I'll bet ya a trip to Sally's we get that money," Connor said, shaving off a long, curling sliver. "That's clean money—Carr's money. If those people are accounting for every penny, it just won't fit anywhere." He stopped carving and inspected his work.

A loud rap on the depot door sent Frank scrambling to his feet. Connor nicked his thumb and dropped the carving while the other two froze where they were.

It was Harmon, and he was alone. He walked in. Gone was the brash, in-charge Pinkerton, in his place the mild and familiar accountant.

Nodding affably, he walked over to the main counter and slapped down a white envelope.

"Bonus money," he said. "Wakefield has a tendency to get caught up in the moment. I read the instructions inside and noted the amount. Sean, I expect Mr. Carr would appreciate you following up on its distribution."

Sean nodded. "How long have you been a Pinkerton?"

"Sixteen months. My accounting background comes in handy where money's concerned. Sorry for the subterfuge. I know I was the worst lineman in the history of railroading, but it wouldn't have worked any other way."

"Are you really Carr's nephew?" Patrick asked.

He shook his head. "Mr. Carr suggested it."

Frank let go of the chair back he was gripping. "Was Miller . . . ?"

Harmon smiled. "Sorry, I'm not at liberty to discuss the investigation, other than to say that we are done here in Nevis and I don't believe it will be necessary to come back. After speaking with Mr. Miller, we feel we have apprehended the guilty parties, and we will prosecute accordingly. I'm here only because I know how much everyone was counting on the bonus money. So, uh . . . here it is. Nice to have met all of you. Regardless of what opinions you likely have of me, I have the deepest respect for what you do. Have a good day."

He tipped his hat and headed out the door, then paused a moment before stepping out. He looked back at Frank. "Mr. Byrne, some three-hundred-year-old advice from Mr. Shakespeare: 'Neither a borrower nor a lender be.'" Then he was gone.

Frank turned pale. "How did he . . . ?"

"Because you are one lucky bastard if ever I knew one." Patrick lunged for the envelope, getting there one step ahead of Sean. He fanned out the money. "Good Lord, there's a fortune in here! You got to get rid of this, Sean, before somebody robs us again."

Sean eased it out of his hand. "My pleasure, Mr. Byrne. Let's see how quickly we can get you to the B and O. And where might you be off to, Frank?"

Frank and Connor drew in close. "There better be enough in that envelope to put me to sea, Sean Murphy."

"Connor?"

"Count first; then I'll tell you."

They sat down in a circle on the floor as they had as youngsters playing marbles in Philadelphia, and Sean began doling it out, one beautiful bill at a time.

CHAPTER THIRTY-EIGHT

Clockwise

S ecurity around the Dentzel carousel had been tight ever since
Sean delivered the three missing pieces. The partnership, apparently dead set on dazzling the public, planned to unveil their
spinning masterpiece of color, light, and music in one magical, heavily
publicized moment. Patrick envisioned that moment perhaps differently
from Carr and his cronies. In his mind's eye, each rotation of the platform showcased a lion, horse, and bunny garishly out of place amid the
rest of the menagerie. The visions kept him a little on edge, but neither
camaraderie nor bribes could get him or his pals within spitting distance
of the carousel.

As soon as the park opened, Patrick, Sean, and Frank headed straight
for the central plaza. The sprightly melody of the barrel organ drew them
along like the Pied Piper.

When they hit the plaza, they joined a jostling, oohing and aahing
crowd of all ages and stations, standing in awe before Dentzel's extrav-
aganza of motion and sound. The pavilion doors of the carousel house

had been thrown open wide to accommodate the throng. If any had bothered to read the placard, they would have learned that thirty-one horses were spinning past them. In the outer row were sixteen standers of every imaginable color, and two gilt chariots of Roman Empire style. Fifteen equally beautiful jumpers made up the central row, including a much-heralded fiery white "king" horse. In the third and inner row strode a menagerie of animals: one tawny lion, a brown rabbit, a goat, a deer, a hippopotamus, an ostrich, a kangaroo, and a pair each of burros, bison, and tigers.

"You see 'em?" said Patrick, craning his head around youngsters sitting on their fathers' shoulders.

"Not yet," Sean murmured, tiptoeing.

"White horse!" Frank shouted, turning a few heads in his direction. He pointed toward the horses coming into view from the left.

It was the king horse, splendid and majestic as it glided past with a crowing little boy on its back. A bit plain, perhaps, but certainly not out of place among its neighbors. It was perfectly acceptable, as were the lion and the rabbit when they, too, swirled by.

The three trainmen sighed and exchanged looks of relief. They had done it—fooled everyone.

"Look, Mom! This one has orange tassels, too!" exclaimed the little boy standing beside Patrick. "Just like the orange ones on the other carousel."

Patrick's stomach dropped. He stooped down to address the little boy. "There is another carousel with orange tassels?"

The boy retreated behind his mother's skirt but nodded before disappearing entirely in the billowing folds of cloth.

"I love tassels," Patrick said to the mother, winking at the tyke as he peeked out. "Where would that other carousel be? Here in this park?"

He nodded politely as she pointed down one of the promenades.

"Son of a bitch!" Sean hissed. "Those sneaky Krauts built the second carousel!"

The three men sprinted down the promenade, dodging in and around patrons, homing in on the lively notes of another barrel organ. Dead ahead, they saw it: the red-and-white-striped canvas of the carousel top. Frank eased his way close to the carousel while Patrick and Sean skidded to a stop in front of the description placard.

"'Winner of Nevis carousel contest: master carver Jakob Koenig, Nevis,'" Patrick muttered. "We've been played, Sean."

The carousel was smaller and simpler than the Dentzel. The rounding boards on top were white and adorned every few feet with carvings of crabs, fish, and seabirds, all framed in clusters of red and yellow flowers. The painted scenic panels hiding the steam engine depicted scenes of bay life: oyster and crabbing boats, the *Chessie Belle,* Tanner's Mercantile, Sollars Ferry, the Chesapeake Railway Express depot, the pickle boat houses on the far side of town, and other familiar scenes of Nevis.

The three rail men watched as fifteen jumpers on the inside row glided up and down on their poles, and eight menagerie figures—two giraffes, two sea horses, two lions, two deer—cavorted on the outer ring. Scattered among them were chariots in the shape of oyster shells. The carousel's ornamentation was a dazzlingly patriotic array of red, white, and blue stars, stripes, eagles, and shields.

Then there was the king horse, a magnificent white Lipizzaner stallion positioned in levade, the orange tassels of its saddle accentuating its gravity-defying pose.

"Son of a—"

"*Shh,* Pat! Kids," Sean said, indicating the dozens of children surrounding them.

"Interesting," Frank said, bending down to see something down low.

"What are you looking at?" Patrick said.

"This one's twirling in the opposite direction from the big carousel. *Clockwise.* Why'd they do that?"

"Do we really care?"

"No," Sean said, pulling on Patrick's arm. "We don't. This has all worked out. Looks like they needed us just as much as we needed them. They built a nice clockwise carousel, and we get to keep our jobs. Who cares about tassels and Krauts? Let's get out of here."

"A good deal for everyone," Michod Zugel said, coming up behind them, his eyes sparkling. "Isn't it lovely?"

"Why didn't you tell us you were building a second carousel?" Patrick asked.

"Would it have mattered? You needed our carving, and we needed your train. Everyone got what they wanted. You have belated misgivings?"

"The orange tassels?"

Zugel laughed and waved him off. "Jakob always carves them. No one cares."

"Well, William Dentzel certainly recognized them," Sean said. "He sends his best to *Jakob Koenig*."

Zugel smiled. "Does he, now? Jakob will be pleased. The tassels are nothing—like hello in a close-knit family. Jakob Koenig and Gustav Dentzel both learned to carve from Gustav's father, Michael, in Kreuznach. Gustav will appreciate the joke. Carvers have their work swapped out all the time on these machines. No one else will ever know unless you tell them."

He turned back to the carousel. "There is motion, fire, beauty in what they carve. Honestly, this is as lovely as the Dentzel, don't you think? Smaller but, with the story it tells about Nevis, so much more appropriate. Yes?"

The three rail men studied the carousel, and one by one, they nodded.

"Yes," Patrick said. It was uniquely Nevis, created by someone who loved the town and who could express it better than they ever could. "But why is it going backwards?"

"Not backwards, *clockwise*. Some European carousels go clockwise."

Sean's face flushed. "But you're not in Europe anymore, are you? All your beer and your sauerkraut and your—"

Patrick put a hand on his shoulder. "Sean, it's time to go. Like you said, we're done here. Good day, Mr. Zugel." He pushed and got Sean walking away.

"Jakob is good with small details," Zugel called after them. "You might enjoy his carving around the bases of the oyster shells."

Patrick was sick of the drama, and he wasn't about to go inspecting any oyster shells. A flash of green on the carousel caught his eye. *Be damned.* Leprechauns, driving a miniature train along the border of the shell base. It was an American carousel with a European spin and an Irish dedication. He looked back over his shoulder to Zugel, who tipped his hat. Apparently, those stubborn, stoical Germans did have a sense of humor after all.

CHAPTER THIRTY-NINE

From Gandy to Sea Shanty

P atrick stood at the bottom of the train steps looking up at Frank. "You're making me nervous. Don't blow it all in one place, okay?"

Frank frowned at his brother. "Is that all you think of me? Some irresponsible doof who blows his paycheck the same day he gets it?"

Patrick arched his eyebrows.

"Well, maybe sometimes, but not anymore." Frank patted his breast pocket and bit his lip to control his huge smile. It's my ticket out, Pat. I'm not gonna blow it. Tomorrow I'll be in the merchant marine, an official member of the Portland crew and out to sea the day after. Be excited for me. I'm off to see the world. No more dirt and smokestack cinders for me."

"No decision you've made that you can't unmake, Frank. If you're really set on it, I won't try to talk you out of it. You're old enough to make your own decisions, but you've had that money less than a week. You sure you don't want to sit on it for a while and look at all your options?

244

Do you really think working in the hold of a ship will be any better? At least, here you're out in the fresh air all day."

Frank took a thoughtful look around the rail yard and shook his head. "I'd rather spend six days in a hold and a seventh in some exotic port than spend another day in a two-street town like Nevis. I'm not going anywhere here, Pat. You got a shot at working your way up—maybe even Broderick's job, if they ever decide to fill it—but I"ll never be anything but just another jerk on the line. You know I don't have the makeup to be a good foreman. Everything's good here now—time for me to skedaddle."

The bell on engine 873 warned of its impending departure.

Frank held up a finger. "Wait. One more thing; then I'm off." He peeled several bills from his money roll and shoved them at his brother. "Not all of it, but a good start at what I owe you. Seeing as how it won't be easy to pay you once I'm off on some banana boat, I thought we could whittle some of it down right away."

"No, go on, I can't take your money," Patrick said. "You'll need a bit extra until you get yourself settled. Promise me you won't go *borrowing* any from the boat captain, and we can call it even." He grabbed Frank and bear-hugged him. "Don't do anything foolish, mick."

"Promise. And same goes for you. Foremen, they direct. Don't overdo it out there. No one will appreciate it if you kill yourself."

"I promise, Frank."

Another warning hoot from the train, this time followed by a loud hiss of steam.

"Gotta move back, Pat. I'd hate for the wheels to get you before something else does. Be good, okay?" he said, his voice cracking. "I'll send you an address once I know how it all works."

He climbed the last step, looked out one more time, and then disappeared inside, appearing again as he picked a window seat on the near side of the train.

The conductor pulled up the step, and the train eased forward. Patrick walked alongside, locking eyes with Frank as the train outpaced him and began to pull away. He waved at the face pressed up against the glass. Then he was gone, the train rumbling away as it had hundreds of times before. Frank was gone. Only this time, it was different. Somehow, *gone* felt as though it was for good.

CHAPTER FORTY

No More Canning Tomatoes

Patrick ran the point of his pocketknife around the bottom of his boot and flicked dried mud from the crevice between the upper and the sole. There was thinking to do, and the steps of Phil's Barbershop were as good a spot as any to ponder his situation. He watched the helix of red, white, and blue stripes twisting around the barber pole. *Counterclockwise.*

Dilly's was across the way. He hadn't frequented the place since Zugel issued his ultimatum or threat or whatever it was. That was about to change. He knew he could be as pigheaded as Frank sometimes, but no one was going to tell him what he could do or where he could go—especially a German, no matter how many leprechauns he carved.

Frank would already have dragged him into the diner by now and had him thumb his nose at Zugel. But the thought of sitting alone in there as he dug into the blue plate special would only compound the empty feelings that swirled around inside him. He hated to admit it, but he missed his brother.

The problems that tormented him involved more than Michod Zugel, though. George Dilly was dead a week now, kicked right into the hereafter by one of his horses. As far as Patrick knew, Dilly had no family, which left the fate of the diner up in the air. He wondered how Anna felt about that.

But even that did not sum up all the turmoil within him. With Frank gone, he spent a lot of time contemplating how *he* felt. In spite of being the younger, irresponsible brother, Frank had taught him a lot: how to lie and keep a straight face, the best way to outrun and evade an outraged German, but most importantly, how to follow through on what you really wanted out of life. He had thought Frank sorely lacking in a life plan, but he was wrong. The merchant marine was just a plan he himself would never have made.

Harry Cooley had tried to clue him in, pointing out that Patrick was never satisfied with what he had. Said all he did was chase things that might never be. And maybe there was some truth in that. God certainly hadn't offered any vision or special insight into it. Getting a desk job at the B&O—a dream that had sustained him for three years now—didn't seem to be in the cards. They weren't even hiring track men, let alone promoting anyone. With Miller gone, Broderick's job might never be filled, or, worse yet, might go to some friend of whoever replaced Miller. He needed to accept that, although getting another medical form past Doc Bagley would be a battle.

He should listen to Harry. There were no guarantees of tomorrow. It was time to stop searching for the elusive. It was dawning on him that his happiness was right here in Nevis, just waiting for him to reach out and claim it.

He glanced over at Dilly's for the hundredth time this morning. A white and green dairy truck pulled up to the diner. Patrick watched Mr. Anderson throw the reins over his horse's head and hop out. The four bottles of milk jiggled and clinked together in their wire carrier as he shooed away the little boy sitting on the wooden milk box at the top of the steps. The dairyman flipped up the box lid and slid in the bottles. He tipped his hat to Anna as she came out, and then urged his blinkered old white dobbin on to the next stop.

Patrick's heart beat double time. Anna's blue checked gingham dress matched the color of her eyes, if memory served him correctly. He watched her pull out the milk and go back inside. He gave himself a moment, patting his pocket to make sure the sealed envelope was still there, and then crossed to the diner. Matthias Koenig was inside at the counter, talking to her.

"Sorry for the interruption," Patrick said, putting the letter on the counter as he passed by. "Saw this come in at the depot. Thought I'd save you a trip to Tanner's to pick it up." He sat down at a table nearby.

Matthias did not miss a beat. He leaned as far across the counter as he could. "Anna, you would have a great time if you came." The young man's smile deepened as Anna's cheeks turned rosy. She shook her head and moved to the other end of the counter. He watched in worshipful silence as she poured Patrick a cup of coffee.

Patrick had seen the young German come in often. He tried to impress Anna but lacked the finesse to overcome her shyness. Patrick admired his persistence, but his efforts seemed in vain. Oh, he made her blush and giggle a few times, and this would have encouraged any man, but it was as far as he got. Patrick watched him give up for the day, the twinkle in his eyes gone, his usual saunter reduced to a shuffle.

Anna picked up the envelope. Frowning, she ripped it open and read the contents. When he was sure she had read it all—twice, as he noted—Patrick drained his cup and returned to the counter.

"Not having any breakfast?" she asked him, setting the letter aside.

"Only have time for coffee."

He put a dime down on the counter. "Good news?" he asked, nodding at the letter."

"Someone has bought Dilly's," she said, her frown deepening."

"Well, then you'll stay open. That's good, right? So why the long face?"

Her lower lip quivered. "The buyer intends to be a silent partner. They want me to run this place. Heavens! What am I going to do? Why me?"

Patrick smiled at her. "Why *not* you? You practically run the place as it is. You do all the baking, and I'll bet you do the inventory, too, don't you?"

"Yes, but how would the buyer know that?" She stopped and tiled her head back, eyes narrowing to slits. "You've never delivered any mail here before, and you look like the cat that ate Uncle Bill's canary. You knew what was in this letter, didn't you? You're the silent partner."

"Oh, heavens no! On a railway man's salary? But yes, you caught me." His smile grew wider, and he shifted from one foot to the other. "I mighta sorta written someone I know to see if they were interested in running a diner with a very capable waitress who is also one heck of a baker. I knew the letter was coming. Let's just say a little birdie told me, and leave it like that."

"But *me*? I'm a woman. I can't run all this alone."

"Anna, there are a dozen crazy suffragettes in Nevis, including my sister, who will make sure a woman's business succeeds in this town. Don't let a lack of confidence stop you from grabbing this opportunity. This isn't a matter of life and death. You might not get a chance like this again."

"Me?" she repeated. She swept her damp cleaning cloth across the counter and sent Matthias's cup skittering, splashing cold dark coffee in all directions across the clean wooden surface.

"Excuse me," she whispered, blotting off the soaked bill for Matthias's coffee. "I must check the oven." She retreated through the double doors to the security of the kitchen.

Patrick sat down on a stool at the counter. She would be back. Anna was too diligent to leave the counter unattended for long.

Several minutes later, Anna returned. The vulnerability in her eyes hit him hard. "Sorry," she said. She picked up the dime and rang the two-cent sale on the cash register.

When she dropped the change in his palm, he closed his hand gently around hers. She didn't resist.

He took a deep breath, then looked deep into those deep-blue eyes.

"Anna, I was wondering if you would come with me to Bayland this Friday. I already have tickets. We can play some arcades, ride the carousels, maybe even hunt down a candy apple. Ever had one?"

His heart began to sink. She would say no and break his heart. It would be karma.

The soft, pink lips moved in an unexpected direction. She smiled. "I'd love to go with you."

"I can call for you at six," he said. *Michod Zugel be damned.* This felt good.

"I, uh, would rather meet you at the park entrance, if that's all right." She looked away. "I was afraid you might have left town with your brother."

"No, still here a while. Depends on how things go."

"Oh," she said, and her face fell. "I was hoping you might stick around a while. You can always pick up and follow Frank . . . if things don't turn out as you hoped."

"We can talk about that someday. A good friend once told me that sometimes you just have to decide what's important to you, and let things fall the way they will. I'm hoping things turn out, so maybe

I'll stick around and watch you make a name for yourself here—'best baker in Nevis.'"

"There's a new name for this place," she said, picking up the letter. "We are no longer Dilly's. From now on, this diner will be known as Betty's—which isn't a bad choice, actually. My mother was an Elizabeth. But we're not going to discuss that with Father."

Well, what do you know? My mother, too. And no, I foresee a few things that we probably won't be discussing with your father. Now, if you have anything that resembles paint around here, I can change that 'Dilly's' sign out front. See? Change won't be so hard. Just take life a day at a time and enjoy each one. Sound good to you?"

"Yes. It sounds really good."

Patrick jumped off the rail runner as it coasted to a halt at mile marker five. The crew had already started hauling and heaving ties, but all activity ceased when he appeared.

"So, boss man, what's it gonna be today?" Mac called out to him.

"Better than it was yesterday. If we want tomatoes, we're going to pluck 'em off the vine. No more canning tomatoes."

Mac and Connor looked at each other. "Come again?" Connor asked.

"Never mind. Let's get everybody dancing, Mac. Full day o' work here."

"Yes, sir," Mac said. He waved the gandies back to work and pulled out his harmonica. Then he gave Patrick a wink and sang:

"Pretty girl down Nevis way,
Boss man said he could not stay.
She said that would be all right,
Make it up to you tonight.

Sliding bars in, bah.
Sliding bars in, bah.
Sliding bars out, bah.
Sliding bars out, bah."

Everybody laughed. Patrick imagined it would get worse as the day wore on, but that was okay. That pretty little girl was not going anywhere, and neither was he.

Continue reading for a sneak preview of

The Pickle Boat House

CHAPTER ONE

Fugue and Exposition

As the orange passenger jet roared overhead, sinking toward the runway beyond, James loosened his grip on the wheel a little. But even the blare of Beethoven's op. 123 Credo couldn't put him in the zone. Pity—it was one of his favorites. Arrival time was 12:35 ... right? It was important; he had a three o'clock meeting. James turned the radio off and pulled into short-term parking. Lucky day! An empty space, right up front. He whipped his car into the spot and headed for Terminal A.

The airport was a sea of faces trailing wheeled appendages. "Sam, Sam, Sam," James mumbled, spinning his key ring on his finger as he surveyed the moving mass. "Come out, come out, wherever you . . ."

"Paging James Hardy. Paging James Hardy."

James whirled around at the sound of the familiar voice and spied Sam in the distance, hands cupped to his mouth. Khakis and a polo shirt—the guy was finally maturing.

"Sam! Great to see ya, bud." James pulled his friend into a bear-hug. "Glad you called. How long's your layover?"

"Let's see, 12:50 . . . got about an hour to kill. I remember you every time I pass through Baltimore, but this is the first time I ever thought about calling. I'm surprised you squeezed me in, being a big-shot lawyer and all. Dressing for success, too," he said, eyeing James's navy suit and mirror-polished Florsheim wingtips. "Looking sharp for a twenty-four-year-old."

"Oh, please! Yours will be the first ass I sue when I get a real job."

"Let's go get you a latte and me a strong cuppa joe, and I'll tell you about the latest corporate shit-fest. You'll soil your legal briefs when you hear what the assholes in my company are trying to do." Sam grabbed James by the elbow and steered him toward the coffee kiosk. "Large dark roast, please." He turned his attention back to James. "Talked to Mark and Jay a few weeks ago. They want us all to meet up in Myrtle Beach in August."

"Not sure about August—may have a job. Interview today," James said, pulling on his lapels. "The place has great credibility. I want this one bad. Small coffee," he said to the barista. He followed Sam to a table at the entrance where they could people watch while keeping an eye on the digital clock on the arrival/departure board.

"So, dressed to *impress*," said Sam. "When's your birthday, August? Expect a Baysox T-shirt. You're gonna need me to keep you grounded."

"Acceptable," James said, dumping sugar into his cup. "Sox are holding their own this year. Don't even think about a United jersey—guys are stinking up the division. They traded everybody away. How are your parents?"

"Good. Yours?"

"Peas in a pod," James replied. "Dad and I are going skydiving on my birthday. Mom's seeing how long she can keep me tied to her apron strings. If she only knew how long ago I cut those!"

Sam laughed. "So this job—you want it, eh?"

"Yep, this is the one—small firm, populist minded. The big corporate offices don't care. If I get this one, I can stay local. I might even be able to live in my great grandparents' house in Nevis, rent free."

"The pickle boat house? Sweet! I loved summer vacations there. Nevis is like one of those fifties sitcom towns, you know? I swear the Beav lived around the corner. Dude, we used to get into such trouble."

"Hah! I remember. It was awesome. We were such idiots—climbing out the window at night. I don't think they knew where we were half the time. Mom still goes down there quite a bit. She's collected a lot of turn-of-the century memorabilia from when Nevis was a hopping resort. She has grand plans to open a museum one day."

"Dontcha miss those carefree days? Hey, check this guy." Sam pointed across the concourse to a well-dressed man with an attaché case. In a hurry, he wove his way in and out of the human traffic on the people mover, with little regard for feet, shoulders, or even small children. "What a dick. If I was in front of him, I'd do my passive-aggressive best to box him in and not let him by."

James laughed. "Always looking for trouble." People movers—they worked best when slowpokes stayed right and the type A's could progress at will in the left lane, like the autobahn. But it took just one jerk like him to give all left-laners a bad name." James watched with fascination as the man bullied a series of people in front of him to move right. He gave the guy the full once-over. "Cold eyes. Wouldn't touch that dude with a ten-foot pole."

As they each reached the bottom of their cups, Sam said, quite out of the blue, "In all seriousness, James, promise me one thing: when you get your job with some hot-shot firm, you won't turn into that guy." Don't ever lose a sense of where you've come from or develop that sense of entitlement. Use your gifts for the good of people. In fact," he said, pulling a pen out of his carry-on and scribbling on his napkin, "put this in your wallet, and when you suspect you might be getting a fat head, read it." He ripped the corner off the napkin and slid it into James's shirt pocket."

"Okay, *Mom,* I promise. Y'know, the dude is probably just late and stressed. Wait until he spends an eternity waiting for his luggage. And speaking of late, Sam, I gotta roll. It's one forty. No rest for the wicked."

Sam grinned. "Gotcha. Only slow down a little, okay? Smell the roses."

"Ah, I'll rest when I'm dead."

"Not planning on dying young, are we?"

James shrugged. "Definitely not in my plans, but time waits for no man."

Sam leaned forward. "Then don't be a man for a while, bro," he whispered, and raised his eyebrows as he extended his hand and gave James the super-secret handshake they had made up when they were kids.

"Grow up, dumb-ass," James said, laughing. "I'll call you."

"Thanks for the company, and good luck today. I'll let you know about August. Text me." Sam watched James move out into the throng of travelers. For the briefest moment, he wanted to ditch his flight and spend the rest of the day with his best friend. Why was this good-bye so hard? He stood rooted, trying to freeze in time the retreating image before it disappeared into the crowd. Jeez, what *was* with this nostalgia thing?

James hit the freeway with the Jeep's pedal down, the road clear, and a lot of information floating around in his brain. Interview suit, check. Directions, check. Plenty of time still? He checked his watch: 1:55. A little close—maybe the visit wasn't such a great idea. He pulled Sam's limp folded napkin out of his pocket and flipped it open. Scrawled in small capital letters were three words: "pickle boat house." He smiled and tucked it back into his pocket, then cranked up the radio to keep his mind occupied. It was almost two; he could catch the news.

James's eyes returned to the road just in time to see the rear end of a stalled car rapidly approaching. "Where'd you come from? Christ!" He jerked the wheel, and the car lurched right, hugging the edge of the asphalt. Hitting loose gravel there, the jeep zigzagged back and forth across the lanes as James fought to maintain control. Careening off the road on two wheels, the car hit an embankment and went airborne, doing a half roll before it came to rest upside down in a creek. It seemed to float on the surface for a brief moment before sinking into the sparkling, flowing water. Then all became strangely quiet.

In those last moments, James had no sudden rush of life's experiences. He just felt himself floating weightlessly, willingly, toward the brightest, warmest light he had ever seen. Confusion . . . somewhere a bus accident, humming lights, frantic medical personnel . . . and through it all, a strange sense of detachment overwhelmed him.

Meanwhile, at the airport, Sam had grabbed a seat at his departure gate, the constant human flow had morphed in new shapes, and the man with the cold eyes had claimed his luggage. As he stepped off the curb toward the rental cars, supremely indifferent to those around him, he never saw the city bus, rounding the corner with its own kind of indifference. As the digital clock on the arrival/departure board changed to 2:00 p.m., the bus hit him and the woman three steps ahead. Floating weightlessly toward the lovely white radiance, in that eye blink, the summed experience of the man's life passed before him. Ryan Llewellyn Thomas had been assessed the price for the life he lived.

At two o'clock that day, the light at the end of the passageway shone for many people. It was certainly nothing unusual for more than one soul to traverse its length at exactly the same moment. But it was rare to have two men so very different in temperament and virtue traveling together. And it was almost unheard of for one soul to be cast back to Earth, into the body of his traveling companion, for a second chance in the world.

If you would like to be placed on a mailing list for future book announcements

http://gordymac1.wix.com/louisegorday

Made in the USA
Lexington, KY
19 November 2019